PRAISE FOR SAV

"John Witzel has written a novel full of action sited in unusual settings. The protagonist is an Air Force Combat Controller, and it seems to me he is a composite of the traits which make this breed of warrior-commandos as a group the most highly decorated in the USAF today. Obviously the writer has first hand experience with these men. A fast paced piece, I recommend it for enjoyment and a glimpse of something new."

— Richard V. Secord, Maj Gen, USAF (Ret.)
President, Air Commando Association

"Witzel takes on the big issues of public education today, articulating the challenges, frustrations, and joys teachers experience daily. This is a real-time adventure of military intrigue, a second career, and the difference a highly qualified caring teacher can make for children with no hope of succeeding at anything!"

— Dr. John Bonaiuto
Former Executive Director
Nebraska Association of School Boards and Lifelong Educator

"I hated to see it end. I wanted to continue with Mr. Madden onto Stanford and beyond. It's a great story."

— T. E. McGinnis, independent reader

SAVING
TRES RIOS
A NOVEL

To The Nebraska Center for
the Book.
   Looking forward to working
with NCB for the advancement
of Nebraska authors
   Enjoy "Saving Tres Rios"

   John White 06/04/14

SAVING TRES RIOS

A NOVEL

JOHN WITZEL

WILDCATTER
PUBLISHING

Omaha, NE

PSALM 118:22

"The stone that the builders rejected became the cornerstone."

Wildcatter Publishing books may be ordered from your favorite bookseller. www.wildcatterpublishing.com

Wildcatter Publishing
c/o CMI
13518 L. Street
Omaha, NE 68137

Because of the dynamic nature of the internet, any web addresses or links contained in this book may have changed since publication and may no longer be valid. Any people depicted in stock imagery provided by iStockphoto are models, and such images are being used for illustrative purposes only.

Certain stock imagery © iStockphoto

Paperback ISBN: 978-0-9911029-1-4
ePub ISBN: 978-0-9911029-2-1
Mobi ISBN: 978-0-9911029-0-7

LCCN data on file with the publisher

Printed in the USA

10   9   8   7   6   5   4   3   2   1

PART ONE

CHAPTER

"Sheriff," she screamed over the phone, "they're back! Do you hear me? They're back!"

The sheriff's dispatcher calmly asked, "Who is back?" knowing full well about the situation at the school.

"Billy Hemrod and his friends are driving up to the school now. This has happened before, and the sheriff promised me it wouldn't happen again," she continued to scream at the man on the phone.

The dispatcher sarcastically advised, "Ma'am, I will contact the sheriff and I'm sure he will be right out."

"Right out?" Crying and stressed, she shouted, "Last time the sheriff was 'right out' took over two hours."

"Ma'am, I will ensure that the sheriff is informed—sorry about any past delays," the dispatcher said, almost laughing. Like the students, the dispatcher had also been through this drill many times with the previous teachers.

Meanwhile, two pickup trucks recklessly made their way to the gravel parking lot of the Tres Rios Rural Elementary School. "Hey, schoolteacher, we're back. Aren't you glad to see us?" Billy Hemrod yelled out the cab of the first pickup as it screeched to a halt, kicking gravel and dust everywhere. Several men in their late twenties and early thirties, all appearing liquored up, jumped out of the trucks, finishing off their bottles and throwing them to the ground.

"Yea, schoolteacher, did you call the sheriff again?" All were laughing now and grabbing more bottles of whiskey and cigarettes out of the cab of the truck.

Racing to the front of the school, Betty Wilson was not prepared for this intrusion and was trying desperately to find help from somewhere. Close to a breakdown, she yelled back to the classroom, "Class, remain in your seats—I'll take care of this."

"Ms. Wilson, what should we do? Do you want me to go for help?" Manuel Cortes excitedly offered.

"No, Manuel. Just stay in your seats!"

Confused and shaking, Betty Wilson prepared herself to confront Billy again when she heard the commotion and yelling from the parking lot. She heard him announce, "Out of the schoolhouse, everyone. Out of the schoolhouse—class is over for the day."

"Students, remain in your seats," countered Wilson. "Billy, get off the school premises now or I'll …"

"I said everyone out of the school now; the teacher and I have some school business to talk over," he laughed. Smoking a cigarette, Billy threw his empty whiskey bottle to the ground and approached Wilson to confront her face to face.

"Okay, teacher, do you really want your young students to stand around while we're here? Because you and I need to talk in private." Billy's crew, an assorted collection of motorcycle-gang wannabes and doped-up society dropouts, began making their way into the classroom shouting at the students, "Now get outta here and go home—now!"

Confused and terrified, the students were quickly leaving the classroom.

"Get out of here now—your teacher needs to give me some private lessons," Hemrod shouted as his crew sat around the classroom smoking.

Finishing off their bottles, they yelled, "Hey, Billy. When you going to have your little teacher's conference?"

Billy's eyes remained on Wilson, making up his mind what he was going to do next. "Schoolteacher, I figure you have wanted it for a long time now, so let's get it over with." Whoops and yells from the crew were heard far away from the school, but no help was coming. As in the past, no help was ever coming for the teachers at Tres Rios.

"Come with me, schoolteacher, let's go back to your office for our little teacher/parent meeting," he said while grabbing Wilson by the arm and pulling her toward her office.

"No! You can't do this! The sheriff'll be here any minute; he's been called," shrieked Wilson, and violently attempted to escape Hemrod's hold.

Laughing, while still pulling and grabbing Wilson, he claimed, "Lady, you don't seem to understand—I own the sheriff."

"No, no, no—it's not true. You'll see. He'll be here any minute and you'll be sorry for this."

Billy pulled the fighting and struggling Wilson to her office while the crew yelled their approval and continued drinking and smoking around the small desks of the departed students. The screaming was heard as far away as the small pueblo community called the Flats, a couple hundred yards from the school. No help was coming, and no one seemed to care what was happening in the little school.

While holding the struggling Wilson down, Billy surveyed the school again to make sure no student stragglers had remained—only his crew, who were putting their cigarettes out on student science projects and writing crude remarks on the blackboards.

"Let her have it, Billy. She's been waiting a year for this, now let her have it. We don't have all frickin' day."

"Get your hands off of me now! Do you hear me?" Betty cried and screamed for help.

Billy grabbed Wilson, roughly manhandled her into her office, and slammed the door behind them. Blood-curdling yells of agony and more cries for help were heard from the small office. As the crew was totally enjoying this entertainment on a warm, pleasant afternoon, someone else was observing the act with stark terror and confusion.

Breathing heavy and very scared, little Ramon Rodriguez had hidden himself in an old wooden storage locker a short distance from the teacher's office. Watching the entire violent act from a small air vent, he was very confused and frightened thinking, *What can I do?*

Ramon liked Ms. Wilson, had always appreciated her kind and caring ways. She treated everyone with respect—something most of them, including Ramon—never received.

The screaming continued from the office with the dull sound of books and papers hitting the floor: "Help me, help me! Please someone help me …"

Only laughter and encouragement came from the crew in the classroom. "Hey, Billy, when do we get our turn?" hollered one of Hemrod's crew.

Scared and trying to control his tears, Ramon could not grasp what was happening, but he knew something was terribly wrong. Trembling with anger, fear, and confusion, little Ramon stayed hidden during the entire ordeal, wishing and praying for a saving angel from the Almighty to help Ms. Wilson and himself.

Tres Rios Rural Elementary School was considered the hellhole by all of the government-assigned teachers, especially the newly recruited. Many rumors and legends were exchanged among the queue of teachers awaiting their first obligated assignments, and it was common knowledge that no teacher ever left Tres Rios for another follow-on teaching position: public, private, or government. The mysterious death of one newly assigned teacher and the alleged rape of another, plus the constant harassment by parents and townspeople, were too much for the aspiring young teachers. All gave up their teaching careers and left, feeling lucky to be rid of that corrupt cesspool called a school.

The school also boasted the worst educational achievement scores ever recorded in the state of New Mexico. It had a mix of students from Indian reservations, mining communities, and Hispanic families working at the local ranches—all left in the care the Calico County public school system. Calico County was indeed going to follow the letter of the law regarding No Child Left Behind.

School officials were well aware of the federal law that governs primary aid for disadvantaged students, based on setting high standards with measurable goals to show specific academic improvement. To ensure the continuous flow of federal funds to Calico County public schools, the school board and administrators had to ensure that all of its students received a quality education. A token attempt was made to include the impoverished and disenfranchised students at Tres Rios Rural Elementary School.

■ ■ ■ ■

"Okay, I understand. I'm heading over to the school now," the sheriff relayed to the county emergency dispatcher. Like so many calls in the past from the teachers at Tres Rios, he was expecting the worst, for he had a good idea what had happened. Arriving at the school, the sheriff found various empty liquor bottles and beer cans littering the lot and vulgar graffiti painted around the classrooms.

"Ms. Wilson, ma'am, are you back there? It's Sheriff Wells," he called.

Making his way back to the teacher's office, he found Betty Wilson huddled on the floor, shivering with fear and crying. The sheriff immediately attended to her and called for an ambulance to transport her to the county hospital.

While being settled in the back of the ambulance, Wilson stared at Wells and with a trembling, sobbing voice said, "I tried calling you, I tried calling you. You know who did this. You know who did this, and you are equally to blame."

Nodding his head and trying to keep his emotions in check, "Yes, I know," a saddened and disgusted Sheriff Wells answered.

Russell Wells had been the elected Calico County sheriff for over thirty years since he was in his mid-twenties. The endless, brilliant New Mexico sun had weathered the man so he now looked like a part of the desolate, sundrenched plains. Married and divorced twice, Wells was now romantically tied to Dr. Helen Kramer, the school superintendent for the Calico County public schools.

Surviving numerous county administrations and through some tough and controversial times, he was the one person the county residents thought they could trust. Wells's plans for an early retirement were put on hold when the local uranium mine reopened and he and his deputies were afforded lucrative part-time jobs by the mine's head of security, Billy Hemrod. Wells reasoned he could stay on as sheriff for a couple more years because the additional under-the-table income from mine security would make retirement a little sweeter. Reflecting back, he knew his association with Hemrod was one of the worst decisions he'd ever made, but it was much too late to back out now.

While recuperating in the hospital, Wilson had just completed all of the formal legal paperwork to charge Billy Hemrod with various major crimes, including assault and rape, while suspecting it would go nowhere. Remembering that during the assault, Billy Hemrod had said he "owned the sheriff" annoyed and angered her. She was sure no one would be held accountable for this action, no one. While completing more county school out-processing paperwork in the hospital's outdoor plaza, Wilson thought about the past and released a flood of tears and anger.

Betty Wilson had prayed daily to leave this earthly purgatory of being a government-sponsored teacher at Tres Rios, but she had indeed volunteered for it. As a new and quite naïve teacher with a brand-new teaching certificate, Betty was overwhelmed with the numerous and unexpected additional responsibilities; basic teaching was the easy part. Mentoring and teaching these underprivileged young children, grades one through six, under the most austere and challenging of conditions took its toll. Her students were below the poverty line at the rock bottom—with uneducated parents who, in many cases, did not speak English. They could not instill even limited social skills or core values in their children. She felt that no one cared for these students except herself and, of course, the law—just as long as they stayed at Tres Rios.

What had brought Betty Wilson to this isolated New Mexico town bordering the La Mesa uranium mine and the Kwanki

Indian Reservation? As a divorcée after four years of marriage to the man of her dreams, she was shocked when he came home early one day to announce he wanted a divorce because "things were not working out to his liking." In layman's terms, he was shacking up with his twenty-two-year-old secretary at his insurance company.

She negotiated a deal in the divorce settlement in which her ex-husband would pay for Betty's continued education, allowing her to earn a degree in elementary education and her teaching certificate. She summed it up as a pretty good deal with him footing the bill for the next four years of schooling and, after that, no ties or obligations. They would both be free to start new lives.

The government pamphlet looked inviting: full tuition, books, and boarding for two years, but only if one agreed to accept a three-year teaching position at a school designated by the Department of Education. Betty remembered mentioning to her sister, "Why not? This looks like exactly what I've been searching for and dreaming of—a fresh start away from Omaha and a chance to do some traveling while I'm teaching."

She was accepted into the program, and the next two years were as advertised: everything was taken care of by the government, and she became a certified elementary school teacher. Betty Wilson was on cloud nine, and the future looked bright with promise. Betty had a bubbly and pleasant personality and could still pass as a college cheerleader. She remained in good shape with daily workouts at the local gym and attracted a fair amount of notice, but she was not looking for romance and went to great lengths to avoid any type of flirting.

She was, however, noticed by several of the men who oversaw the government's teaching program. This group included Ralph Beller, her assigned mentor and manager. On several occasions, Beller had made unwanted passes at Betty, and she either turned them down or ignored them. He often warned Betty that it would be best for her career to "play nice" with him. Betty ignored his advice and warnings, naïvely thinking that government officials would treat her fairly.

"Betty, good morning. This is Ralph." Betty was now used to the numerous unwanted calls.

"Ralph, good morning to you also. How can I help you?" she had replied, trying hard to be cordial and professional under the circumstances.

"Betty, the assignments just came in, and I thought I'd be the first to give you the word."

Very excited now, Betty was anxious to find out about hers. Would it possibly be a government school in Europe, South America, or maybe in Asia? A new life and a new start—where would it be? Ralph was no longer the menacing womanizer, but the holder of her career and happiness.

"I'm pleased to inform you that your first teaching assignment for the Department of Education will be the county rural school at Tres Rios, New Mexico. Good luck, Betty, I'm sure you will enjoy it immensely—glad to have helped."

Betty Wilson was released from the hospital and escorted to the Albuquerque International Airport where she boarded a plane back home to Omaha. Viewing the glorious mountains and enchanting landscape from her window seat on takeoff, she realized it would take a long time to heal from her experiences in Tres Rios. She was also sad to be leaving the poor students she so desperately tried to help, teach, and mentor.

"Could anyone save them?" she murmured, shaking her head and turning away from the window.

Little Ramon Rodriguez kept secret what he had observed while hiding in the school's storage locker, but he had recurring, traumatic nightmares of the assault on Wilson. His family was concerned about the abrupt change in his behavior and noticed he spent many hours hiding in their home's closet. Keeping quiet about what he observed, Ramon continued to put his hands together in prayer and ask for a savior. As fate would have it, Ramon did not realize his prayers would be answered.

CHAPTER

"Madden, you have fifteen minutes to the landing zone. Better get your people ready," shouted the Colombian Army pilot in Spanish.

Madden gave the pilot a thumbs-up as the two Black Hawk helicopters skimmed the beautiful, awakening Colombian jungle below. Surveying his combat-controller team, he loudly commanded, "Get ready, equipment check." After a few seconds, everyone onboard gave the thumbs-up. All was good.

Senior Master Sergeant Rob Madden was just under six feet tall with a lean body and features weathered by his months of service in the South American jungle. Even at thirty-eight, Madden's piercing blue eyes and light brown hair gave him that "All American Boy" look but with a dangerous edge. Besides being fluent in Spanish, he was respected and liked by all—from Army Green Berets to the lowest private in the Colombian Army. Always the optimist in an unpleasant and dangerous world, Madden was the one professional everyone wanted on his or her side.

Madden double-checked his party that included elements of the Colombian military and national police, Colombian Air Force, U.S. Drug Enforcement Agency (DEA), and his own team of U.S. Air Force advisors. Madden's team were hand-picked Air Force Non-commissioned Officers (NCOs), sergeants who were considered specialists in their areas of responsibility.

Some often kidded Madden that his group looked like a flying circus act. As one of the most seasoned and experienced combat controllers in the U.S. Air Force, Madden and his team were training the Colombian military in daylight and night infiltration/deployment operations. They were establishing helicopter-landing sites in the jungles and rugged terrain of

Colombia for follow-on helicopters to land. Madden had learned it was the most effective (and maybe the only) way to find, fight, and destroy the Revolutionary Armed Forces of Colombia, who are the terrorist rebels and their drug-producing friends better known as FARC.

"Another walk in the park and a free ride to paradise," Madden said to the group, smiling. He always had a big smile on his face and was constantly building up his team because he understood their nervousness; they had dangerous jobs. He watched Special Agent Bonnie McCord, one of the DEA newbies, constantly tying and untying her boots to mask her excitement. The DEA agents were not afforded the opportunity of much military training in air-assault operations, so Madden understood their apprehension.

As in past operations, McCord settled down, remembered her training, and proved to be one of his most valuable and dependable team members. Madden frequently and affectionately described her as a "pretty tough broad" because she had held her own in a few unexpected firefights in the past.

Sergeant Will Little, Madden's deputy team leader, was strapped to his web seat next to the copter's crew chief position. He was rechecking his rifle's ammunition clip when Bonnie McCord nudged his side.

"Sergeant Little, what do you know about Senior Master Sergeant Madden? How in the heck did he end up here in Colombia?" McCord yelled over the rushing wind of the helicopter's rotors. "He knows what he's doing."

The helicopter doors were now open, and over the wind driving through the crew compartment and sound of rotors, Little answered, "Agent McCord, Senior Master Sergeant Rob Madden will probably be one of the most interesting people you will run into on this planet."

McCord looked perplexed. "How so?" she asked.

"Rob Madden may be the most experienced special-tactics sergeant in the Air Force. His parents were what he calls 'oil-field trash' because he was born and raised in the oil fields of

East Texas. When Rob was ten, his father was transferred to Venezuela to operate oil-field operations for a large oil drilling company. Going to school was tough there, especially for an American. That's where he learned so much about street fighting and gained a command of the Spanish language more than anything else. As Rob puts it, 'Surviving the streets had priority over mathematics.'"

McCord sighed and said, "He must feel right at home in Columbia then."

"That's not the half of it." Little went on, "After Venezuela, his father was transferred to work the oil fields in Kuwait, again making Rob the new kid in school, which meant daily fights and learning Arabic just to get by."

"He also knows Arabic?" McCord asked in awe.

"Yes, and I must say, Rob's life appears to have mostly been about getting into fights and learning languages. He was also a decent soccer player to boot. Believe me, lady, we're blessed to be on his team. He'll see us through."

"Get ready to rappel from the helicopter. Five minutes. Check your gear," Madden yelled above the whine of the helicopter engines, "and sit in the door." The assortment of team members positioned themselves in the door with their feet out on the helicopter skid. Madden could sense the balance of excitement and fear as his team prepared to rappel into the trees and jungle below.

"Drop rope," he ordered. Ten ropes were now deployed from the Black Hawk, all straight down to the jungle floor below. "Position!" All members then pivoted 180 degrees on the Black Hawk's skid bar, facing the inside of the helicopter. It quickly became obvious that one of the Colombian police members was having, what Madden recognized as, a panic attack. Madden saw this all the time with his new members. He felt it was no big deal and could easily be defused.

In perfect Spanish, Madden said, "Hey, Rafael, how ya doing, man?"

"Rob, I don't know. Not sure if I'm doing this right, what if …"

"Hey man, you're doing fine. No problems, looks good." Madden always gave the vote of confidence. "When we get on the ground, I need you to help me with setting the C-4 explosive charges. You're the best there is at setting the switches. Let's you and I work on this together. I'll rappel down with you, okay?"

Looking at Madden and nodding, Rafael gave Madden a thumbs-up. Madden patted him on the back and said, "Go on, friend, let's do it!"

Raising his fist in the air, the pilot pointed to Madden. The Black Hawk was over the planned exercise-landing zone (LZ). Acknowledging his signal, Madden yelled, "Go!" and his assorted team of combat controllers and their equipment immediately rappelled to the jungle. Flexing their knees and jumping backwards, they expertly let the rope run through both the brake hand and the guide hand.

"Keep your feet together and your legs straight," shouted Madden as he monitored his team's uneventful deployment from the Black Hawk. With the Black Hawk directly above and spraying the team with a strong rotor wash of wind, jungle debris was flying everywhere. Madden accomplished a quick head count and found Sergeant Will Little.

"Sergeant Little, what's our status?" Madden instinctively asked his top NCO upon hitting the ground.

"Rob, we have ten members on the ground, and all of the equipment has been accounted for."

"Okay, Will. Get everyone going. Looks like we've got a lot of work to do here. Make sure everyone gets a chance to fuse the C-4 explosives."

While the Black Hawk continued to hover over them, Madden made sure that all of the ropes and lines were free of personnel and equipment. Looking up to the pilot, Madden checked in on the radio and gave the all-clear sign for the Black Hawk to depart. In a few seconds, it was gone.

"Heads up, heads up, everyone. The follow-on assault team will be landing here in fifteen minutes. Let's get to work," Madden ordered. In a matter of minutes, a thick Colombian jungle spot was transformed into a cleared landing zone suitable for helicopter landings due, in part, to a little elbow grease and C-4 explosives.

"Thank God for C-4," mumbled Madden to one of the Colombian airmen on his team. The C-4 was a plastic explosive encased in what looks like a garden hose. Wrapping this hoselike explosive around trees, vines, and other obstacles made it possible to clear an area of jungle in a matter of minutes—and Madden's team did just that.

"Team, excellent job on the LZ. Now let's secure the area and start our air-traffic job." Besides clearing the landing zone, Madden's combat-controller team now took on the role of pathfinders, and Madden became a mentor to his young team. He allowed each of them all of the necessary experiences—from leading the team to clearing the trash. Each member was going to know how to complete every task without hesitation.

"Well, schoolteacher, going to be setting up your little schoolhouse now to make us all intelligent and brave pathfinders?" Sergeant Little poked a little fun at Madden.

Clearing more fallen trees and shrubs around the landing zone, Colombian Army Sergeant Raul Lopez heard this remark and asked Little, "Hey, why'd you call him schoolteacher—is he really a teacher?"

"Yeah, Madden is a certified schoolteacher, believe it or not. I think he's going to do some teaching when he retires next year."

"I don't know squat about teaching, but I guess Madden does have a knack for it, or from what I can tell anyway," commented Lopez.

"Hey, Little, Lopez, if it's not too much of a problem, would you mind marking the initial assembly points for the incoming troops and equipment?" Madden asked sarcastically.

"Okay, boss. We're on it, schoolteacher. Sorry, I mean Senior Master Sergeant Madden," Little remarked with a big smirk on his face. Madden just nodded as he walked over to the command radios to notify the follow-on helicopters that the landing zones were ready and secure.

Madden's team followed National Security Presidential Directive 18 as the orders and mission that directed their actions. This order officially widened the role of the U.S. military in South America to include assisting Colombia with tracking down and wiping out rebel groups and drug cartels. The initial cadre of Special Forces was assigned to advise Colombia's elite 18th Brigade—the country's tip-of-the-spear in fighting terrorists. The Special Forces' current responsibilities included assisting with training the brigade on mobile tactics, operations, and intelligence.

Upon completion of an exercise, Madden routinely conducted what in military terms is called a "hot wash" or critique of the exercise: what went good and not so good. This hot wash was no different from the ones held in Colombia over the past few months, usually in an open area near the landing zone. Madden would critique the rappelling, the clearance of the landing zone, sharing of responsibilities, and the marking of the troop-assembly areas near the zones. Madden now reemphasized the need for security around the zones.

Wrapping up the hot wash at a small hangar next to the airbase runway, he said, "We've had several live-fire exercises like this one in the past few months, and you can see for yourselves the Colombian police and Air Force are taking the lead with some assistance from our DEA friends." Madden added, "We need to place more emphasis on securing the landing zones against hostiles. And to our DEA *compadres*, I'd like to express our respect and appreciation for all of your hard work and dedication these last few months of training."

The team members all nodded their heads in approval and a short round of applause followed. It was obvious: the DEA team was glad to be part of it all. "Thank you, Agent McCord, for not making one of your spirited speeches after this exercise,"

Madden said teasingly to McCord. "Granted, we all know that in your previous life as lawyer you actually got paid for speaking, but for now, let's forgo the speeches."

Being of good nature, McCord laughed and replied, "Sergeant Madden, I defer all motivational talks to your discretion."

"Thank you, Agent McCord. Anything else for the good of the team?"

"It's remarkable that we've not run into any FARC or drug operators in our last few exercises," voiced Captain Fernandez of the Colombian national police.

"We all know Colonel Sanchez isn't scheduling all of these live-fire exercises for our health," concluded Madden with a sense of apprehension about the future.

The next day, at the Colombian Army 18th Brigade forward command center in Saravena, Colonel Ricardo "Ricky" Sanchez was preparing his staff for another live-fire exercise near the border with Venezuela. Live-fire exercise was just another name for "search and destroy," but was more politically correct to outside observers—especially the U.S. military advisors, who were prohibited from engaging in any type of fighting with the rebel forces. The target for the upcoming live-fire exercises was the FARC, a continuing problem for the Colombian government.

For years, the FARC had waged a bloody guerrilla war against the Colombian government by crossing back and forth between Colombia and their sanctuary in Venezuela to harass the border villages. The FARC achieved only minor results in persuading the local populaces of these impoverished small towns to accept their idea of socialism. Funding for the FARC's war of terror mostly came from the production, cultivation, and sale of illegal drugs. The profits from selling these drugs went to buy weapons and equipment from neighboring Venezuela. Now the momentum had shifted due to the backing and support from the United States, which included advisors and technical assistance. The Colombian government was gradually eradicating the killings, kidnapping, drugs, and, most important of all, the FARC.

The central irritant for the Colombian government was the strip of jungle on the Chancer River along the border of Colombia and Venezuela. Venezuela had become the safe haven for the FARC rebels who traded their illegal cash crops, haggled with the drug dealers, and harassed the local governments on a routine basis. If attacked or pursued by the Colombian military, the FARC would simply turn north, wade across the Chancer River, and wait for another day to return.

"Another great opportunity for a live-fire exercise," announced Colonel Sanchez to his staff. "Prepare the necessary orders, and contact the usual team leaders to include commanders of Bravo and Charlie companies. Briefing tomorrow at 0900 hours here at HQ," ordered Colonel Sanchez to his executive officer. The staff busily began preparing for another live-fire exercise. There was much to do.

At 0900 hours on Thursday, the team leaders gathered in the briefing room of the 18th Brigade headquarters that also doubled as a makeshift supply/break room. As the team leaders were coordinating details with the HQ staff, Colonel Sanchez bellowed, "Come on people, let's get going with the briefing. Five minutes. Clear!"

The leaders and staff took their usual places around an antique dining table and sat on the worn-out card-table chairs. The large chalkboard at the front of the table contained typical operations data for the upcoming exercise, including units, timing, call signs, and radio frequencies. On the side walls of the room were large, colorful maps showing the varied topical features of the 18th Brigade's area of responsibility.

During the past few months, the briefing room and maps were used with increasing success for the numerous exercises and daily operations conducted by the local units. Colonel Sanchez was becoming a folk hero and a household name among the locals as well as the Colombian military. He liked the fame and notoriety, which is not surprising for a senior officer on the move up. He was preparing to expand and upscale his live-fire exercises with more soldiers and advisors.

"Attention!" was loudly shouted by the brigade executive officer as Colonel Sanchez entered with his staff.

"Please, gentlemen, take your seats. This morning we will brief the planning and execution of exercise 11B, if it's okay with my American advisors, of course?" Sanchez said sarcastically to the American advisors who were now taking on a more augmented versus advisory role. Even though Sanchez had been repeatedly warned by his superiors against using his U.S. military advisors in any possible direct action against the FARC, he clearly ignored those warnings.

"Major Domingo, would you please brief us on the details of 11B to ensure our friends have the total picture." It was another jab at the advisors for their propensity for details.

"Good morning, Colonel Sanchez, gentlemen. The exercise for tomorrow is 11B, and it's built on the same footprint as 9B: an air assault on a suspected rebel outpost near the town of Puerto Rancho. Our friends in Columbian military intelligence inform us that there appears to be newly built makeshift roads to the Venezuelan border and a well-used trail to our interior," Major Domingo surmised. "This certainly appears, by our analysis, to be drug and rebel operations. However, we consider 11B to be another live-fire exercise."

The staff operations and military advisors all looked uneasy when the operation was defined as an "exercise." It looked more and more like a risky search-and-destroy mission to them—especially so close to the Venezuelan border.

"Any problems, gentlemen?" Sanchez asked those in attendance, sensing issues with his American advisors. There were no replies.

"As in previous exercises, the operations plan calls for two helicopter-landing zones south of the crossroads. Bravo Company and their advisors will land on the north LZ, and Charlie Company will land on the south LZ, squeezing any activity in the area." Major Domingo continued, "The two LZs are different. The south LZ is located in what looks like an old farm field approximately three kilometers from the crossroads. However, the proposed north LZ is a different story—located in what appears to be a jungle clearing adjacent to one of the newly constructed roads near the Venezuelan border. No doubt, quickly clearing the north LZ for troops disembarking from the helicopters will be challenging."

The advisors were now showing their concern and frustration. They had been lucky in the past with these exercises, but tomorrow would be, regardless of what Colonel Sanchez called it, the real deal.

Major Domingo completed his briefing with, "As before, the troops will depart the LZs and join at the crossroads for reconnaissance into the town. Again, the key to this exercise is the operational status of the LZs for follow-on troop reinforcements and the speed of our troops in reaching the crossroads."

"Thank you, Major. Well it appears our success tomorrow depends on quickly clearing the helicopter-landing zones, and do we have anyone familiar with landing zones here?" Colonel Sanchez laughed sarcastically as he continued, "Well, look who we have in our little briefing today, Senior Master Sergeant Rob Madden. Good morning, Rob. Are you and your little circus of Army wannabes ready for some action and real work?"

Madden was used to this type of reception, and he took it all in stride. It was obvious the Colonel liked Rob and felt comfortable in his presence. "Colonel Sanchez, has my band of combat controllers ever let you down? Granted, you may have had some rough landings now and then, but remember, we're just advisors—the 'Christmas help,'" answered Madden. The rest of the officers, staff, and advisors in the briefing always got a big laugh at the exchanges between the 18th Brigade Commander and the senior Air Force NCO.

Sanchez smiled and answered, "Ah yes, Rob. You can create landing zones out of nowhere and secure them so well that I had to escape and evade in the La Paz jungle a few weeks ago. You know the story."

Rob remembered all too well. Again, it was another case of a Colonel Sanchez live-fire exercise turning into a live fight with the FARC. Madden was in no position to comment on Sanchez's decisions. However, his Special Forces detachment commander, Captain Lewis Jeffers, was—and he continued to remind Sanchez that his two training companies and assortment of paramilitary trainees still required more training before taking on further engagements with the FARC. Jeffers's concerns fell on the Colonel's deaf ears. He was moving forward.

"Rob, help me out here again. Where did you receive your wonderful training in working landing zones? From the Army?" Colonel Sanchez was always deliberately referring to Rob as an Army man, which usually got the expected rise from Madden, who just sighed and shook his head.

After leaving the briefing room to head back to his team barracks, Captain Jeffers stopped Madden just outside the door. Jeffers and Madden had worked together in Iraq and now for more than six months in Colombia. Both men liked and respected each other, which was not that common among different rivalries of the elite Special Forces branches. Both men spoke fluent Spanish and had previously lived in South America.

"Rob, I'm probably thinking the same thing you are. This 'exercise' as Sanchez calls it looks dicey. The FARC knows darn well what our air-assault operations are like, and if they happen to be entrenched near that crossroads tomorrow, it will be a bloody mess," said a frustrated Jeffers.

"Lewis," Madden said, "have you spoken to Sanchez about the dangers and uncertainty of tomorrow, and will there be any air support or a mobile force backing us up?"

"Rob, I've spoken with him about it until he told me, 'Shut up—I'm tired of hearing it.' He still believes that tomorrow will be just another exercise, and if any situations develop, we can handle them. One more thing, Rob, make sure your teams cover and secure those damn LZs. They just might be our only salvation tomorrow," said a worried Jeffers.

"Different subject, how are your DEA training augmentees working out? Do you think they are up for tomorrow's exercise?" Jeffers inquired.

"Yes, I do. They've accomplished much in the last three months and have successfully completed all of the training I could throw at them. However, they lack a lot of soldiering skills that our teams possess," Madden commented. "No fault of their own; they're just working with some of the most experienced operators in the business—so we'll cut them some slack."

Jeffers agreed nodding his head and asked, "How about the female agent? What's her name again?"

"Bonnie McCord," answered Madden, "She is one tough broad and has performed exceedingly well during the past two months. But I must say that she is definitely career minded and has a few distractions."

"Is this your first female trainee?" asked Jeffers.

"Yes, and I treat her no different than anyone else on my team. She wouldn't want it any other way. You know, Lewis, she came from a military family, so she's a brat. Plus, she graduated with an accounting degree from Louisiana Tech University while her dad was stationed at Barksdale Air Force Base in Louisiana," Madden relayed. "She earned a scholarship from the Air Force to attend law school at LSU and served out her commitment as a lawyer with the Staff Judge Advocate."

"So, what in the hell is she doing here? We need shooters, not lawyers," Jeffers said while smiling at Madden.

"I understand she didn't exactly relish lawyering and wanted something more adventurous and exciting. So she applied to all of the federal law enforcement agencies and was accepted by the DEA. As a new special agent, she's paying her dues with some challenging assignments including our little jungle party here," Madden explained.

"Rob, who knows? We might just need a lawyer when this thing is over," laughed Jeffers.

Madden nodded his head and saluted Captain Jeffers before returning to his team's barracks across from the 18th Brigade headquarters.

Colonel Sanchez outwardly and proudly admitted to his superiors in Bogotá that his helicopter-assault operations against the FARC were enormously successful. He maintained that the live-fire exercises had become routine tactics—although Jeffers and Madden believed a little too routine. However, the Colonel's promotion to general was certainly not a routine matter. Also, Captain Fernandez, the Colombian Army officer in Madden's team, smelled a big fat promotion if they could successfully complete the final live-fire exercise. Fernandez was pinning his success on the back of Senior Master Sergeant Rob Madden.

Directly after the exercise briefing with Colonel Sanchez, Madden asked Little to have the combat control team meet at their makeshift briefing room in the unused hangar by the runway.

"Could I have your attention please?" Madden asked.

"Sergeant Madden, I'd like your input on this operation, and I will follow with my comments," said Fernandez. Madden heard the same old song and dance from this very ambitious captain.

"Thank you, sir, with your permission …," continued Madden, who was always respectful to the captain and ensured all knew that the captain was senior and in charge. Everyone knew who really called the shots, though: Madden. He had grown up in South America. Plus his language skills and courtesies paid huge dividends with the Colombian military officers and police. They trusted him.

"Yes, we're going into an area heavily influenced by the FARC, and I can guarantee you that caution will be our number-one concern in dealing with this area." Reassuring his team and group, Madden went on, "Listen, we've all worked well together with many successes in the last few months and, frankly, we're at the top of our game. We should be able to handle any contingency that comes our way. We can work this." The tension around the table eased up with Madden's words.

"Our strengths have been our teamwork and 'let's show them' attitude. So let's show these prima-donna Army guys who's really leading the way in this fight—Colombian combat controllers with DEA assistance." Madden's attitude was that the Colombians were in charge. He and his team were, as previously described, the "Christmas help."

"We'll be working exercise 11B and using the same template and tactics from the past exercises." Like the schoolteacher he was, Madden methodically briefed the mission to ensure that all team members knew their roles and responsibilities while calming any concerns.

Pointing to the open map on the wooden table, Madden said, "Tomorrow morning, with operations beginning at 0600, we're going to be clearing, maintaining, and securing two maximum-effort landing zones for Black Hawk and Huey copters. Landing zones north and south are located near the Venezuelan border a few kilometers from the Chancer River, approximately here."

"So close to the border?" was heard in low murmurs after Madden placed the wooden pointer on the map. The group was stunned and immediately turned silent, all trying to comprehend what Madden just conveyed.

"Sergeant Madden, I take it this may be different from our past landing-zone exercises?" asked DEA agent Bonnie McCord while nervously adjusting her briefing notebook and tightening the straps on her boots. "So close to the Venezuelan border—why an exercise, an exercise of all things, so close to the bad guys?"

Madden knew the answer but did not share it with the team. The other members had a good idea, though: someone's pride and ego was involved. "Okay, my friends. Let's get down to the nuts and bolts of tomorrow's exercise," said Madden who then turned to Captain Fernandez, "Sir, I recommend, with your permission, that we front-load and augment the north landing zone with more assets and resources due to its obvious sensitive location and probable heavy FARC activity there."

Fernandez nodded his approval, and the entire group was now focused on Madden's words. "Sir, I recommend that four Colombian controllers, four Air Force controllers, the Colombian police, and the DEA agents work with me on the north LZ. Also, sir, I recommend you take the remainder of the controller forces and work the south LZ," he continued while staring at the map.

Captain Fernandez gave a sigh of relief knowing he would not be responsible for the north. It didn't take a village idiot in the group to determine the south LZ was going to be a cakewalk as compared to the north in securing for the follow-on Army Special Forces and Colombian training companies.

CHAPTER

As planned, the following morning at exactly 0600 hours, the Colombian Black Hawk and Huey helicopters loaded with the maximum number of combat controllers and DEA agents gradually rose in the early dawn morning above the Saravena airport tarmac. Slowing rising and banking left, one headed for the north landing zone while another Black Hawk immediately followed carrying Captain Fernandez and his combat controllers to the south landing zone. Not a word was spoken while the controllers checked and rechecked their equipment. Madden made sure they were kept busy and their minds off the upcoming assault.

Through the continual whooping of the mighty Black Hawk rotors and the constant vibration of the helicopters, theirs was a cautioned optimism that this would be just another uneventful exercise. Madden thought differently; a sixth sense from soldiering around the world told him that something was terribly wrong. He continued to instill confidence in his controller team, however.

Madden was now working an informal inspection of equipment and controllers. "Okay, everyone, please listen up and finish your equipment checks. Again, we'll be working this landing as we have in the past. Let's drop the equipment ASAP and follow it down. You all have your assignments." Madden emphatically stressed, "Monitor channel four for landing communications and channel six for the assault tactical frequency. Do not use the radios unless absolutely necessary."

More last-minute equipment checks were made by the members—it helped relieve the tension. Madden was proud of his team, in particular the DEA agents who literally had no formal military skills prior to arriving in Colombia. They had come a long way and could be counted on if the going got rough.

"Let's have a clean and secure landing zone for our friends coming in. Rendezvous at the southeast sector of the north LZ near the dirt road," Again, Madden stressed, "Secure the landing zone. We can't afford to let the bad guys have it." A thumbs-up was given by all. The U.S. Air Force controllers were now looking at Madden and nodding—they were a close-knit family.

The Colombian pilot looked back at his passengers and raised his hand showing five fingers, which meant five minutes until ropes would be thrown out the side of the Black Hawk. Everyone was in position, a little tense, but confident. Madden was not. He could see the river a few miles ahead, and on the other side was Venezuela, his old neighborhood. *God, I hope this little hamlet is as nonthreatening as Major Domingo said it would be in the briefing*, he thought.

While they approached the landing zone, Madden noticed the area appeared to be quiet—too quiet for his taste. No farmers or peasants were visible, which was unusual. A disturbed Madden was beginning to read the signs and shouted, "Everyone, listen up! Change of orders." The new command got everyone's attention. "After we level the LZ, take up defensive positions near your areas of responsibility. Make reinforced shelters to the north of the LZ. If anyone comes toward us, they will come from the river. Ensure your weapons are readily available and carry as much ammunition as possible. You just may need it."

"What is Madden so excited about? Why is this exercise any different from the past?" asked one of the DEA agents.

"Listen, pal, Madden is pretty good at sensing things from doing this for tons of years. If he has concerns, I would recommend that you have concerns," answered Air Force combat controller Sergeant Sam Satterwhite.

The pilot's fist went up, and the giant Black Hawk hovered directly over the LZ with the dirt road and hamlet just in sight.

With precision speed, the combat controllers cleared the north LZ in short order. They were becoming experts in this line of work. Madden found the headset for his Mark V radio, made sure he was on the mission frequency, and contacted the follow-on helicopters.

He advised them the LZ was ready for hard landings—the winds were 240 degrees at 10 knots and visibility was unlimited and marked by purple smoke. Madden pointed at Sergeant Little to pop a couple of purple-smoke canisters to assist the follow-on copters in correctly identifying the LZ. The first two Colombian helicopters made perfect landings at the LZ, and the off-loaded troops were guided to the assembly area at the direct crossroads.

With the inbound copters uneventfully deploying their troops and equipment, Madden turned his attention to his main concern, securing the LZ. Placing his combat controllers in an LZ defense configuration, he radioed his team, "If we're attacked, the FARC will come en masse with light weapons and keeping the river to their backs for a quick escape. They'll wish to fight another day if shit hits the fan."

The Colombian police and DEA trainees on his team were asking each other, "What is Madden so excited about? Everything's going well, this is just another exercise."

"You'll rethink the word *exercise* when the bullets start flying!" yelled one of the Air Force controllers.

The Colombian military companies in training and the U.S. advisors assembled and moved quickly up the road to the hamlet. Converging no reserves, and like the other live-fire exercises, they always pushed forward at full strength.

"Task force lead, this is homecoming. Reporting status 0845L. Operations normal. All troops have disembarked at north LZ heading for assembly point. The wind is ..." In the middle of his radio call, Madden was suddenly hit with the deafening sounds of hundreds of small-arms fire rounds coming from the direction of the hamlet. Large explosions and the rattle and thud of heavy machine guns immediately caused Madden to hit the ground just outside the LZ. Most of the Colombian controllers and DEA agents had never experienced such an intense amount of fire, especially on the receiving end.

Madden immediately regained his senses and began to rally the scared and nervous controllers back to life. "Stay put in your positions and be ready to defend yourselves from the front. Hold the LZ!" Madden screamed over the radio to his team. Grabbing his government-issued M-4 rifle and Beretta 9mm pistol, Madden didn't know what to expect. He only knew that the LZ must be held.

"Strike lead south, strike lead south, this is homecoming. Over. Strike lead south, strike lead south, this is homecoming. Over," Madden repeated. He immediately went to the secondary-strike frequency and again attempted to raise strike lead south. No reply from either strike team set Madden's mind racing. The intense firefight in the hamlet just over the ridge was now a deafening roar with the horrific explosions and smoke rising above the jungle.

"Homecoming, homecoming. This is Chief Warrant Officer Baker in strike lead south. Can you hear me? Over."

Madden grabbed the radio, "Strike lead south, this is Madden. Chief, what the hell's going on?"

"Rob, we were ambushed coming into the hamlet. Both sides of the dirt road are filled with bad guys, believe FARC. Hold on …" Madden heard more automatic small-arms fire and explosions in the direction of the south LZ.

"Madden, Sergeant Madden!" a Special Forces advisor came on the frequency and screamed, "Rob, we are being hit by strong forces from both sides of the dirt road and a small force behind us. Lots of causalities—any words from the north?" Madden's mind was racing trying to work a plan of action with the resources he had on hand. Again, the advisor came on the radio, "Rob, can you get us some fire support on either side of the road?"

The sounds from the hamlet were nearly deafening, "Baker, this is Madden. Any strikes available will be close to position. Can you fall back and escape and evade to the safe area? Over."

Baker was now visibly excited and yelled, "No, damn it. Where the hell is strike north? Danger close!"

The rising smoke and explosions from the north company's positions confirmed Madden's worst nightmare: another terrorist force had ambushed the north Colombian company and its advisors. Madden now recognized the severity of the situation and was bewildered, scared to be exact. He mumbled to himself, "Get over this you piece of shit," slapped himself across his face and scolded himself for being such a worthless coward. Soon, the shaking and quivering subsided, and he was back to his old sergeant self.

"Strike lead north, this is homecoming. Over." Madden was back on the radio trying to make contact with anyone in the north LZ company, which was several hundred yards from the south LZ, and continued to observe massive explosions in the direction of the hamlet.

The radio finally crackled with, "Madden, this is Sergeant Peters. Over."

Madden recognized the voice as one of the Special Forces advisors with the north company. "Peters, this is Madden. What's your status? Over."

"Madden, the company was just entering the hamlet when we encountered regular FARC forces in fortified positions. We're stuck with heavy casualties. We need air support. Over."

Madden was frustrated and mad. He thought, *Damn it, air support! In all of our contingencies and planning since we've been here in Colombia, there was never any mention of close air support during live-fire exercises, and now half the world needs it.* After coordinating countless combat air support missions in Iraq and Afghanistan, Madden knew it would take hours to work any type of air strike. And under the circumstances, the Colombian Air Force could not be expected to generate such sorties—they were never expected to.

"Peters, this is Madden. Negative on close air support. It appears strike lead south is bottled up. Can you support the south with a flanking maneuver? Over." Madden knew that would probably be impossible, but he was required to ask.

Suddenly the radio crackled with advisor's detachment commander, "Rob, this is Jeffers. We're pinned down with no room to maneuver. I understand the south is in the same situation. Over." Jeffers urgently asked, "Any word on air support?"

Madden said to himself, "Air support?" He shook his head in disbelief. *What the devil are they talking about? Do they expect me to pull air support out of my ass? We're not back in Afghanistan or Iraq where the sky was filled with U.S. aircraft. We happen to be in the middle of the Colombian jungle.* Madden was abnormally tense and frustrated, still working on a plan in the back of his mind. The Colombian military company commanders were also on the radio ordering Madden to provide some sort of air support.

"Standby," was the reply he gave the commanders while he continued to work the problem. Madden knew, as did the others, that any type of close air support would be suicidal because the engagement was so close. The Colombian Air Force, as good as they were at drug interdiction and border security, was in no way prepared or trained for supporting ground troops with air support. Period.

"Take cover, controllers, and prepare to defend yourselves and the LZ," Madden advised. He was working his way around the LZ positions with his radio and encouraging his people to get ready for a fight. "Strike lead south and strike lead north, this is Madden. Over." Quickly, Madden was in contact with the acting commanders and advisors, "Air support is negative, I repeat negative. And mobile reinforcements are being worked on with HQ."

The ground commanders expected Madden to pull off some sort of air-support miracle while the firefights were still intense with sporadic fire coming down on his own LZ. The controller team appeared to be in position with the LZ closed to heavy-weapons fire. Madden had a plan to break the deadlock until reinforcements could arrive. He didn't like it, but it just might work.

"South and north companies, this is Madden. I have a plan, ready to copy!" The Colombians and the advisors were relieved that someone was planning something, anything, to get them out of this impasse. "Sir, I see this as the only way of dislodging these assholes on your front. The only way, as I see it." Madden continued with the details of the plan, "I'm taking what force I can spare here at the north LZ and move up behind the enemy line in front of you. These ranch hands don't expect any action behind them. If we can get in close enough to start lobbing smoke grenades into their positions, they may think we are setting them up with an airstrike."

Madden and his Air Force controllers had used colored smoke in the past to mark targets and trick the enemy into thinking there was an imminent air strike. "After we drop the smoke, we'll start yelling, 'Stay down! Air strikes coming in, stay down.' After the smoke is popped, my team will begin using small-arms fire to possibly ignite the route and panic among the FARC. I'll have my sniper target the FARC officers and sergeants. Let the others panic and run for the river. North and south, I need your permission to execute this plan now, over!"

The radio frequency was unnervingly quiet for the first time, when Captain Jeffers finally broke the silence, "Rob, sounds like a long shot, but it may be our only option. Good luck to you and your team. Out."

"North and south companies, this is Madden. Request you continue return fire for the next fifteen minutes until my team can get into position. I'll tell you when to begin popping smoke. Over."

Captain Jeffers came back on the radio, "Rob, what about communications out—if we lose contact with you?"

"Sir, if you don't have contact with me by 1410 hours, request you cease fire until we get the smoke into their positions. When you see the smoke, have your troops begin yelling in Spanish and English, 'Airstrike coming in. Airstrike, keep down.'" Captain Jeffers and the Colombian commanders immediately began passing the word down their lines about the upcoming plan. Madden and the advisors knew it was a long shot, but they had to try it.

Madden was trying hard to keep his emotions in check. He and his team were in all probability going to be murdered by this stunt, but it might be the only way out of this damned live-fire exercise. After briefing his team in the north LZ on the situation and upcoming plan to dislodge the terrorists, most did not want to even think about leaving the confines of the LZ, especially with the fight going on so near them in the hamlet area.

The DEA agents were extremely apprehensive about staying behind to secure the LZ, given the FARC's hatred of DEA agents. Madden's emotions were strained as he said, "Listen up, everyone. You can go with me to the firing line or stay here and secure the LZ for reinforcements. Our best chance of success rests with you staying here." The agents were resigned to the fact that Madden was correct. They prepared their LZ positions for an imminent fight with their old nemesis, the FARC.

Madden was almost shouting now due to the added horror of mortar bombs dropping close to the LZ area. "Okay, controllers, here's the plan. Load up with smoke grenades and ammunition. Drop everything else and prepare to move fast." As Madden was ridding himself of unnecessary equipment and loading up with grenades and ammo, he viewed the brave Colombian controller trainees, who had always been highly motivated and proved themselves, also loading up with only the essentials. "Team," Madden was now getting his spirit and confidence back, "we're going to follow that ravine, which should take us pretty close behind the FARC line. Get close enough to lob smoke grenades into their positions."

The controllers looked at him as if he had gone completely mad. "Sergeant Madden, are you expecting us to risk our lives just to throw some smoke grenades at the FARC?" asked one of the confused trainees.

"Sergeant Espalda, that's not the half of it. After we throw the grenades into their positions, we're going to begin yelling for the world to hear, 'Keep down, airstrike on the way!'" The faces of his team said it all. They understood completely that Madden was planning to trick the FARC into thinking a massive airstrike was on the way and create a panicked route.

"North and south strike, this is Madden. Controller team on the move to target area. Will contact you when in position. Over." Securing his mobile radio, Madden led the way, moving rapidly with his little army up the ravine while watching for anything that resembled a FARC rearguard.

The firefights remained as intense as ever with the ravine affording some cover for their movements. After ten minutes of moving low, the team stopped and surveyed the enemy lines— they were close. Madden whispered, "Okay, team. Look, we have good cover behind theirs, thank God." Using infantry hand signals, Madden directed the team members to their positions and stressed that no action was to be taken until Madden started the fight. Slowly and silently, the controllers took their positions on the line, readying their smoke grenades and weapons for a quick response.

Madden positioned himself in the middle of the line also preparing for action with one last radio call to the besieged companies. "North and south," he quietly called, "executing in one minute. Over." Both companies acknowledged.

Madden specifically tasked Sergeant Pepe Vale of the Colombian Army to join him on this mission because he was one of the top snipers on his team. "Pepe, we need you to find yourself a good position overlooking the line of FARC, a concealed location where you can get possible shots at their officers or NCOs."

"What?" asked Pepe, who was a little confused.

Madden instructed Pepe in a hushed tone, "Listen, when the FARC believe a strike's coming in on their positions, I'm guessing that they'll all want to get the hell out of their holes and head back across the river—I know I would. I want you to set up a sniper position where you feel you can get some good shots at the officers and NCOs who are trying to stop the panic. Let them run to the river and keep on going. Don't let the officers stop them. Take them out."

Pepe nodded his understanding with a smile and his usual, "Okay, boss." Soon he was off finding a good shooting position with his World War II vintage sniper rifle, an M-1 Garand. Pepe considered it the best rifle for long-distance targets.

Madden waited several minutes for Pepe to get settled, pulled the safety pins on two smoke grenades, and began tossing them into the FARC positions. The other team members immediately followed with a most unusual color of smoke drifting above the FARC positions. Stunned by the sudden appearance of smoke and the ensuing confusion, the enemy fire became sporadic, almost ceasing, along the line.

With the grenades now spewing smoke above the jungle canopy, Madden began screaming in perfect Spanish, "Keep down. Airstrike on the way, keep down!"

His other team members were also now yelling at the top of their lungs, "Keep down. Airstrike coming in with napalm. Stay low!"

Madden detected a lot of commotion and nervous chatter from the FARC positions. Suddenly, the sound of sporadic rifle shots was close and nearly over his head, "Good ol' Pepe," he thought, "has found some targets." Suddenly, Madden could make out the distinct uniforms and scarves of a few FARC soldiers running south on the dirt road, and more shots were heard from Pepe. More and more FARC followed, jumping out of their positions and racing for the border and river. It was a complete rout of the FARC's northern positions.

"Let them run, do not open fire! I repeat, do not fire." Madden did not want the FARC to turn and try to fight it out, he wanted them to run.

Madden signaled his team to make for the cleared positions and push the remaining die-hard FARC out into the open. Also, the remaining would take a chance to run for it or be taken prisoner. They were now running for the river and Venezuela.

"North and south, this is Madden. Teams are in position pushing east. Appears FARC is scattered and running toward the border." Madden shouted on the radio, "North, this is Madden.

Do not open fire on the forward positions. We are still in position and continuing to push the FARC east."

The north company commander contacted Madden, "Rob, great work. We'll be working toward the east to assist the south company. I have several causalities. Can you assist when you neutralize their positions? Over."

"Negative, sir, I need to get back to the north LZ. I left a skeleton force there of DEA and Colombian police, and I need to get back there now. Also, sir, recommend we only use north LZ for reinforcements and casualty evacuation until we get a clear picture of the south LZ. Over."

Madden was praying that the DEA and Colombian police were able to hold the LZ against the escaping FARC headed for escape and the river. The intense gunfire was now confined to the ambushed company in the south, but that too was subsiding with the newly arrived segments of the north company. The rout was now complete.

An extremely heavy and loud firefight was now evolving at the north LZ held by the Colombians and DEA. "Get as much ammunition as you can find. We're going back to the LZ," Madden ordered his small team. They looked at him with amazement and shock.

Madden could see the bewilderment in their faces, "Listen, we don't have a choice. No one is available except us—we have to go back. Get ready, we'll be moving fast."

"North company, this is Madden. Sir, imperative that you watch out for my team on your right side. We're moving fast back to the LZ." Madden lost them for a minute but came back, "Request support from your company at the LZ. Status of defenders in doubt. Over."

Captain Gomez replied, "Rob, just as soon as we join with the south company, I'll send a force over to the LZ, and see you there. Out."

"Okay, let's move, controllers." Madden took a short pause to look over his little team of Colombians and Air Force controllers. All were about as dirty and banged up as possible, but they were in good order. Madden noticed Pepe making his way back from his sniper position, "Great work, Pepe. Get some good shots in?"

Pepe nodded and said, "We sure got the officers out of the way, those mean bastards. While I was taking down their officers, they were taking down their own privates for running." He added, "It was a good idea, Rob."

The small controller team didn't have time to reflect on what they had just accomplished that morning; there were problems at the north LZ. "Let's go team, let's finish the job!" cried Madden, leading the way back to the LZ down the hill into the ravine. All knew it would be a risky fight at the LZ, and they prayed and hoped that the Colombians and the DEA agents could hold until they arrived.

The fighting on the dirt road to the far left was now subsiding as the FARC were literally running for the safe haven of Venezuela. The north company immediately took chase toward the south company and overwhelmed the fleeing FARC. A small force from the dirt road was racing toward the LZ.

"Move, move, move!" Madden shouted as his team burst into the LZ perimeter and immediately saw three terrorists firing their weapons while approaching DEA agent Bonnie McCord's position. McCord was putting up a good fight against several FARC from her position, but it appeared she would soon be overtaken. In a matter of seconds, Madden and Pepe fired on the FARC threatening McCord. The team's return changed and swung the initiative, and the FARC raced toward the river again.

A sudden mortar-bomb explosion threw Madden and Pepe to the ground. "Rob, I've been hit!" Pepe yelled. In a daze, Madden tried to turn around and assist Pepe but found that he was hit in the leg.

Madden had been wounded several times in the past in different wars. "I'll be okay," he said. "Pepe, hold on to my shoulder, I'm going to try to get you over there for now." Madden laid Sergeant Pepe Vale behind a clump of trees and administered what care he could. "You'll be okay, just stay here and don't move," he ordered.

Madden tied a large first-aid patch onto his own leg wound and slowly went back to the fight, checking on the other positions at the LZ. In silence and with tears, Madden found his loyal friend, DEA agent Hank Lee, dead just outside his hole with several dead and wounded FARC soldiers. The other three DEA agents, including McCord, sustained wounds.

A force of Colombian soldiers and advisors raced to the LZ while pushing the remnants of the FARC attacking force back to the river. The Colombian and Special Forces medics created a makeshift aid station at the initial rendezvous point, a few yards from the LZ. Madden found Pepe and painfully carried him to the aid station.

He also began searching for those in need—both Colombian and FARCs. Having grown up in Venezuela, Madden knew the FARC privates were just peasants who were drafted or "shanghaied" into filling the ranks for the FARC leaders. Madden had a lot of empathy for these poor, young people. Oh God, he hated to see such a waste of life.

"Madden, get your banged-up, dirty little ass over here now!" Special Forces medic Bill Lipscomb ordered Madden.

"Good idea, glad you thought of it," replied Madden.

Sergeant Lipscomb had Madden put on a stretcher while he cleaned his wounds and applied the necessary stitching and bandaging. "Bill, how'd we do today?" Madden was afraid to ask the question and did not really want to hear the answer, but he had to know.

"Rob, it appears we have a total of ten dead and around twenty wounded. Of the twenty, six were advisors plus Agent Lee." Lipscomb added, "It was bad, but it could have been a lot worse."

Madden was now close to tears and shaking. He nodded his head and repeated, "It could have been a lot worse."

The past action was catching up with Madden to the point where he felt like just walking out to the LZ to find a place to let his emotions out, but that would have to come later. After all they'd been through this day, his team was still responsible for the incoming relief helicopters due to arrive at the LZ. Madden mustered his team together while limping around with the aid of a sturdy stick.

"All controllers to me," Madden began rallying his team. Gradually, the familiar, dirty, and grimy faces began moving to Madden. "Team, copters are coming in—let's set up the LZ for their arrival."

In the late afternoon at dusk, Madden broadcasted, "Roger, homecoming."

"Expect arrival in fifteen minutes. Over," relayed the incoming flight of helicopters as they were nearing the north LZ.

Madden's team was in their expected positions and very thankful to hear the whooping noise of the incoming helicopters. The company of soldiers and advisors were being organized into their prospective deployment positions off to the side of the LZ. Soldiers began taking the body bags of the fallen soldiers and advisors to the edge of the LZ. The wounded followed, all to be taken to the Colombian military hospital at Santa Rosa. Regardless, Madden and his team would be the last to leave—it was the nature of the job. *So goes the life of an Air Force combat controller,* Madden thought to himself.

Late in the afternoon, the sun was gradually falling below the twisted jungle canopy over the rise from the LZ. Suddenly, the jungle came alive with the rapid, thumping sound of rotor blades and the appearance of the first two medical evacuation helicopters. "Homecoming, this is angel five. Have a good visual on the LZ. Request permission to land. Over."

Madden's team popped green smoke grenades to assist the chopper pilot in identifying the LZ and to gauge the wind. "Angel five, this is homecoming. You're cleared to land and begin immediate evacuation of the wounded. Over."

Madden returned to the radio to check the guard frequency and broadcasted to all aircraft, "Break, break—to all flight elements using the north LZ, homecoming is operational for all landings and takeoffs. Acknowledge by exception. Over."

No one answered meaning everyone understood. The loading of the dead and wounded took less than thirty minutes, and the rest of the companies began filing to the incoming troop utility helicopters for extraction. The sounds of the officers and NCOs could be heard pushing and encouraging their men and women to care for their weapons and inventory their equipment. Ultimately, they wanted to keep their teams busy and occupied.

After a matter of two hours, the only personnel left at the LZ were the two company commanders of the Colombian Army, two Special Forces detachment commanders, the remainder of the original controller team, and Madden.

"Rob, you saved our asses out there today. If you and your team did not move when you did, the training companies would have been spread all over the place." Captain Jeffers held Madden's arm, "Those of us left owe our lives to you." Emotionally drawn and tired, Madden looked at Jeffers and just nodded.

Waiting for the last two copters to transport them back to La Paz, Captain Fernandez gave Madden a big hug and with tears in his eyes stuttered, "Thank God you were here today. The Colombian military is very grateful."

Madden thought, "Leave it to the captain to give such an inspiring speech in the middle of this shit." Getting the hell out of the forward operating area, and alive, was the team's priority at the moment. Madden and the rest of the wounded were loaded first and air evacuated to the Colombian military hospital. The Colombian military and U.S. advisors, as protocol and tradition dictated, were loaded in the last copter headed back to La Paz.

Flying out on the departing Black Hawk in a web troop seat with side hatch open, Madden peered down at the LZ and the battle area. He was in awe that just a few smoke grenades and the bravery of his controller team might have saved the day. They had been very lucky today. The Black Hawk gained altitude, and Madden could see a few muzzle flashes from across the river very far away.

As he sat back and reflected, he thought of the old Barry Sadler Special Forces song, "I have fought in many places, seen wars a thousand places, but after this my wars are through, and I'll, I'll come home to you." Madden repeated to himself, crying now, "And I'll come home to you," while fixated on a now dirty and torn picture of his wife and two daughters. They were his life and his reason for living. *I have to take care of my girls when I get home*, he thought as tears streamed down his face.

CHAPTER

04

Word of Senior Master Sergeant Madden and his team's performance spread quickly among the Colombian military and the various advisors from several different countries and agencies. The U.S. Embassy in Columbia was kept abreast of the stories with pressure from Washington asking what military personnel were doing in a full-blown firefight with the FARC, especially with so many U.S. casualties. After debriefing the company commanders and the advisors, Colonel Sanchez was on the carpet to explain the rationale behind his so-called live-fire exercises when in reality they were "seek and destroys" involving U.S. advisors.

The Colombian officers and U.S. Special Forces commanders were emphatic that if Madden and his LZ team had not acted on their own and when they did, two Colombian training companies and two Special Forces detachment teams would have been forced to scatter and escape and evade back to friendly turf—if that was even possible under the circumstances. After ensuring an accurate report on the exercise was forwarded to his superiors at the military headquarters in Bogotá, Sanchez debriefed the remaining members of the companies and allowed them to rest.

Colonel Sanchez notified his commanding general that he would like permission to nominate Sergeant Madden for a decoration. "General Menendez, based on the accounts I am receiving from our field commanders and advisors, I would like your authorization to nominate Madden for an Air Force medal, possibly the Air Force Cross. My staff will do the paperwork and coordination with the U.S. Embassy."

General Menendez nodded his head in approval and asked, "Have you talked to our military attaché friends at the embassy about this? Last time I heard they wanted to give Madden a medal, they took a stripe and a promotion from him instead."

"Yes, I know the story," replied Sanchez. "Permission to move forward."

"Yes, of course, and I'll endorse it," added Menendez. "Oh, by the way, Colonel Sanchez," he continued, "you were very lucky the other day. Those eight FARC prisoners your people captured sang like song birds with tons of good information."

When the U.S. Embassy in Colombia got word the Colombian military wanted to begin the process for the award of the Air Force Cross to Madden, the embassy lights stayed on late into the evening. Sergeant Madden was a hero and legend among the military's Special Forces members. Many at the State Department considered him an out-of-control rogue, however.

One week after the deadly exercise, the Air Force military attaché to the U.S. Embassy, Colonel Ted Tuckerman, had just received the Colombian after-action reports and request for a decoration for Sergeant Madden. Colonel Tuckerman knew Madden only by reputation. Granted, he had met him at various embassy briefings and found him to be very professional, quiet, and polite—not unlike many of his counterparts in the Special Forces world.

Colonel Tuckerman walked the short corridor on the fifth floor of the embassy directly into the ambassador's office and waited for the receptionist to authorize his entry.

"Mr. Ambassador, good afternoon, sir. I need to speak with you concerning …"

"Ted, are you talking about that little incident that happened recently, something about a live-fire exercise and our guys being involved?" interrupted Ambassador Benton, who was on edge over this incident. "What's going on out there? We lost six of our advisors and a DEA agent with God knows how many wounded. Damn it, those advisors know they're not to get involved in any type of combat action. Is anybody even listening to our instructions?"

"Sir, our people were simply following orders from the Colombian brigade commander, Colonel Sanchez." Tuckerman continued, "I don't know how many times we've politely reminded him that advisors are prohibited from accompanying Colombian troops into potential conflicts."

The frustrated ambassador shot back, "Let me guess, another live-fire exercise right into the heart of FARC country. Correct, Tuckerman?" He fumed, "We lost six of our best soldiers and friends in a live-fire exercise. Well that's just great. Somebody had better start reigning in this Colonel Sanchez, because the shit has just started rolling down from Washington. Damn it, six of our best! This has got to stop now, do you read me Colonel?"

Colonel Tuckerman was used to the ambassador's temper and outburst. However, he knew Ambassador Benton was 100 percent correct. "Mr. Ambassador, one other issue that's going to be coming across your desk that you need to be aware of …"

"Yes, what now, Colonel Tuckerman?"

"Sir, during the engagement, it's reported that Senior Master Sergeant Rob Madden, the Air Force combat-controller advisor under Captain Lewis Jeffers's Special Forces detachment, saved the day for the Colombians and our advisors."

"Yes, Sergeant Madden. I do remember him from years past; what a character. How could he have saved the day?"

"Mr. Ambassador, I don't know the specifics, but the chief of staff for the Colombian military is working with my staff in processing an Air Force Cross for Sergeant Madden."

"What?" The ambassador jumped out of his seat shaking his head and shaking his finger at his attaché.

"Who in God's name is going to write the recommendation from our end?"

"Mr. Ambassador, I understand Captain Lewis Jeffers, who was with him, will be writing and endorsing the citation for Sergeant Madden. I've been briefed that the Colombian military chief of staff is also pushing it."

The ambassador could not believe what he was hearing. "Get Jeffers and Madden here immediately. I'm going to have a long talk with both of them."

"Sir," said Colonel Tuckerman attempting to control his sarcasm, "both Captain Jeffers and Sergeant Madden received serious wounds in the conflict and are recovering at the military hospital at Santa Rosa. Do you still want them to come here now?"

"Of course not," he replied after calming down and realizing the gravity of the situation. "Ted, please keep me advised on any paperwork the Colombians submit about Madden while we try to explain to Washington what our advisors were doing in a firefight with the FARC." Tuckerman nodded.

"That's all, Colonel. And keep me advised of what our Colombian friends want to do about decorations for our other men who were involved in this so-called exercise." Colonel Tuckerman saluted smartly and hurriedly left the office.

Ambassador Benton sat back in his chair and gazed out the window of his office facing the main cathedral in Bogotá. Madden's name evoked a few unpleasant and controversial times in his career as a diplomat. He had forgotten that Madden was working as a military advisor in Colombia.

Ambassador Benton reflected back to the middle of 2004 when he was an assistant to the ambassador in the Arab United Republic (AUR) and the CIA had roving clandestine Special Forces/CIA detachments scattered around the Middle East to hunt down and kill terrorists. The most effective weapon the teams could use was the Predator Unmanned Aerial Vehicle (UAV) drone that delivered two Hellfire air-to-ground missiles to literally anywhere in the world with deadly accuracy. The Hellfire was the preferred air-to-surface strike weapon launched from drone UAVs. The ambassador recalled that Madden was the Air Force combat controller on one of those teams and was responsible for coordinating and executing all Predator operations.

Madden was the only Air Force member he had ever met who spoke near-fluent Arabic, making him an invaluable asset on any Special Forces team—especially in the Middle East—and in particular, Afghanistan and Yemen.

Benton vividly remembered the morning the incident happened. *Why did he do it?* the ambassador continued to repeat to himself. *Why?*

During the spring of 2004, the Special Forces team received good CIA intelligence that a top al-Qaeda leader, Anwar Aldawasari, was meeting with other al-Qaeda leaders at a small airstrip in central Yemen. Weeks of planning and moving brought the American team to a bluff overlooking the airstrip near a cluster of small huts in the summer of 2004. The usual command-and-control bunker was immediately established, and Madden ran radio communications with the Predator pilots who were stationed halfway across the world at a small Air Force base in Indian Springs, Nevada, flying the Predators remotely by using satellite communications.

Both the State Department and the Department of Defense gave the order to take out Anwar Aldawasari—he was on the administration's target list to be killed or captured. Captain Jim Morton and his team were in a good concealed position to begin the operation. Sergeant Madden was in contact with the Predator's pilot passing checklist information such as temperature, wind, and target confirmations by lasers for positive accuracy.

A small stream of light pickup trucks led by a sedan could be seen by the sophisticated onboard cameras on the Predator and through the binoculars of the team members on the ground. Ambassador Benton had almost memorized the after-action report. Anwar Aldawasari and several of his lieutenants were positively identified. Madden passed on to the pilot that the targets were confirmed and then began the tedious process of gaining approval for the execution from State Department and Department of Defense.

During the coordination process with the State and DOD, a small turboprop passenger airplane buzzed out of nowhere and circled the small airfield looking to land. After it stopped on the small tarmac near the group of huts, the team noted visible Arab United Republic (AUR) markings on the plane—royal AUR markings, in fact.

The ambassador was again reliving those moments. He remembered the excited and intense radio traffic from the team regarding this surprise arrival of an AUR royal prince. *What the hell were they doing there?*

Madden was in contact with the Predator pilot advising him of the arrival of an unexpected AUR airplane. The pilot, monitoring and flying the Predator from his controls in Nevada, replied that it had almost hit the Predator while coming in for a landing. The pilot also advised that the Predator was running out of fuel and if Madden wanted to execute this mission, he'd better do it quickly.

Through CIA sources, it was quickly discovered that a member of the AUR royal family was there to meet Anwar Aldawasari for a hawk-hunting trip. Both the CIA ground team's steady binoculars and the cameras and sensors on the drone confirmed the AUR royal deplaned at the small airfield and began hugging his guests including Anwar Aldawasari. The State Department instructed the onsite Special Forces commander, Captain Morton, to "standby" while they sorted things out.

According to the reports, Madden was in no mood to sort things out and instructed the Predator pilot to continue to stay on station—a decision was immediate. Madden asked Captain Morton to check the radio frequencies again in the well-hidden, camouflaged pickup truck parked a few yards from the bunker. When the captain was out of sight, Madden authorized the Predator pilot to proceed with the mission and execute by placing one Hellfire missile in the group of huts and the other on the royal AUR aircraft parked at the edge of the field.

The pilot placed the cursors on his assigned targets according to the checklist and, using lasers, reconfirmed the target with Madden. Captain Morton was just returning from checking the radios when he saw two missiles streaking down to earth in the early morning skies. The shock of massive explosions was heard in the valley below.

The huts and aircraft were now balls of fire with thick black smoke rising on the horizon. Not a soul walked away from the carnage—it was over for Anwar Aldawasari, his lieutenants, and an AUR royal prince. Captain Morton returned to see that the strike in the valley was a success, but was confused about why, of all people, Madden executed the strike without his permission.

Ambassador Benton had filed the official government court of inquiry report on the Yemen strike and had kept it in his classified safe since its final legal review in January 2005. He had all but forgotten it, but now in 2007, it meant something— Madden was back. In simple terms, the inquiry stated that Madden asked Captain Morton to check the frequencies to ensure positive communications. However, the court of inquiry, all senior military officers and noncommissioned officers, knew Madden's motives were to save his captain and the rest of the team from having any culpability in the execution of the strike. Madden made sure that he, alone, was responsible for the strike.

The State Department and the AUR royal family were furious, demanding an explanation and justification for such an attack. When the Predator photos taken just prior to the strike showing an AUR royal prince embracing Anwar Aldawasari and his terrorist associates were delivered to the AUR embassy and the State Department, the clamor for retribution calmed to a point of embarrassment. The senior leaders at DOD were thrilled with the results of the strike, but expressed their regrets that a senior Air Force NCO would take action into his own hands that resulted in the death of a member of the royal family.

During the inquiry into the Yemen strike, officials from the State Department, DOD, and AUR diplomats met to resolve the situation on the diplomatic level. After the formal protests and posturing, it was agreed by all parties that the Yemen-strike incident never happened. Going public with it would have been a great embarrassment to both the AUR and the United States. The politically correct version of events indicates that a royal AUR aircraft crashed into a group of huts at a small Yemen airport killing several people. End of story.

However, the State Department and AUR pressed DOD to take some sort of judicial action against Sergeant Madden, even though the incident officially never happened. The AUR wanted a punishment so the royal family could save face. Given the encouragement from the State Department and demands from the AUR ambassador, the president of the United States personally contacted the secretary of defense and instructed him to take Uniform Code of Military Justice (UCMJ), the law that applies to all military members, action against Madden. The secretary of defense knew this was just a show by the president to accommodate the AUR ambassador. So, yes, the DOD would have to come down hard on Sergeant Madden.

Weeks after the incident and the inquiry, the assistant secretary of defense and the U.S. Air Force chief of staff scheduled a meeting with Madden at a small private office in the Pentagon. To them and anyone who knew about the Yemen strike, Madden was a hero who literally took the hit for the team. The assistant secretary informed Madden that due to the political sensitivity of the raid and his acknowledged participation, his promotion to chief master sergeant would be redlined, meaning cancelled. According to the chief of staff, this action would satisfy the AUR's quest for justice.

The chief of staff relayed to Madden that the U.S. Central Command (CENTCOM) commander explained to the royal family that being denied his promotion to chief master sergeant was an act worse than death for Madden. He was given his just punishment according to the commander. Everyone from the administrative clerks up to the generals knew that this was as bogus as it gets, but the royal family believed it. Rob Madden took one for the team by taking down Anwar Aldawasari, but now he would have to remain a senior master sergeant for the remainder of his career.

"No good deed will go unpunished," stated the Air Force chief of staff as he handed Madden a cold beer after their meeting at the Pentagon.

Now, as he placed the inquiry file back into the embassy safe and spun the combination dial, Ambassador Benton mumbled again, "No good deed will go unpunished."

Returning to his desk, Benton picked up his phone. "Colonel Tuckerman, would you please check with our friends in the Colombian military and get a status on Jeffers and Madden at the hospital in Santa Rosa?"

"Yes, sir," replied Tuckerman, "Colonel Sanchez relayed to us that he is going to the hospital this morning to check on them—will keep you advised, sir."

"Colonel Sanchez, good morning, this is Colonel Doctor Francis at the Santa Rosa military hospital returning your call." Colonel Sanchez was emphatic about getting the best possible care for his people. "Yes, Madden will be fine, but will require a few more days of care before sending him back to the United States on the military medical evacuation flight."

The doctor briefed, "His wounds are out of critical condition, but we'd like him to remain here for another week— just to be on the safe side. Okay with you?"

Discussions at the highest echelons of the Colombian military, U.S. Embassy in Bogotá, and the United States Southern Command (the military command that includes Colombia) were now centered on what to do with Sergeant Madden and his Air Force combat-controller team since the recent live-fire exercise. The Colombian military were thankful and in good faith stressed that Madden's actions warranted the Congressional Medal of Honor, and the rest of his team deserved Air Force Crosses for valor and selfless acts of bravery. To their credit, the Colombian military brass were unfamiliar with the various citations and awards earned by U.S. service members, but they wanted Madden's team to have the highest citations—regardless of what they were.

"What the hell happened at a live-fire exercise that we're looking to nominate advisors, who technically should have only been advising on base and not in the jungle looking for a fight, for the Medal of Honor and Air Force Crosses?" roared Lieutenant General Buck Baker, Commander of Southern Command.

"Sir, from our reports, it sounds like two Special Forces detachments were working with two Colombian Army companies in training when they accidentally ran into an unknown heavily armed FARC force and Madden ..." briefed Colonel Tom Zink, Southern Command's chief of legal affairs.

"Yes, yes, I know all about Sergeant Madden. What's his status?" asked Baker impatiently.

"General, it's reported he is doing fine and recuperating well from his wounds in a military hospital in Colombia. Sir, what are your intentions?"

Removing his reading glasses and raising himself from his chair, General Baker took a moment to look out the window and reflect on his days working with the Colombians early in his career. "Okay, Tom, please relay to our friends in Bogotá that we will work the paperwork for an Air Force Cross and Silver Stars. Yes, our guys certainly earned them from the various after-action reports we are receiving." Sitting back down at his desk, the general added, "Tom, please let me know when the doctors feel that Madden and the rest of his team can safely deploy back to home station."

"Will do, sir. And, sir, just a reminder, our people in Colombia have an informal rule that if they fight and train alongside the Colombians, they will also use the same hospitals and facilities. There will be no special treatment because they are Americans." Colonel Zink saluted smartly and departed the general's office.

Placing his reading glasses back on, General Baker again studied the reports and understood completely the importance of equal treatment for the Americans living and working in Colombia. "Captain Jeffers and Sergeant Madden, may God help you and your people," whispered the general.

CHAPTER

"Colonel Sanchez, good morning, sir. This is Sergeant Madden returning your phone call." Madden was instructed to contact Sanchez as soon as he felt up to it.

"Rob, I'm happy you're feeling better and will be out in no time. If you have some time in the next few days, I'd like to talk to you about the recent exercise. I hear you and your team played a major part in the success of the exercise, and there may be some awards coming your way." Colonel Sanchez knew very well what was happening but did not show it to Madden.

Madden already had more awards and citations than he could have ever imagined. There were more pressing issues on his mind that included returning home and retiring from the Air Force. "Thank you very much, Colonel. I look forward to meeting with you soon. We learned a lot of lessons in that exercise." Madden replied with a smirk but also thought, *I'm sure the Colonel learned many lessons himself.*

The Colombian military medical staff were outstanding during the week after the live-fire exercise. Special Forces doctor Captain Juan Ricardo continually checked on the progress of the advisors and team members wounded during the exercise. All were looking well and preparing for their return back to home base, Hurlburt Field in Florida.

Madden now focused on after-action reports and, most important, the letters home to family and friends of his wounded and deceased team members.

One letter began

"Dear Mr. and Ms. Milam,

It is with pain and sadness that I inform you of the loss of your son Kevin. I was privileged to work with Kevin as an Air Force combat-controller senior advisor in Colombia and ..."

Madden disliked writing the letters home about the losses of his team members and people he worked with in the field, and he openly cried when writing them. He felt the families deserved to know firsthand that their sons and daughters made a difference in the world as volunteers and were enthusiastic about their work and missions. Madden knew that someone else could have been writing a letter home about him, and so he always kept in mind the sorrow and pain of the family. He could not explain why the family lost a member, only the fine qualities and selfless spirit of the deceased. They all died heroes, they truly did.

Moving out to a small patio near the hospital, he found an empty spot where his emotions and thoughts caught up with him. He became emotional, naturally thinking that maybe he could have done something differently that would have saved his fallen team members. Madden tended to blame himself.

Later that day, Madden was very smooth and accustomed to hiding the truth from his wife and daughters when speaking to them on the phone for their own peace of mind. "Yes, sweetheart, I'm okay. It's just a scratch—something I ran into at a local park."

"Daddy, when are you coming home? I miss you terribly!" his daughter Angela excitedly yelled.

"Honey, I got my leg banged up a little playing soccer with some fellows in a local park. So, just as soon as my leg is better, I'll be home to my girlies."

His oldest daughter, Katy, grabbed the phone and said, "Dad, are you going to bring us back something from Colombia?"

"Have I ever forgotten my girlies, Katy? Absolutely—you know I always bring back the best of surprises." Both of his daughters were smiling and very excited to have their dad back home and, of course, with the surprises.

"Rob, we're all looking forward to your homecoming," said Madden's wife, Nancy, who was now smiling. "We girls have a lot of work for you to do when you get home. We need you here."

"Okay, honey, I'll be home soon. Miss and love you," Madden replied with tears.

"Rob, one other thing. The wing executive officer came by asking when you will get back. They're coordinating and scheduling your upcoming retirement ceremony," his wife added. "Oh, and honey, Dr. Tessa White, the school superintendent called and wanted to know if you'll be ready to start teaching this fall?"

The long talks with his wife and daughters about coming home and retirement brought Madden's spirits up while he recovered in the hospital. The family's dreams of Madden teaching school and completing his master's degree in teaching would soon be realized. Madden's wars were through, and he was going home to his girls. "Oh, how I miss my girls," Madden constantly commented while stationed in Colombia.

Waiting to return to home to Hurlburt Air Force Base in Florida, his team would still be responsible for accomplishing some overlap training and briefings with the newly arrived combat control team that was to replace them.

During one last conversation Nancy said, "Rob, the wing executive officer has been calling every day to ask about any retirement ceremony plans you might have. What should I tell him?" She continued, "Rob, he also said something about you being awarded an Air Force Cross for valor. I thought you said you weren't doing much in Colombia but training Colombian Air Force people in loading helicopters?" Madden did not know how to respond and was sure Nancy was misinformed about the Air Force Cross—the executive officer must have confused Madden with someone else he reasoned. Eventually he would tell her the whole sad story, but not now—it could wait.

To retire from the Air Force at thirty-eight years old and start a second career as a local elementary schoolteacher was his long-sought-after dream. Madden and his family had sacrificed their time and effort to ensure Madden earned his degree and teacher's certificate. The world was bright with great expectations in the Madden household. Madden was now more than ever anxious to get home to his family, get retired, and get back to teaching.

CHAPTER

"Come on, girls, if you want to go to the beach," Nancy Madden yelled to her daughters who were working on a new dance routine for an upcoming school production. Nancy wanted a break from grading papers for her summer-school classes in June 2007. She always looked forward to a relaxing afternoon at their favorite beach spot near their home in Mary Esther, Florida—next to Rob's home military base at Hurlburt Field.

"Let's go, Mom. We're ready," Katy eagerly announced as she hurriedly dragged her younger sister, Angela, to the kitchen where their mother worked on the kitchen table scattered with piles of papers.

Looking up from the table, Nancy asked the girls if the dance routine was looking good for the big performance, and both girls smiled and nodded their heads. "Okay then, let's get our suits and towels. Off to the beach we go," Nancy said.

They loaded up the Honda Civic and headed to the beach—one they had gone to at least twice a week for many years. The routine was normal for the Madden girls when Rob was away on assignment. After Nancy parked the Civic in their usual spot, the girls unloaded their towels, umbrella, and most important of all, their books. The Madden family loved to read while listening to the rhythm of the surf as it rolled in and splashed against the shore.

On the other side of the beach's parking lot, two men in the front seat of a nondescript white Ford van focused on the movements of Nancy Madden and her two daughters. Watching through binoculars, they observed the family making their way through the sand dunes to the trail leading to the beach.

"Let's move," commanded the van driver as he maneuvered to park it directly next to the Maddens' Civic. The men immediately got out of the van, locked its doors, and were picked up by a waiting Mercedes sedan. The Mercedes departed the parking lot and headed east toward Ft. Walton Beach.

Two hours later, Nancy Madden looked at her watch and called to her daughters playing in the surf, "Okay, girls, time to go. Get your stuff and let's head back to the car." While walking back, they sang songs and recounted their day at the beach, looking forward to the day when Rob would return and they could go to the beach together. But for now, life went on.

Nancy noticed the white van parked next to her vehicle and wondered why it was parked so close when the lot was practically empty. She immediately thought something was wrong, hurriedly gathered the girls, and inspected the Civic for any type of damage or break in. Seeing none, she quickly ordered the girls in the car, locked the doors, and started the engine.

The explosion created a huge fireball above the beach parking lot and a deafening concussion that spewed hunks of metal and debris hundreds of yards away. The Ford van and Honda Civic were gone in a fraction of a second, and the gas fire from the explosion was seen as far away as Ft. Walton Beach. Beach goers witnessed the explosion, and many were severely injured from the blast.

The medical, fire, and police first responders arrived immediately after the explosion with sirens blaring and various colored flashing lights illuminating their vehicles. The entire beach area was cordoned off by the police while the local investigators and federal agencies began their investigation. Fragments from one vehicle showed it was registered to a Nancy Madden from Mary Esther, Florida. Finding the owner of the white Ford van would be extremely challenging—it was scrubbed clean of any type of identification markings or ownership—"very professionally cleaned," one federal agent noted in his report.

Watching the law enforcement agencies at the blast site from a towering apartment building, a man on a high balcony said to his partner in a thick Middle Eastern accent, "It is settled now, Madden."

Rob Madden was giving ground-school instruction to several Colombian lieutenants at the airbase near the military hospital. "It's essential to keep that backup-guard frequency open with the lead pilot during the initial approach to the …," Madden stopped in midsentence because he noticed some unusual activity at the base operations building.

Official vehicles were slowly making their way to his location carrying what appeared to be high-ranking military officials and Colonel Sanchez. Next, two official embassy helicopters landed, and key embassy officials, including Ambassador Benton, were being escorted to the operations building. Madden and the lieutenants got up from their map-filled table and observed the sudden arrival of so many officials with curiosity. *But what the heck,* Madden thought, *this is Colombia.*

"Lieutenant, sir, I have no clue what's happening, but it's sure attracting a lot of important people," he said to the group. The officials slowly headed for the little ground school in the south hangar.

"Sergeant Madden," one lieutenant commented, "maybe they want to talk to you about the crossroads exercise."

"Yes, Lieutenant, but I hope not. We need to get you trained." All of the energetic lieutenants were nodding their heads in agreement. The official caravan slowly made it to the front of the hangar.

"Attention!" Madden announced at the entrance of the unexpected party. Madden and the lieutenants stood at attention, and Colonel Sanchez asked the lieutenants to return to base operations and remain there until released.

"Yes, sir," replied the lieutenants as they left the hangar. Madden had no clue what was going on, but he somehow expected the worst. His sixth sense told him something was horribly wrong; he could just feel it.

Ambassador Benton approached Madden with the Southern Command Chaplain Colonel Joseph Boone and Command Sergeant Major Jim Vick. Madden noticed there were tears in the eyes of all present. "Ambassador Benton, sir, I'm honored and surprised to see you. Colonel Boone and Command Sergeant Vick, good to see you too." Madden went back a long way with Boone and Vick. The seconds felt like hours while he tried to determine what was going on.

Still standing, Madden was trying to control his emotions, as he'd done so many times in the past when facing adversities around the world, when the ambassador placed his arm around Madden's shoulders and said, "Rob, why don't we sit for a minute." Colonel Boone seated himself next to Madden, while Sergeant Vick stood behind him.

No, no, not this. Oh God, please not this, thought Madden reading their faces. *Not now, God. Oh my God no, please no.* Madden had been through this ritual a hundred times in the past when caring for his airmen and troops who were being notified of the loss of a loved one. He had been on the receiving end twice for the sudden deaths of his father and mother. He still carried the pain of those losses. "Please, sir, tell me straight up. What happened?" Madden asked, as usual quickly regaining control of his emotions.

"There was a horrific tragedy at home. Rob, your wife and two daughters are with our Lord," Colonel Boone sadly stated while trying to get control of his own feelings. Madden could not grasp the impact and severity of what he had just heard.

"What do you mean? Are you sure? No, no, certainly there's a mistake," said a confused Madden. "No, no—not my girls!" he cried, now comprehending the magnitude of the few words from the command chaplain. Madden, now with tears flowing down face, kept asking, "Who's going to take care of my girls?" Little more was said in the hangar—they all had been through this many times and knew the protocol, including Madden.

"What happened, what happened?" a frustrated and confused Madden asked Colonel Boone.

"Rob, from what the Florida authorities are telling us, Nancy and the girls were killed when a large explosion occurred next to their vehicle while they were at a beach near your home.

It appears someone, and they don't know who yet, parked a van full of explosives next to their car and ignited it when they got in," explained Boone.

"In other words, my family was specifically targeted and murdered. Is that what you are saying?" a stunned and shaken Madden asked.

"Yes, Rob. It looks that way right now, but the incident is still under investigation." Boone added, "I know this is a sad and difficult time, but it is essential that you speak with the feds as soon as possible regarding who you think might have been behind this."

"There is no doubt in my mind who is behind this," yelled Madden attempting to control his rage. "I'll contact the authorities on what I know on the flight back to Hurlburt."

"Okay, Rob. Let's get you back to Florida," Boone said while helping Madden to his feet and holding his shoulder.

"Rob, we have a plane waiting for you at Bogotá that will carry you back to Hurlburt." The ambassador continued, "Arrangements are being made as we speak."

"Thank you, Mr. Ambassador. I'll be ready to go," Rob said while trying to gain some composure and patting Benton on the back.

"Sergeant Madden, all of the members of the Colombian military feel your loss. You're a member of our family," offered Colonel Sanchez, who was deeply moved by the tragic consequences facing his friend.

"Command Sergeant Vick, would you please assist Sergeant Madden with getting his affairs in order and his bags packed for the trip home?" requested Colonel Boone.

"Absolutely, sir. Rob, how about you and I see what needs to get done now?" Vick also was trying but failing to hold back his own emotions. Tears were flowing from this hardened combat veteran of several wars.

"Ambassador Benton, Colonel Sanchez, Colonel Boone, and Command Sergeant Vick—gentleman, would you excuse me for a few minutes? I'd like to go outside and be alone for a while."

"Please, Rob, take your time. We'll be up at base operations," replied Colonel Boone.

The officials returned to their vehicles and made their way back to the operations building while Rob, holding back an immense, bottled-up grief, headed for a path near the edge of the base. He had traveled this path before when looking for a little tranquility and reflection. In the past, he had hoped and prayed for great things in the future for his girls and himself. Sitting on a stump near the tree line, Madden's grief was so intense that he could no longer hold it. Memories of his family flooded his mind and he could not imagine life without them. They were his life; they were his only world.

He questioned himself, *What happened? Could I have prevented this? Why wasn't I there? Why, oh God, why?* The natural response to a tragic loss was taking its toll on Madden. *Life is not worth living without my girls,* he kept thinking. On his knees, Madden prayed to the Almighty God for the final peace of his girls and asked for the strength he needed to get through this ordeal and avenge their murders. Madden took a small bible he had always kept in his shirt pocket and began to read Job in the Old Testament.

In the distance, Command Sergeant Vick had a good view of Madden making his sad and painful journey down a path next to the tree line. Vick did not like seeing his old comrade of many years in this state. Experience, however, had taught him that anything could happen. He especially did not want his friend to do anything stupid in his distressed state of mind. Vick watched from a safe distance just to ensure his safety.

At noon, Madden suddenly stood up from the stump, looked up at the sky for a moment, then put his hat back on his head, and headed back up the path to the hangar where Sergeant Vick waited. Madden looked at Vick and nodded, knowing full well that Vick had probably been watching him from a distance, a standard procedure.

"Rob, let's get you on the flight back to Hurlburt Field. The ambassador's arranged for the diplomatic plane out of Panama to take you back this evening." Vick gave Madden a quick pat on the back and said, "How about you and I get your bags packed?"

Working their way back to the operations building, they saw Colombian soldiers and airmen in a loose formation on the field tarmac. Everyone was saddened by their friend and advisor's tragic loss. The senior NCO called the group to attention and presented Madden with a Colombian military banner that he tearfully accepted. He said goodbye to each individual soldier and airman and recounted small tales of their adventures together. A small contingent of DEA agents in training also stood with the Colombians to say their farewells.

The Colombian Black Hawk helicopter was starting to make its whining startup. "Senior Master Sergeant Madden, we took the liberty of packing your personal items and gear for you. Hope you don't mind," said Special Forces Detachment Commander Jeffers and DEA Agent Bonnie McCord while both giving Madden a hug.

"Thanks, Lewis. Thanks, Bonnie. I'm sorry I have to leave you all sooner than expected."

With tears in her eyes, McCord grabbed Madden's hand and gave it a firm hold before letting go and said, "Rob, please call me if you need me for anything. I mean it." McCord had a special place in her heart for Madden and, at that point, she realized that she always would.

"Rob, we'll see you at Hurlburt," said Captain Jeffers.

With the Black Hawk rotors idling, Madden was escorted to the copter by the ambassador, Colonel Boone, Colonel Sanchez, Command Sergeant Vick, and a few Special Forces advisors, DEA agents, and Colombian sergeants. Attempting to hold back a stream of tears and trembling, Madden gave a final salute to his escorts and said, "Wherever I go, I will always recall with great fondness and affection the family I got to live with, work with, train with, and fight with here in Colombia."

Madden was aware he did have a rough side to him and had many faults of which he relayed to his friends and comrades, "Thanks for putting up with me, and good luck to each of you."

With that, Madden's gear and equipment were secured in the helicopter as the currents picked up from the powerful rotor blade spinning above them. Madden instinctively took his pathfinder seat in the Black Hawk as he had done so many times in the past with Command Sergeant Vick joining as his escort. Glancing at Vick, Madden wondered, "How many times has he served as an escort under similar circumstances? Probably too many to count."

With the sensation of the Black Hawk lifting up and the blast of air from the whipping blades, Madden waved a final goodbye to his friends. The gravity of the situation reentered his mind, and his thoughts now turned toward the tragedy at home. Home, where was that now? In all his years of working around the world in the Air Force, home had always been where his loving and patient wife and his daughters were.

Everything they'd planned for the future was now gone: no love, no future, no promise. His mind was now flooded with memories—possibly nature's way of trying to keep his girls alive, his only way of connecting with the loves of his life. *If only I'd been there. If only I'd opted out of this assignment. If only,* he kept thinking.

The Black Hawk landed at the military base in Bogotá, where the diplomatic jet was waiting for Madden and the American military advisors wounded at what was becoming known around Colombia as the "live-fire exercise crossroads." A small group of teachers and students from the local mission school gathered in the parking lot with one student holding a Colombian flag and the other holding the Stars and Stripes of the United States. Others held small bouquets of flowers in their hands.

Madden and his Air Force combat controllers, who were all fluent in Spanish and certified Air Force instructors, spent their off-duty time in the local schools, teaching English and math or assisting in rebuilding classrooms. Whatever assistance the local teachers needed, the controllers were always glad to help. Granted, the controllers were not all choirboys, but they all had good hearts.

Command Sergeant Vick oversaw the transfer of Madden's equipment onto the jet while Madden was quite moved to see the little school group saying goodbye and paying their respects. Madden walked over to the teachers and students and immediately embraced them and wished them the best of luck in the future. He felt honored to receive the students' little self-made display of flowers.

"Many thanks, my friends. Study hard, listen to your teachers, and pray to God every night." Madden looked at every child as if they were his own and thought to himself, *Oh God, please care for these children. Please watch over them.*

"Rob, we need to go, your gear is on board," Vick patiently reminded him. Madden took one last look at the gathering and waved his final goodbye. In a matter of minutes, the jet was in takeoff configuration and heading down the lighted Bogotá runway for Hurlburt Field, Florida, Madden's home base.

"Sergeant Madden, welcome aboard. Our flight time is estimated at eight hours and twenty minutes," the steward warmly briefed him. "I have a cell phone for your use, and I will assist you in obtaining any numbers you may need. Please do not hesitate to ask for anything. Oh, one more thing," said the steward while reviewing his checklist, "your gear is located in the aft storage compartment, and you can have access at any time during the flight. Again, Sergeant Madden, it is an honor and pleasure to have you onboard." The steward returned to his galley.

Left alone with his thoughts, Madden's mind kept repeating the same themes: seeking revenge for the murders of his girls and how he might have prevented this tragedy. Madden felt it was entirely his fault because he wasn't there to protect them.

"Rob, I'm sorry to bother you, but it's imperative you speak to the federal authorities and local law enforcement regarding the people who might be responsible for this action," said Command Sergeant Vick. He was in contact with the FBI and Florida State Police who wanted to speak with Madden as soon as possible about potential suspects.

"Jim, I'm ready now. Let's get a conference call patched to the FBI, and I'd greatly appreciate you monitoring the call just in case something happens to me," Madden concurred.

Vick nodded his head and began setting up a conference call with appropriate points of contact within law enforcement and the federal agencies.

"Good morning, Sergeant Madden, this is Special Agent Frank Sullivan at the FBI district office in Ft. Walton Beach, Florida—can you hear me okay?"

"Yes, sir, I read you loud and clear, and I also have with me Command Chaplain Colonel Boone and Command Sergeant Vick," Madden replied.

"Sergeant Madden, besides myself, I have Special Agent Denny Wilkins, Colonel Brad Tullis with the Florida State Police, Deb Houghting with the CIA, and our respective staffs also monitoring this call. Okay with you, Sergeant Madden?" asked Sullivan.

"Okay, let's proceed," Madden acknowledged, "I will provide you with any information you require. Let's find these godless butchers."

"Every available asset has been committed to finding these terrorist murderers—and with your assistance, we will find them," Sullivan affirmed.

"Thank you, Frank, and please call me Rob," Madden replied while trying to temper his righteous anger.

"Rob, we are aware of your background and history overseas while working many special-ops missions. We understand some groups have identified you as being responsible for killing many of their members. Could you provide us with more details and information on these groups?" asked Sullivan.

"Yes, thanks to our State Department, it was intentionally released that I, alone and acting as a rogue Air Force sergeant, was responsible for the deaths of al-Qaeda leader Anwar Aldawasari and a royal prince from the Arab United Republic." Madden continued, "I am sure al-Qaeda, the AUR, or both are responsible for the murders of my family."

Not a word was heard on the conference call as the agents and their staffs were attempting to comprehend what Madden had just said.

"Also, I understood through CIA intelligence sources that the brother of Anwar Aldawasari, Humza Aldawasari, has let it be known through al-Qaeda circles that he will seek a holy revenge against me and my family as soon as he is released from Guantanamo," Madden recounted.

"Yes, Rob, we can confirm your information," said special agent Sullivan. "Any other suspects?"

"Just coming from fighting the FARC with the Colombian military, I believe it obvious that they also might want some retribution against me," Madden added. "Colonel Sanchez had a habit of bragging about the wonderful U.S. advisors working for him. I'm sure the FARC took notice and remembered our names," concluded Madden.

"Rob, we cannot express our sympathies enough to you for your loss. However, rest assured, we will find those responsible for the murder of your family," promised Sullivan.

"Frank, from your initial assessment, who do you think did this?" asked Madden emotionally. He wanted a straight answer so he could make his own plans for revenge.

Knowing Madden's reputation as a seasoned, professional special-operations operator, Sullivan decided it was unwise to tell Madden what they already knew about the explosion and who they believed were their primary suspects. Sullivan also did not mention their suspect already in custody: a terrorist who was interrogated with startling results.

"Rob, we're still working the investigation and will keep you updated as we get closer to a determination and please, Rob, please, don't take any action on your own. It might corrupt our work and identify our sources," Sullivan asked.

"Okay, Frank. Do what you have to, but please keep me advised."

Shutting down the conference call at the FBI district office, Frank Sullivan looked around the conference room at his staff and asked, "Any questions or thoughts?"

"When will you allow Madden the information we've already gained from the terrorist?" asked a young new agent.

"When the time is right, Madden will be provided the information he is seeking. For now, the data received and the sources are classified top secret. It cannot be divulged to anyone outside of the Bureau who does not have a need to know," Sullivan warned. "This terrorist attack on Madden's family has international implications and appears that it may be part of an even bigger plot currently unraveling."

"Do you consider Madden in any type of danger from the same terrorists when he returns from Colombia?" asked Special Agent Wilson.

"No, probably not," answered Sullivan. "According to what we've gathered from the interrogation of our terrorist, the only goal for this particular mission was settling an old score with Madden and making him suffer on earth from the loss of his family.

"However," Sullivan warned, "if Humza Aldawasari is ever released from Guantanamo, Madden's life would definitely be threatened and he would need to be monitored."

After getting off the conference call, Madden disciplined himself by grabbing a legal notepad and a pen from his uniform pocket. *Okay, Rob,* he thought, *let's get a hold of things and quit feeling sorry for yourself. We've got work to do.* Madden began diligently writing checklist items, the things that needed to be accomplished, on his legal pad. The items included funeral arrangements, calls to family, travel plans, and disposition of the estates. It was second nature for Madden throughout his career— either he was writing checklist items as an instructor/advisor or following checklist items. For Madden, following the checklist was gospel.

After a few hours, Colonel Boone worked his way back to Madden's little table and asked how the arrangements were coming. Both Boone and Madden were professional military and each knew his responsibilities and protocol. As sad and tragic as the situation was, they both wanted to see this through for the dignity of the families and military members.

As the diplomatic jet flew north on a moonlit night, Colonel Boone patiently worked with Madden on the fact-of-life details immediately facing Madden. For hours, Colonel Boone and Madden discussed items such as funeral arrangements and retirement plans. Boone knew Madden would be facing a tremendous cultural shock from losing his family to retiring from the Air Force. Madden could not see the impending shock, but Boone could. Finally, Madden was able to sleep.

"Sergeant Madden, excuse me, sir," said the steward trying to wake Madden from a deep sleep. "Sergeant, we'll be landing at Hurlburt in a few minutes."

Coming to his senses and hoping he was waking up from a bad nightmare, Madden instinctively looked at his watch preparing to execute some team action. But he wasn't with his team—he was very much alone.

Seeing Madden was awake, Vick took the seat across from Madden and said, "Good morning, Rob. Did you get some sleep?"

"Never miss the opportunity to take a nap—wherever you are," chuckled Madden.

Vick thought to himself, *Okay, let's get Rob focused here.* So he said, "Rob, I remember you telling me a while back you had promised your wife that after retirement, you would teach full time and work on getting your master's degree, a pretty noble goal. Rob, you're a gifted instructor, and I've earned the right to say it," Sergeant Vick whispered, knowing Madden desperately needed something to live for, something to hold on to.

Madden grinned and nodded his head, acknowledging his love for teaching and the many challenges that went along with the responsibilities, especially in today's world. "Ah yes, the promise to my wife and kids, the promise. Can't go back on the promise," repeated Madden.

The diplomatic jet landed at Florida's Hurlburt Field during a heavy rain shower. Madden's family members and representatives from his unit awaited his departure from the jet. Madden greeted each while attempting to hold back his tears.

"Whatever you need, do not hesitate to ask," was the standard and universal phrase spoken by those greeting Madden. He appreciated their thoughts and efforts, but nothing could relieve him of the burden he carried, and they knew it. Again, standard procedure.

All agreed, especially his superiors, that Madden had to constantly be kept busy the next few weeks until his retirement. Colonel Jerry Barton, 1st Special Operations Wing Commander, knew the feeling so well after losing his parents and brother while deployed overseas. Keeping Madden busy was the best medicine, and Colonel Barton was going to do just that.

The funeral for Madden's wife, Nancy, and his two daughters was planned for three days after Madden's return to Hurlburt. It took place at the Hurlburt Field Chapel where Nancy and Rob were married more than fifteen years earlier. The Madden family was popular, and the chapel was filled to capacity with their many friends and relatives. During the funeral, Madden reflected on how his life had truly started here with his wonderful wife and how it now felt as if it were ending here as well. Madden was learning more of the circumstances surrounding his family's death, and he also realized he was being given vague information—the officials were short on details. Fueled by the need to avenge the murder of his family, Madden was convinced it was one of two organizations—maybe both.

As soon as the funeral was over, Madden would begin debriefing Air Force Special Tactics members (combat controllers) and Special Operations command officers on his experiences in Colombia. Colonel Barton tasked Madden with authoring a complete report on Air Force combat-controller operations in Colombia to include the infamous live-fire exercise at the crossroads. Besides being a fair and compassionate commander, Colonel Barton was an ambitious career officer who recognized the value of riding Madden's current star power.

Senior Master Sergeant Madden's Colombian report was considered by many in the Special Operations community to be a colossal surprise. Most had no idea of the types of tasks the Army and Air Force Special Operations were conducting with the Colombian military. From testifying before a Congressional committee to briefing cadets at the United States Air Force Academy, Madden became a briefing (basic teaching) zealot in this environment.

Colonel Barton ensured there was no rest for his rising star, Madden. Next stop: briefing the Air Force elite at the Air War College in Alabama. The military audiences were impressed by Madden's briefings and exploits paying particular attention to his language skills and background, with fluency in both Spanish and Arabic. Also, many remembered the controversy surrounding Madden's call, in 2004, to strike al-Qaeda terrorists in Yemen along with an AUR prince, who happened to be at the wrong place at the wrong time.

The audience was warned by the Air War College superintendent not to question Sergeant Madden about his involvement with the Yemen operation; that topic was off limits. However, the superintendent did have a private meeting with Madden to learn all the details of the well-known takedown of one of the world's most-wanted terrorists.

When asked by senior officers where he received his training in languages, Madden often replied, "Arabic and Spanish are the languages of oil-field trash like me. I'm just a product of my environment."

During the briefing at the Air War College, a colonel asked, "Sergeant Madden, we understand you will be retiring from the Air Force soon. What are your next career goals? CIA, DIA, defense contractor?"

"Thank you for asking, but I'm proud and privileged to be a certified schoolteacher. I am going back to teach school."

This response stunned the audience of high-ranking military officers from all branches of the service. They couldn't fathom his answer. "Here's a guy who has most of the medals and badges authorized by the Air Force and he is going to hang it up and teach school kids. Why?" they whispered.

CHAPTER 07

After a rewarding and exciting twenty-year career in the Unites States Air Force, Senior Master Sergeant Rob Madden was finally retiring. The shock and sadness of losing his wife and two daughters was always on Madden's mind where he knew it would stay until his own passing. Like his retirement from the Air Force, their deaths were just another tragic and sad passage in his life.

"Come on, Rob, snap out of it," Madden yelled at himself in the mirror one night. "Get your shit together, you whiny baby." Clumsily getting up and half dazed, he looked for another bottle of his favorite whiskey in the kitchen to replace the empty one. Finding it, he opened the bottle while crying and screaming, "What was I thinking? Where are my girls?" Madden finally came to when the phone rang in the morning.

"Good morning, Rob. Tony St. Amant here. Are you ready for your retirement ceremony next week? We've got to get rolling with the paperwork. Now." Madden knew Chief Master Sergeant Tony St. Amant from the old days in the combat-controller arena. St. Amant was now serving as the senior enlisted advisor for the 1st Special Operations Wing, making him the top enlisted man at Hurlburt.

"Hey, Tony. How in the heck are you?" Madden worked at trying to make normal conversation even though, at the moment, he felt like throwing up. St. Amant knew Madden well and was aware of the tragic deaths of his girls.

"Rob, things are good. Of course, the wing is stretched all over the world and losing you to retirement isn't helping our cause now, is it?" St. Amant came to his real reason for the call, "Rob, I'd like you to meet me at my office today at 1500. Can you make it?"

Feeling quite sick now, Madden agreed, hung up, and immediately went to the toilet to throw up. Getting back to his sofa, Madden mumbled, "Whoa, I wonder what I just agreed to? Okay, better sober up."

Being a professional, Madden soberly walked straight into the headquarters of the 1st Special Operations and tried to hide his previous night's drinking binge. Upon entering, colonels and airmen, alike, wanted to talk with the now-famous Rob Madden. All showed respect and sympathy for his loss and congratulated him on his upcoming retirement. They would miss him— everyone liked Madden.

Amid the commotion of Madden's arrival at headquarters, a large crusty old sergeant embraced him and said, "Rob, great seeing you. You sure haven't gotten any prettier."

"Neither have you, Chief St. Amant. Neither have you," he replied.

Walking down the illustrious hallway of honors won by the wing since its creation during World War II, St. Amant had his arm over Madden's shoulder on the way to his office. Both men found themselves seated in a small conference table located in the chief's large office.

"Airman Hunter, would you please get Sergeant Madden and me some coffee?"

Like so many other senior personnel in the military, Chief St. Amant had an extensive "I-love-me" wall that perfectly reflected a large and extended ego. Madden mused over such displays and often kidded officers and sergeants alike about such walls. It was known throughout the organization that Madden's "I-love-me" wall consisted of a family portrait of his wife, daughters, and parents. That was all, just his family.

While Airman Hunter served the coffee, St. Amant requested that he and Sergeant Madden were not to be disturbed.

"Rob, it's great having you back. We know all about your actions in Colombia, and you've done a great service to the wing." Madden continued to regain his senses from the night before and

St. Amant recognized his condition—after thirty years in the Air Force, he had seen it all. "I have all of your retirement paperwork here. The wing's executive officer Captain Sullivan is working out the ceremony and protocol. Everything is scheduled for the end of this month."

Madden nodded his head in agreement.

"Frankly, Rob, we, meaning the wing commander and the command, would like you to reconsider your retirement. We need you now more than ever."

Madden was expecting this conversation. Special Operations had carried the lion's share of responsibilities for the global war on terror since 9/11. There just were not enough experienced combat controllers or special-tactics members for all of the theaters of operation: South America, Iraq, Afghanistan, and now Yemen. Madden was blessed with the number of controllers he'd had in Colombia.

"Unofficially, the commander of the Special Operations Command and the wing commander would be very grateful if you would pull your retirement paperwork in the name of national interest and security."

"Wait a minute, Tony," Madden said, "you know damn well I've served more than my share of deployments overseas to some of the most bullshit and screwed-up places on this planet. And what do I get for it? They denied my promotion to chief master sergeant for killing the most-wanted terrorist." Madden was letting his emotions get the best of him.

"Rob, you and I both know you pulled the trigger without authorization, and in doing so, you killed an AUR royal prince. If my memory serves me right, AUR is an ally of ours."

"Damn it, Chief. God knows how many more people that asshole would've killed if we didn't take him down when we did." Building into a rage, "I can't help it if that prince had murderers and terrorists as friends."

"Yes, I know you took the hit for us. We all wanted him down. Listen, Rob, I understand you have your heart set on teaching school when you retire." St. Amant continued, "However, if you're still intent on retiring, we'd like to make you an offer. Immediately after your retirement, the command has authorized us to award you a government civil-service position as a general schedule pay grade, GS-14. The pay is equivalent to that of a lieutenant colonel, and you would be doing the same combat-controller duties as if you were still on active duty military—except that you would be paid a heck of a lot more, plus your retirement check. What do you think, Rob?"

The offer and pay were certainly enticing to Madden, however, the promise to his wife and daughters was firm. "Tony, I greatly appreciate your interest and the offer, but I still plan to retire and teach school. That's always been the goal and is still the plan." He couldn't live with himself if he didn't follow through on the pledge made to his late wife: to be the best schoolteacher possible.

"Okay, Rob, we're trying extremely hard to assist you in your future plans. Are you familiar with STOP GAP?" St. Amant's mood now switched from ol' buddy to hard-core salesman.

Madden's heart sank when he heard St. Amant mention STOP GAP, which is a measure where selected service members can, by law, have their retirements or separations postponed to an indefinite date. Madden was familiar with STOP GAP and had many fellow special-ops friends who were denied retirement due to their critical career field, especially given the continuing war on terror.

"The way it looks, Rob, is that you can remain with us either as a senior master sergeant or as a civil servant GS-14. What do you think?"

Boiling mad, Madden kept his composure, not particularly liking the hand he'd just been dealt. However, Madden was good at playing hands with bad cards. Trying to reason with St. Amant as a longtime friend was out of the question, and Madden knew there was pressure from above to keep him in the service.

Madden moved his chair closer to St. Amant and lowered his voice so they would not be heard by anyone eavesdropping. He looked directly at St. Amant and warmly stated, "Tony, you and I are old friends. We've been around the world together and lived potentially dangerous and adventurous lives by most standards. As a friend, I believe it to be in your best interest to allow me to retire on the planned date this month." He continued, "Tony, you recall a while back when your son and daughter were attending a public school with a few bad apples in it, and those bad apples were involved in drugs and gangs? You recall those days, right?"

St. Amant almost immediately knew where the conversation was heading. Staring at Madden and nodding, he agreed, "Yes, Rob, I do recall."

"And, Tony, do you recall asking me for help with resolving any problems at their school—as a concerned citizen of course."

"Yes, Rob, I remember. Can I ask where this is going?"

"You knew that due to some of my past experiences with such situations, I could possibly see if those drug and gang problems could go away. Sure enough, after a couple of weeks, no more drugs or gangs in the school. I wonder how that happened. Oh, and one other thing: Tony, do you remember telling me that you owed me big time for taking care of that little problem?"

Sitting back in their chairs with hands folded, both men sat silently with their cards laid on the table. There had always been an informal barter system within the noncommissioned officer ranks, where favors, both professional and personal, were considered bargaining chips to be paid off at a later date. This system had worked since the creation of the armed forces, and they were always honored—or at least every attempt was made to honor them. Now Madden was cashing in an old bargaining chip, hoping this would ensure his road to retirement. There was no disrespect pointed toward his friend, Chief St. Amant, however, Madden knew how to play the game to win.

"Teaching school is that important to you, huh, Rob?" St. Amant was resigned to the fact that Madden had him over a barrel with that one favor.

"Tony, it's a promise I made to my late wife and kids: I would be the best teacher possible and we ..." Madden stopped midsentence to reflect for a moment.

"Okay, Rob, there will be no STOP GAP for you now, and you can go ahead with your retirement at the end of the month." St. Amant warned Madden, "However, remember this. If we get to a point where your skills are critical for national security, you will be immediately recalled to active duty. No ifs, ands, or buts about you coming back."

"Thanks, Tony. Again many thanks."

"Forget it. We have a clean slate now and, you're correct, I didn't forget what you did for that school. Run on down to the personnel office and start your out-processing. Here is your retirement package," he conceded and handed Madden a large folder containing his service and retirement records. "Oh, by the way, Rob, did you know you'll be receiving a pretty high medal at your retirement ceremony?"

Madden had more citations and medals than any other sergeant in the Air Force, and he was always modest about receiving them. He was prouder when his people won awards; like the nurturing teacher he was, their awards reflected well on him.

"Oh. Let me guess, the good ol' Meritorious Service Medal," Madden said, which was amusing due to the fact that the Meritorious Service Medal was the standard retirement medal for nearly all enlisted personnel.

"Rob, you will be awarded the Air Force Cross at your retirement ceremony."

Madden almost fell off his chair, "You have got to be kidding. For what?"

"Apparently the Colombian military took how you handled that live-fire exercise pretty seriously and requested, then literally demanded, you receive the award. Well, Rob, look at it this way, we denied your promotion to chief master sergeant because you took out a terrorist and a royal prince. Now, you're receiving one of the highest awards for killing terrorists. Is that justice or what?"

Madden thought this was the craziest thing he had ever heard. *Just another day in paradise,* he thought as he shook hands with St. Amant and began his out-processing from the United States Air Force.

CHAPTER

"Attention to orders!" barked the wing adjutant as he began reading the citation for the Air Force Cross to the audience and assembled airmen at Madden's retirement ceremony.

On the beautiful morning of the last day in July 2007, the Hurlburt Field parade grounds were filled with the pageantry of the 1st Special Operations Wing. The commanding general of the Air Force Special Operations Command and the wing commander served as officiating officers, whose protocol was to provide nice going-away speeches and present decorations for the retiring members. Also in attendance, in full-dress uniform and regalia, was Colonel Ricky Sanchez, the Colombian 18th Corps Commander who was instrumental in Madden receiving the Air Force Cross.

Those in attendance were in high spirits. As fellow NCOs came up, patted Madden on the back, and spoke of the good ol' days, the officers were mingling with their wives in the normal politics of working every angle to get ahead or the appearance of such. One would have thought Colonel Sanchez was running for governor of the state with the charismatic and smooth way he worked the crowd. The wing executive officers were now busy trying to get everyone seated to begin the ceremony. Both commanders took center stage at attention with Madden at their side.

"Adjutant, read the orders," instructed the wing commander.

"The president of the United States of America, authorized by Title 10, Section 8742, United States code, takes pleasure in presenting the Air Force Cross to Senior Master Sergeant Robert C. Madden, United States Air Force, for extraordinary heroism in military operations against an opposing armed force while serving as a combat controller with the 1st Special Operations Wing, supporting the National Security Presidential Directive 18, direct military support to the government of Colombia.

Senior Master Sergeant Madden was the senior combat controller supporting two companies in training from the Colombian Army and two United States Air Force Special Forces detachments searching for terrorist and rebel bases. While he and his team established helicopter-landing zones for the incoming Colombian helicopters, he led his team in securing the landing zones against an overwhelming number of hostile combatants. During the engagement, the two training companies unexpectedly encountered entrenched, regular hostile forces of approximately battalion strength. While the two training companies were overwhelmed with mortars and crew service weapons, he led a controller team forward directly in front of the rebel lines and single-handedly deployed airstrike smoke grenades against hostile positions.

As a result, with the perception of an incoming air strike, the hostile forces departed their positions and retreated to a neighboring country. While seriously wounded, he risked his life as he led his team back to the helicopter-landing zones and immediately engaged rebel forces attempting to overrun it. With fighting at close quarters and hand-to-hand, his team fought off the rebel forces and reestablished the landing zone for critical incoming helicopter support and reinforcements.

It was his superior airmanship and his
resourcefulness and masterful techniques
at orchestration that made this operation
successful—a first in the history of combat
controller-special tactics. Through his
extraordinary heroism, superb airmanship,
and aggressiveness in the face of enemy forces,
Senior Master Sergeant Madden reflected the
highest credit upon himself and the United
States Air Force."

The troops were standing at attention while the commanding general of the Special Forces Command pinned the Air Force Cross on Madden and whispered to him, "Shit, Rob. Three years ago we took a stripe from you for killing terrorists, now we're giving you the Air Force Cross for doing the same thing." For everyone to hear, the general commented, "We all know him, worked with him, and were always blessed to have him on our teams. Many thanks, Rob, and good luck in your second career as a schoolteacher." The entire audience stood and applauded.

One old seasoned combat controller commented to an Army Special Forces sergeant, "Old Madden's teaching school?"

The sergeant replied, "Sure as shit, there won't be any discipline problems in his class. That's for sure."

After the retirement ceremony, the officiating party and all attendees were invited to the Hurlburt Base Club for a lunch and reception. All were saddened about the tragic loss of Madden's family, but they greeted Madden warmly and made no mention of the tragedy. Occasionally, Madden could be heard saying, "Yes, I wish the girls could be with us today. They would have loved to see you all." Typically, Madden held back his enormous grief and sadness.

While all of the guests finished their meals and were saying their farewells to Madden, a few people arrived unexpectedly to give their respects. Madden recognized his old friends, the DEA agents he had trained and worked with in Colombia. Immediately giving each a huge hug and a slap on the back, they were glad to see each other again. Madden had nothing but respect for these agents, especially their performances while protecting the helicopter-landing zones during the live-fire exercise. With no ground-combat experience or training, the agents were able to improvise on their own and defend the vital landing zone.

"Rob, congratulations, you finally made it to retirement. How does he do it?" a smiling Bonnie McCord announced. She still had a small scar on her face from her fight with FARC terrorists in the Colombian jungle.

Madden was amazed by McCord's transformation. He remembered her mostly wearing a Colombian military jungle-fatigue uniform with a jungle hat that hid her curly chestnut hair. Now she looked like she had just stepped from the pages of a fashion magazine, wearing a nice-fitting blue dress, a stylish hairdo, and subtle makeup that highlighted her jade green eyes.

"Thank you, Bonnie, and whoa, don't you look sharp," Madden observed while marveling at the "new and improved" Bonnie McCord. "Glad we were able to get back to the landing zone in time to chase off those FARCs—hate to think of you being carried across the Venezuelan border and ending up in some Army brothel," Madden joked. McCord just grinned and squeezed his arm; she was so happy to see him again.

"Hey, Bonnie, what does DEA have you doing after Colombia? You going back to practicing law?" Madden jokingly asked McCord.

"Nope, I begin my undercover training next month, and God knows where I'll end up," replied McCord.

"In all honesty, if it hadn't been for each one of you, we wouldn't even be here today," Madden acknowledged.

"Okay, Rob, we can live with that. Now, where's the food and drink?" the agents asked. After a few beers and warm buffalo wings, the agents directed Madden to a corner table where they could talk in private.

"Listen, Rob, the DEA kingpins were impressed by your leadership and performance in Colombia. It was first rate and produced results," Senior Special Agent Bill Wagner stated. "So much so, that the agency would like to hire you as an advisor, possibly a government service pay grade 12. What do you think? You'd be stationed out of Miami and work Central and South American issues. You speak perfect Spanish and know the turf. The job was made for you."

"GS-12? The Air Force offered me a GS-14," Madden replied laughing. The DEA were now backtracking and were preparing to make a revised offer to a GS-14.

Madden thought for a minute and said, "Yes, it would be perfect, and I'm honored and flattered to be asked, especially by this team." All eyes were now on Madden hoping he would accept the assignment. "After living with you all in Colombia for the better part of four months, you know my goal, better yet my promise, to my family of beginning a second career in teaching."

The DEA agents knew in their hearts that Madden would end up teaching school, but they still could not figure out why he'd want to be in a classroom with a bunch of snot-nosed kids given his vast experience and language skills.

"Hey, let's get back to what's left on the buffet table," Madden chuckled as he grabbed his beer and led the agents back for seconds of meatballs and chicken wings.

The day had been a long and emotionally draining one for Madden. After the retirement ceremony, the large reception, and the sad farewells, Senior Master Sergeant Rob Madden was officially retired from the U.S. Air Force—his home and family for over twenty years.

Madden had been to hundreds of retirement ceremonies and often thought of them as train rides coming to an end. Retirees departing the warmth and security of the train were now going in a new direction while watching the train depart from the station with all old friends and comrades continuing their journey onward. The retiree watches and waves to the people on the train, but suddenly feels lonely and may wish to be on the train. Madden's time had come to retire, though, and start a new life.

Feeling the humidity of the sunny Florida afternoon, he was now Mr. Rob Madden, public school teacher. His second career had just begun, and his life would be changed forever. Looking at the watch his wife had given him for his thirty-fifth birthday, he noted the inscription: "The angels have chosen to fight their battles below," a line from the play *Camelot*.

Leaving past the main gate of the base with tears in his eyes, he yelled out the window of his car, "See ya, Sergeant Madden, and many thanks."

CHAPTER

Madden had earned his teaching degree and certification while on active duty at the expense of the government through the Troops to Teachers program sponsored by the Department of Defense. In return, however, he was expected to accept any teaching assignment the sponsoring school district offered upon his retirement. In most cases, the worst schools in the district were reserved for the Troops to Teachers graduates. The Crestview Public School system, located just north of Hurlburt Field, hired Madden to teach full time at the Roosevelt Hills Elementary School. "The Hills" was considered the very bottom in all school-graded categories. From test scores to attendance, the Hills was the abyss of Florida schools.

Roosevelt Hills averaged a state high of more than 80 percent of the student population enrolled in the National School Lunch Program that provides low-cost or free lunches to children at or below the poverty level. The 80 percent served as an indicator of the economic status of most of the students' families or guardians. The ethnic population of Roosevelt Hills Elementary School was 50 percent black, 20 percent Hispanic, 20 percent white, and 10 percent Korean. Madden's fourth- and fifth-grade classes predominantly reflected these percentages.

Madden was ready to fulfill the promise to his late wife, who had also been a teacher, that he would become the best teacher possible. He had wanted his girls to be proud of him, and he wanted to be the center of their world—as the proud father. The only possible flaw that Superintendent Dr. Tessa White observed in Madden during his first few months of teaching was his method of discipline.

Initially, there were some complaints from both students and parents. He assigned extra work and responsibilities to those students whom Madden described as "slackers or trouble makers." He also formed learning teams in the classroom and rotated the team leaders every month to provide the opportunity for all students to be team leaders—whether they liked it or not. Amazingly, the team concept worked with results including higher test scores and better class cohesiveness.

The students rebelled at his unorthodox teaching methods at first, but they gradually learned to respect and like him. He demonstrated daily that he cared for them when few others did, including their parents, if they even had parents. From early mornings to late afternoons, Madden mentored and encouraged these students with limited resources and opportunities to "dream big. This classroom is just a stepping stone for better things and a better way of life. Raise the bar of achievement."

Madden worked with local juvenile courts and the jailed parents of his students. He loaned money to deserving students in need and held after-school homework sessions. Madden was becoming well known in the community for his extraordinary ability to motivate his young students—continuing to press them forward. Most important to Madden's plan for the advancement of his class was teamwork, something so important to the military units he had worked with in the past. He knew that teamwork could not be taught; it had to evolve.

The Crestview Public Schools board of education initially received numerous letters of complaint about Madden because he required all of his students to complete their homework and learn the lessons, unusually high standards for the district. As one frustrated mother, Ellen Robson, stated at a school board meeting, "This man Madden is making my son do more work— you know he'll never be able to do work like those white kids!" She continued, "Why make Jesse do all this work? Is he being punished? He's been punished enough during his life, and I certainly can't help him with all that schoolwork."

All of the board members politely listened to Ellen Robson and came to the same conclusion: apparently Mr. Madden was trying to help her son and, perhaps, get him to succeed.

"Well, maybe you're right," a now calmer Ellen Robson said. "I'm just not accustomed to a teacher taking that much of an interest in my son's future and pushing him like he does."

"If we receive any more complaints like this directed at Mr. Madden, that will be fine with me. I wish we could get more teachers just like him," the school board president said in one executive session.

After his first year of teaching, Madden received numerous citations and awards for his performance and that of his students. Surprised at receiving such honors, he explained, "Hey, I was just doing my job—no more." He was also known for getting along well with his fellow teachers and administrators. Madden surmised that first-year teachers were much like second lieutenants in the military, who are not expected to know much or do much. If they did, however, it was a real eye-opener, and Madden was opening a lot of eyes at the Hills.

Roosevelt Hills' principal, Dr. Cindy Pearson, reviewed the year-end statistics and required test scores of all of her teachers. She found that Madden's numbers were phenomenal, especially considering he was responsible for classes with a history of low achievement, a high rate of absenteeism, trouble with the juvenile authorities, and limited parent participation. That is, until Madden was assigned as their teacher.

The No Child Left Behind law measured school perform-ance by "adequate yearly progress." The gold standard for any teacher was an incredible 10 percent rise in test scores over the previous year. Madden's progress with his students reflected that 10 percent increase. Also striking was the attendance record for his students, now one of the best records in the school district.

Dr. White and Dr. Pearson were ecstatic when reviewing the year-end results but wondered how a first-year teacher working full time and taking master's courses at night and on weekends was able to meet those numbers. Dr. White was well aware of Madden's past in the Air Force, his reputation as a hero, the loss of his family, and his command of both the Spanish and Arabic language. Not knowing much about military culture, Dr.

White decided it must have something to do with his military training. She had taken a chance by hiring Madden from the Troops to Teachers program and had placed him in the most challenging school in this part of the state. It appeared to her that Rob Madden brought many intangible gifts to the students as a role model: success, compassion, empathy, resilience, integrity, perseverance, and, most important of all, faith in their future—hope.

"Never in a million years would I have thought this mild-mannered yet charismatic, soft-spoken man could be dedicated to teaching given his background and baggage," explained Dr. White to the Crestview board of education at the annual teacher evaluation meeting. Dr. White added, "Comparing Mr. Madden to my current and past teachers, I have never come across such a teaching oddity like Madden." The school board concurred with Dr. White's review and designated "the Hills" teacher as "a comer," meaning a teacher destined for greater responsibilities and higher pay.

Longtime board member Blake Rhodes asked at the end of the meeting, "Was this year just a flash in the pan and will he burn out too quickly? Or can he positively affect the morale of the other teachers?" Other board members agreed with the questions.

"Time will tell," replied Dr. White, "but I must say his test scores speak for themselves."

Madden's second year began much like the first with numerous complaints from parents regarding the immediate enforcement of discipline and high expectations for achievement.

"Dr. White, ma'am, please help me understand these complaints. I have all of my disciplinary problems under control—well, most of them, anyway." Madden stopped for a second to look at the small bruise he received when a student challenged him with a knife.

"Well, Rob, I'm glad you survived your attack without incident. Where is the student now?"

"Dr. White, after you authorized the law enforcement call,

I restrained the student, took away his knife, and held him until the security guards showed up." Madden added, "I do think he's a good kid and making progress, and I cannot for the life of me figure out what made him turn on me like that. I'll check on him at the juvenile facility after school. Will you authorize his return to school?" Madden asked.

"Rob, a student pulls a knife on you and now you're talking about getting him back in the classroom—have you got rocks for brains?" replied White.

"Dr. White, I would greatly appreciate it if we could give him another chance—you can hold me accountable for his actions," Madden pleaded.

Staring at Madden with disbelief, she said, "Okay, Rob. I'll authorize him back in, but I don't want to hear anything further about knives in classrooms or both of you are out. Do you understand me?"

"Yes, ma'am, it won't happen again," replied Madden.

"Tell me, Rob, how do you know it won't happen again?"

Staring at Dr. White with a childish grin he said, "Now, Dr. White, we all make mistakes. I promise you I won't let it happen again."

Dr. White abruptly stopped the discussion on discipline; she did not want to hear anymore.

As the second year passed, Madden's test scores were up again, student attendance remained high, and parental sentiment had swung from skepticism and defiance to appreciation. The parents and relatives began to see positive changes in their sons and daughters. At first, they didn't understand or accept it, but now they saw something different that this Air Force Sergeant was instilling in their children—hope.

Dr. White had her year-end critique and appraisal with Madden in June. He again earned high marks and unusually glowing statements for a second-year teacher. There were a few items Dr. White wanted Madden to work on, but all in all, Madden was a prize teacher. Much like the ambitious military officers in

Madden's past, Dr. White also wanted to ride Madden's rising star for her own purposes and agenda—she wanted to move up the education ladder in the state hierarchy. White thought to herself while reading his test scores, *My boy, Rob, we're going places.*

"Rob, tell me how your master's degree is going? Are you about to finish?" Dr. White had an ulterior motive for asking, and Madden read her like a book.

"Tessa, I just finished my thesis last month, and I feel confident it will pass muster," Madden answered. "I only have a couple more requirements to complete this summer, I see no problems. If all works out with my advisor, I will probably graduate this August." Besides the pride in earning his master's in education, he was looking for a significant pay increase with the added degree.

"Rob, if you were given the opportunity and resources, would you consider going for a doctorate in education?" she asked, knowing Madden was just finishing his master's degree and probably needed time to catch up and breathe again from all of his duties.

Madden knew that eventually he would need to begin a doctorate program but not right now. And where in the heck, he wondered, was Dr. White going with this "opportunity and resources" thing.

"Your name was submitted by me and Dr. Pearson and you were endorsed by our school board for the prestigious Distinguished Veteran educational scholarship from the Hoover Institute at Stanford University in California." Madden was shocked as White continued, "Each year the Hoover Institute grants ten full free-ride scholarships to the top-ten military veteran candidates from all over the United States to pursue their doctorates in education. We nominated you at the beginning of the school year, and we were just notified of your selection. How does that sound to you?"

Madden was dumbfounded. Yes, this was a dream come true, but there were so many details and questions to answer. He asked, "How long? Who would take my place at Roosevelt Hills?

Would I come back to Roosevelt Hills?"

"Yes, yes, Rob. Lots to discuss. We'll get all details and questions answered tomorrow."

In his wildest dreams, Madden could not comprehend what had just happened and what he was being offered. He thought, *What the hell's going on here? A full ride for a PhD at Stanford University?* Reflecting back, how could a product of oil-field trash and an Air Force sergeant, now a new public schoolteacher, earn such a scholarship?

Returning to his apartment with its cluttered desk of unread school assignments and his own studies, his eyes focused on the pictures of his wife and daughters, "What if? What if?" kept racing through is mind. Dropping into what he referred to as his "dark zone," a natural state of sadness, self-pity, and depression, he thought, *No, no, don't go there, don't Sergeant Madden. Snap out of it and get your shit together. People are depending on you, so move forward.* His mind went back to the Stanford scholarship and eyeing again the photo of his girls, he knew how proud they would be of Dr. Madden.

Madden looked around his cluttered apartment filled with hundreds of books, files, reports, and, as usual, stacks of homework assignments awaiting his review and grading. Stacked in the corner were a few boxes filled with his many awards presented him the last two years. Grateful for the awards, he felt awkward in accepting them. His goal was not chasing trophies like so many in his profession. His rewards were in the development of his students deemed to be in the slow track of life, the ones who showed no promise or potential for a better life. Madden, a daily bible reader and Sunday School teacher, always remembered the bible passage: "The stone that the builders rejected became the cornerstone."

Growing up as an underdog himself, he was given numerous second chances in life by his personal savior, Jesus Christ, loving parents, caring teachers, and strict but fair commanders. Madden particularly enjoyed the informal competition between the underdogs and the privileged fast trackers in life. *Enough reflecting,* Madden reminded himself. *What's it going to take to make a move in August to California?* Beginning to plan, he thought, *Let's see, I need to* ... For the next two days, he planned to phase out of the Roosevelt Hills Elementary School and into a full-time doctoral studies.

"Rob, how's the planning for the move coming along? I have some more information on the scholarship, do you have some time?" Dr. White asked Madden as he was cleaning his classroom at year-end.

"Dr. White, please come in. I was just completing my final student evaluations. Would you like some coffee?" Madden graciously asked his boss and mentor, who had given him a second career in teaching.

Looking around the classroom smiling, she commented, "You've really done the impossible in this classroom. No one in a million years would have predicted this outcome, including myself."

Madden greatly appreciated the compliment, smiled, and nodded his head in agreement, "It's been a very interesting two years, to say the least. I believe everyone learned something important in this classroom, especially me."

"You've paid your dues," she replied. An awkward moment of silence ensued as teacher and student thought about parting ways for a few years. "All right, Rob, enough of this wonderful reminiscing. Let's get back to your plan for the move."

"Tessa, it doesn't get any easier. In August, I'll pack up the Honda Element with everything I own and head west to California for a good ol' West Coast education."

"Rob, I suspect you know it's not really going to be that easy, correct?" Madden felt a little uncomfortable at Dr. White's reply. "Let me lay it out for you, Rob. We just received the package from Stanford," as she handed the heavy assortment of papers and forms to Madden. "Contact the Hoover Institute scholarship coordinator when you arrive on campus. I understand a graduate apartment will be assigned to you, plus your graduate sponsor will show you around. You know, give you the dollar tour. Also, I don't think we covered your salary," White noted.

"Salary?" Madden looked surprised but calmly asked, "What salary?"

"Rob, the school board knew that even with your scholarship, you're going to need something to live on, so they voted to continue your regular salary," Dr. White added, "of course under the condition that you will return to Crestview and Roosevelt Hills upon your completion of the doctorate."

Madden wanted to burst out and yell his happiness. However, he calmly replied, "Dr. White, that's very generous of the Crestview board of education, thank you." Naively, Madden also asked, "But aren't you going to need that money for my replacement?"

Dr. White laughed at his uncommon sincerity, "Rob, there's a ton of grant money involved in this scholarship, and, trust me, the school board knows what they're doing. I don't think, as generous as the military retirements are, the pay for a retired Air Force sergeant is going to get you very far on the West Coast."

Madden was so excited, he quickly rose from his chair and gave Dr. White a hug, "Thanks, Tessa. I'll do the best I can for you all."

"Remember, Rob, you come back in two years and you have a five-year commitment with us. See you at the going-away party," White reminded him before leaving.

Outside Madden's classroom, Dr. White was extremely happy that her protégée was going to earn a doctorate in education. However, she was concerned about Madden's mental state away from the classroom. Granted, Dr. White knew Madden had his vices, but his biggest fault was his uncanny ability to get into situations he had no business in to protect, or side with, the underdogs. Dr. White had witnessed various counseling sessions with students' parents and guardians. Madden refused to believe the parents who thought their children were hopeless—and in some cases "no good." He could see the goodness and potential in all of his students. Madden would not tolerate anything but a safe environment for his students to learn and live. He could never turn his back on an obvious wrong directed at one of his students because he felt as if they were his children too.

"What a do-gooder," Dr. White thought and smiled as she returned to her office. White recalled seeing "The angels have chosen to fight their battles below" on Madden's watch and had a strong suspicion as to why it was there.

CHAPTER

10

The banner above the gymnasium stage read, "Good Luck Mr. Madden!" His going-away ceremony was filled with parents, students, and teachers in the small school gym. Decorated tables overflowed with potluck items that included fried chicken, potato salad, beef tacos, and apple pie—various types of food were everywhere in this festive atmosphere.

Wanda Salvador approached Madden while he was eating the wonderful food and mingling with everyone. "Mr. Madden, you have been a godsend for my child. Thank you, thank you so very much," she hugged Madden and squeezed his hand.

Madden, feeling the warmth of her hand, nodded his head and added a soft, "My pleasure, friend."

Madden's going-away party was an ethnic melting pot of white, Hispanic, African-American, Asian, and Arabic parents praising him for making positive changes in their children's lives. The school had never had a reception enthusiastically attended by so many parents, however the school had also never had a teacher like Madden. For the Hispanic parents, his knowledge of the Spanish language and culture assisted students working the challenges of English as a second language.

Madden conducted parent/teacher conferences with immigrant parents in Spanish, and in most cases, they were relieved and happy to have the opportunity to communicate their concerns and challenges for their children. "*Mucho gusto mi maestro—me alegro mucho para su ayuda,*" was often heard at the conferences and Madden would reply, "*No es gran cosa.*"

Equally surprising for most parents was that Madden understood Arabic. He also won praise from those parents for assisting their sons and daughters to adjust to the American culture and learn the English language.

Dr. Tessa White and Dr. Cindy Pearson made their formal farewell comments to the gathered crowd and presented Madden with several school plaques and letters of appreciation. Madden was asked to say a few words to the enthusiastic gathering.

"I'm so grateful for the opportunities here at the Hills to work with the best teachers and staff in the world and to teach some of the brightest students in the State of Florida. We've all come a long way together."

One older teacher said to another while eating the last of the meatballs, "I don't understand why he got a scholarship when the rest of us have been struggling here for more than twenty years with the worst kids in the district." She sighed, "I'll say this about Rob, though, what he did in that classroom with those students, well, maybe he does deserve a break."

"Did they ever determine how his wife and two daughters were killed?" one teacher asked.

"Not sure. However, the authorities say Nancy and the girls just happened to be next to a terrorist's bomb that went off near Ft. Walton Beach. Apparently they had been to that same beach a thousand times without incident."

"My son is a state police officer here and he told me, unofficially, that there's something suspicious about the explosion."

"You mean how could a van full of explosives just coincidentally explode next to Nancy Madden's car?"

"That's what's on the record and what was reported to Madden, but my son seems to believe there may have been ulterior motives for the explosion."

"As if it was planned?"

"Yes, and you keep this stuff to yourself or I'm going to be in some big trouble. Just forget what I said, okay?"

"But why would anyone in their right mind want to harm Madden's family?"

"Now don't be saying this to anyone, but they think the explosion might be related to an incident that happened with Madden and some pretty bad people when he was stationed overseas."

"Terrorists?" the younger teacher whispered.

"Something like that, I think. He apparently had something to do with killing a few of them overseas, and this explosion was something of a payback. But this is all speculation, and it's still under investigation. So please don't repeat this," she warned her friend again.

After eating the last piece of pecan pie, Madden worked his way around the gym embracing and shaking hands with all present. He wished his girls were with him today. *They would have enjoyed this immensely,* he thought. Madden figured that when he saw his wife and two daughters in the afterlife, he would go into detail about the dreams they had started together but never had the opportunity to finish—the doctorate was just another step in the dream.

Packing up his many gifts from the party, he headed out to the parking lot and loaded his cargo in the back of the Element. "Holy shit, my car looks like a storage shed with all that crap filled to the roof," Madden commented to another teacher leaving the school.

"Hey, Rob, where you going now? Want to go play a few holes of golf? It looks like a great afternoon."

"No, Bill. I appreciate the offer, but I'm going out to visit my girls one last time before I leave for California. You understand."

Bill nodded his head, patted Madden on the back, and left the parking lot.

Madden made the trip every day since the funeral. Winding across the small road lined with silver oaks and through the cemetery's heavy iron gate, he slowly approached the designated parking area and sat alone in the car getting his thoughts together before he met with his wife and daughters.

Getting out of the car and walking to the grave site, he sat down on the ground next to his wife's headstone, and with tears running down his face he began talking to her about the day's events. He turned to clean the little headstones of his two daughters, brushing away any dirt or dust as if he was patting their heads telling them how much he loved them and that he would join them soon so they could all be together again. Relaying all of the day's events to his girls as if they were there with him, he got down and began a long prayer to his savior asking for the comfort and well-being of his family in heaven.

He explained the scholarship and the doctoral program in detail as if they were alive and well and right in front of him. In his mind, they were. Hearing their voices and still sobbing, Madden answered their many questions and promised them he would bring them something back from this trip like he had done so many times in the past. He could hear his daughters tell him what they would like from his trip while his wife smiled and said, "Rob, just bring yourself back—we'll be here waiting."

Standing now over the headstones, he thought, *Girls, I'm heading out now, not sure when I'll be back but suspect possibly two years.*

Rob, we'll be here waiting for you—study hard.

"I know you will, sweetheart. I know you will."

Goodbye, Daddy, bring us back something really neat, okay? his daughters added.

"I will sugar, I love you all so very much. Hear me now, I love you and will be with you soon. Girls, let's finish this dream we started as a family several years ago," Madden ordered as he got up from the grave site and headed back to his car.

Surveying the cemetery as he had so many times in the past, looking for a place for himself so he could be close to his girls when the time came.

PART
TWO

CHAPTER

11

"Stanford, here I come. Get ready for the best doctoral candidate in education you have ever seen. Nothing can stop the U.S. Air Force, oops, I meant Roosevelt Hills Elementary schoolteacher," Madden laughed at himself for being so giddy. He headed out early in the morning on Interstate 10 in his fully loaded Honda Element and a small U-Haul trailer. This was the first break Madden had experienced in years, and he began to loosen up and enjoy the early morning drive westbound.

Passing state line after state line in his quest west, Madden took every opportunity to see all of the points of interest along the way. As a young child and then growing up, he barely knew America and was determined to see and embrace his long-lost home. Admiring the piney woods of East Texas and the high plains of Oklahoma, he was truly excited about discovering his own native land. Passing cars might have heard Madden yell with excitement, "Look what I have been missing all of these years! Whoa, what a country—my country" or "This sure ain't Venezuela or Kuwait, thank God." For Madden, a sense of promise was in the air.

The "Welcome to New Mexico, the Land of Enchantment" billboard met Madden as he crossed over the Texas state line into New Mexico on Interstate 40 heading for California.

"Flying Buffalo Casino—a Place to Stay, a Place to Eat, a Place of Action, the Kwanki Indian Tribe. Turn Right at Exit 81, Grants. Go North 5 Miles on Highway 605."

Madden had been noticing these billboards for the past few hundred miles on Interstate 40, which was once Route 66, with the intended purpose of drawing his attention. "Oh, heck, why not? Might even be fun," he decided. "Who knows, they might have a buffet. Yes, sir, a genuine all-you-can-eat buffet."

Madden was still feeling the high of cross-country travel and was now looking forward to a little diversion at an Indian casino. The signs indeed served their purpose as Madden was imagining what he might find there: a cold beer, a few rolls of the dice, and a never-ending buffet. *Doesn't get any better for an ol' retired sergeant like me,* he thought.

The sun was just setting in the western desert sky as Madden approached Exit 81 and followed the directions to the casino parking lot. Just over the bend, he saw an oasis in this dry and barren land where a brilliantly lighted complex of buildings surrounded the main casino entrance with a huge, glowing sign, "Welcome to the Flying Buffalo Casino."

Surveying the beautiful high plains and the background of mountains, he was struck by the small shantytown located a few miles away in a barren, dried-up river valley. *Wonder what that is,* Madden thought as he viewed what appeared to be some sort of mining operation located up the valley from the little town. Having grown up in all sorts of oil-boom communities around the world, he was familiar with the basic layouts of mines and their supporting facilities. This was nothing new to him, but it sure looked like whatever they were mining for was in full production. He continued to stare at the mining complex that brought back memories of his childhood in the oil fields and what a tough life it was.

"Okay, let's get to the business at hand here, and I'm hungry," he concluded while approaching the entrance to the casino.

"Welcome to the Flying Buffalo Casino, young man. Here ya go, a booklet of lucky bucks and a dollar off on the grand buffet, western style," the smiling lady said as she passed Madden a booklet. He eyed the casino but was more interested in the buffet.

"Good afternoon, ma'am, what a place you have here. Who owns this casino?" Madden asked, not knowing the relationship between Indian casinos and Native American reservations.

Looking at him as if he had just fallen off a hay wagon, she answered with a smirk, "Sir, the Kwanki Indian Tribe owns the land and the casino, but a casino management company from New Jersey actually runs the casino. Any other questions?"

"You're so very kind," Madden acknowledged. "I'm somewhat curious about a small town I noticed with some sort of mining operation in the valley below. What type of mine is it?"

"Sir, the little town you saw is Tres Rios, population two thousand, and I live there." She continued, "The mine is the La Mesa uranium mine. Why are you so interested?"

"Just curious. I know a little about mining. Now, where's that buffet?"

The greeter smiled at Madden, amused by his silly questions. She began to take a liking to this rather straight and naïve man. "Sir, just follow the row of slot machines to the change cage and make a left. You'll run right into it," the greeter pointed as she innocently held Madden's arm.

"Oh, by the way, my name's Sarah. Would you like a little company tonight? I can be very friendly," Sarah questioned with her overly made-up face, intentionally getting closer to Madden as the casino patrons passed by.

Madden was amused at Sarah's approach, so like the many "working women" he'd experienced around the world. "Sarah, my name's Rob, and I am flattered you would consider me for companionship, but I need to get something to eat and get back on the road."

Sarah showed some disappointment about not getting to know Madden better, especially instead of some of the mine workers and truckers she was expected to provide company for. "Well, Mr. Rob, if you change your mind, you know where I'll be. Hey, is that a book in your hand?"

With a wink, Madden explained, "Sarah, I'm a schoolteacher, I always have a book in my hand."

Sarah looked surprised and with a curious smile asked, "Schoolteacher? Maybe you can teach me something, Mr. Rob, the schoolteacher."

Madden and Sarah both let out a big laugh and as he left for the buffet line, he commented to Sarah, "Maybe we could teach each other some lessons."

On the other side of the gambling floor, a tall, pretty female blackjack dealer observed Madden enter the casino. She discreetly turned away to avoid any accidental eye contact with him. Also, she did not want to raise any suspicions with the security camera directly above her table. "Oh Rob Madden, what in the hell are you doing here? Oh please get the hell out of here," the dealer whispered to herself.

Madden went through the buffet line and was seated at a table near the kitchen door—noisy but okay. "Oh, the price paid for not being a preferred casino member," he surmised but he still thought the buffet was great.

Eyeing the dining room, he found it interesting that one section was devoted to everyday tourists like himself, while the other section was designated for the casino regulars. A different, secluded section was reserved for the high-rollers and VIP guests of the casino. Madden was having fun watching the stream of interesting people coming and going. The people in the reserved section got him wondering for a second about who they were and what was considered high-rolling in this small town. Madden sat back with his cold beer, enjoying the buffet and thinking, *Life is good now.*

Then he heard, "You stupid bitch, what do you mean you don't want to go?" loudly coming from a corner booth in the VIP section. Suddenly, Madden and the entire casino heard a thunderous whack and observed a man slapping a woman with two young children. Another loud whack quickly followed as casino patrons and visitors were looking the other way or leaving the casino.

The man was built like a tank, short and squat with plenty of muscle, and he could easily destroy the woman he was abusing. His long, stringy black hair and evil sneer made him look like a low life, except for the fact that he was dressed expensively, and Madden noticed a Rolex on his right wrist. He also observed a pistol in a belt holster on his right side covered by his black leather jacket.

Begging him to stop and with tears streaming down her face, the woman pleaded, "Please, Billy, please stop. We'll go, we'll go now."

"You're damn right you'll go, you useless slut, and when I tell you to," the brute slurred as he slapped the woman again.

Madden was trying to comprehend what he saw as it brought up memories of his own late family, his girls. *What about those poor children seeing their mother receiving this horrible treatment. What if they were my girls crying for help? What would I do?* Madden immediately thought.

"Help me, Daddy, help me," he had heard so many times from his daughters. Who would help these poor children? Madden sat motionless almost in tears remembering how precious life was and watching this animal-gone-wild publicly beating up his wife, especially in front of children. One thing was absolutely clear to Madden: those kids were in trouble.

"You've been playing around on me, haven't you, you cheap whore?" Billy Hemrod screamed at the woman and then directed his attention to a small boy and girl, "Don't ever grow up to be like your stupid mother."

Now grabbing his son, he screamed, "Do you hear me? Don't ever be like your screwed-up mother."

The woman was still pleading with Billy to stop tormenting her and hurting the children. Another loud whack was heard along with more screams and sobbing.

Madden instinctively surveyed the casino dining room trying to gauge whether others were listening to the same commotion he was. "Waitress, excuse me! Is anyone, I mean security, going to do something about the disturbance in the VIP section?" he asked while pointing directly at Hemrod.

"Listen, mister, if you're smart, you won't get involved. Trust me, don't get involved—things happen here."

Checking the reactions of the other customers and employees, nobody was paying any attention or appeared to care about the awful scene in the VIP booth. The abuse continued and intensified as Madden became even more confused about the lack of concern. He noticed that the casino security patrol had conveniently moved out of the dining room area, leaving this man to his unchecked violence.

My God, isn't anyone going to stop this? he thought. Madden stared at the hurt and screaming woman who reminded him of his deceased wife, and the children could have been his own. Madden's guilt from not always being there for his own family was catching up with him. *The paybacks for their deaths are now. Madden, there's no one else to stop this shit. You're elected,* he reasoned.

"I can't believe I married such a slut," Billy again yelled while throwing a drink in the woman's face.

"Please Daddy, please Daddy, don't hurt Mommy anymore, please!" cried the two small children.

For Madden, this was the point of no return. He would handle this situation and make it right for this family, even though he couldn't make it right for his own girls. Madden made a beeline to Billy's booth in the VIP section. The casino patrons, employees, and tourists silently watched in amazement. "What's he doing? Is he crazy?" they said to one another. Casino employees from the kitchen and the back office were now watching to see how this tragedy would unfold. They were in awe of this man who had the guts to approach Billy Hemrod.

"Excuse me, sir. I couldn't help but notice the screaming and hitting here. Could I be of some assistance in stopping it now?" Madden asked. During his military career, Madden had stopped hundreds of personal dust-ups and he knew that anything could happen. Be polite, but be prepared was his motto.

Billy turned around and looked at Madden in disbelief, "Who the hell are you, Boy Scout? And get the fuck out of here before I kick your ass, too."

"Sir, I would be grateful if you would stop this excessive violence against your family. Now!"

Billy moved face-to-face with Madden. It was obvious; Billy smelled like a brewery and was loaded up with fool's courage.

"Excessive violence, huh, Boy Scout? I'll show you 'excessive violence.'"

Billy awkwardly reached for something on his waist, and in a flash, a Smith & Wesson was pointed at Madden's face. Madden had sized up Billy and knew it was coming like in so many past confrontations—from Iraq, Afghanistan, Colombia, and now the Flying Buffalo Casino.

"Please, mister, just go away. You don't know what you're doing, just go away. We'll be okay," pleaded the woman. She was sobbing with pain and repeated, "Mister, just go away now!"

Hemrod still had the pistol pointed at Madden's head, "Come on, Boy Scout. You want to interfere in my life, you'll have to pay the price."

Madden's past training and instincts took over. He quickly surmised, *Let's see here, I have a crazed drunk beating his wife up in public, and now I have a gun pointed at my head. Dangerous situation.*

The crowd of casino bystanders, including security, watched with excitement as the drama unfolded, "Who is this nut? He sure isn't from around here..."

"Mister, I recommend that you drop the gun now, or I'll take it away from you. I do feel threatened," Madden stated so the entire casino could hear. Just legally covering his ass for the expected outcome.

"Why don't you try and take it away, Boy Scout?"

This was just what Madden wanted to hear. His blow was immediate, knocking the wind out of Billy's lungs. He grabbed Billy's hand holding the pistol, and with another blow to the stomach, Madden gently took the pistol out of his hand. He dropped the magazine on the floor, locked the safety, and set the pistol on the floor of the dining room.

Grasping for breath and shocked by the sudden impact from Madden's blows, Billy lay motionless just trying to breathe. After regaining his senses, he struggled to get up, clumsily pulled a knife out of his pocket, and pointed it at Madden.

Anticipating a possible threat from a hidden knife, Madden calmly instructed, "Sir, please put the knife down, or I will take it away from you."

Billy yelled, "Oh shit," as Madden employed a blow to his hand and knocked the knife to the floor. It skidded across the dining room floor and hit the ice cream machine. Billy dropped again with a painful thud, not daring to get up for another blow from this crazy stranger. Billy's wife and children were staring in disbelief at Madden and then back at Billy.

The wife turned to Madden trembling, "You'd better get out of here, we'll be okay."

Billy was still lying on the floor, and the large crowd was stunned into silence after what they just witnessed. Madden slowly went back to his table, set a twenty-dollar bill on it, picked up his book, and headed toward the exit murmuring, "Well, it's been real. It's been fun. But it hasn't been real fun."

Sarah, who was still standing at her assigned station and greeting people at the door, instantly grabbed him and in a low tone warned, "Rob, you'd better get the hell out of here fast. I don't think you realize what you've just done, you truly don't."

"Thanks, Sarah, good idea. Glad I thought of it." Madden promptly headed for his car in the casino parking lot. Everyone, from the dishwashers in the kitchen to the casino pit bosses knew the consequences facing this crazy stranger.

The attractive female blackjack dealer was also watching the commotion of the stranger leaving and thought to herself, "Rob, you stupid son of a bitch. Sorry I can't help you now— good luck."

Madden quickly reached his Honda Element, only now beginning to realize the amount of interest he had attracted. The entire population of the casino, both customers and employees, was standing outside in the valet parking entrance watching him reach his vehicle. As he headed for the exit street, the mob of people in front of the casino shouted, "Good luck, you'll need it!" It was very obvious to Madden there was something amiss with the recent events. *Keep your cool,* he thought, *you've handled worse situations before. Just keep your cool.*

Heading south on Highway 509 to the Interstate, Madden reflected on the tragic events he had just witnessed and participated in. He suspected this guy, Billy, was some sort of high-rolling rich kid who was linked to either drugs or a gang—maybe both. Madden reasoned that regardless of how much money or power Billy had, it didn't give him the right to abuse his wife, especially in front of their children.

CHAPTER

Madden's rearview mirror revealed an ambulance heading for the casino, and he knew who it was for. Directly behind the ambulance, several fast-moving police cruisers with blaring sirens and flashing lights were flying at top speed. They passed the casino and headed straight for Madden in his green Honda Element trying to get out of town.

From his experience with the overseas federal police and his prisoner-of-war training, Madden was mentally prepared for the worst-case scenario and was ready to play the model citizen for his meeting with the police. The Honda Element was pulled over on the shoulder of the highway; Madden put on this emergency blinkers and prepared the necessary papers for what was sure to follow.

"Out of the car with your hands where I can see them," bellowed a loudspeaker while various uniformed officers came from behind the cruisers and approached the Element. Madden slowly climbed out of the car and raised his hands while holding his registration, license, and proof of insurance. He was amazed at the different array of police uniforms and weapons confronting him. He stood with his hands raised as directed.

"Keep those hands raised, you son of a bitch," a rather overweight deputy sheriff yelled at Madden while two uniformed Tres Rios police officers cautiously approached Madden. In an instant, they grabbed him and threw him on the front hood of the first cruiser.

Keep your cool, keep quiet, don't say anything, he thought to himself as the officers placed the handcuffs on him showing some delight by ensuring they were tight enough. Madden winced for a moment as another officer slammed a nightstick across his knees.

Madden was shoved into the backseat of a cruiser with tight cuffs and excruciating knee pain and given several more blows to his face and head. Through the fog of pain, he heard "You have the right to remain silent. Anything you say can and will be used against you in a court of law. You have a right to an attorney. If you cannot afford an attorney, one will be appointed for you."

"Yes, I would like an attorney," Madden said. That statement resulted in more quick blows to his ribs. Madden thought it best not to ask what the charges were. He suspected he already knew and no need to provoke these bubbas into more blows. Remaining silent while still taking the verbal insults and physical pain, he was preparing emotionally, mentally, and physically for what he thought might come his way.

"What about my vehicle, officer?" Madden broke his silence.

"Listen, you bastard, you got a lot more problems to worry about than your stinkin' car." The officer thought for a moment and added, "It'll be towed to the city lot tonight at your expense. Now, shut the fuck up." Another blow was dealt to Madden's side.

During the short drive to the Calico County Correctional Facility, Madden kept wondering who this Billy was and realized that he must have some very powerful friends. Madden's trademark was his ability to find some levity in a bad situation, but he had a tough time finding anything to laugh about here— he was hurting badly.

In the early desert twilight, three law enforcement cruisers approached the Calico County Jail located near the courthouse. Madden arrived in the first cruiser at the main entrance to the jail, where a large reception committee was waiting. He observed the "committee" to be an odd assortment of uniforms and civilians from surrounding communities. There were officers from the Tres Rios police, Calico County Sheriff's Department, Kwanki Reservation police, La Mesa mine security, and casino security. They were of every type and size, and Madden judged them as not the most professional officers he'd ever observed, maybe even the worst.

Madden heard a couple of the officers in the reception committee comment admirably, "So that's the bastard who beat the crap out of Billy at the casino?" Again, Madden, through his pain, wondered who this minor-league thug was.

"Get that son of a bitch into interrogation, now!" yelled the deputy sheriff while two officers pushed Madden into a large room with the harsh, putrid smell of urine, vomit, and cigarette smoke and a few scattered folding chairs around a small table.

When all of the officers gathered around a barely standing Madden, the interrogation began. A Tres Rios police officer shoved Madden against the wall and demanded, "Okay, asshole, what in the fuck gave you the right to come to our peaceful little town and beat the hell out of one of our leading citizens?"

Out of nowhere, a deputy sheriff's nightstick blow to the stomach forced Madden to the ground. He tried, but failed, to get up.

"Mr. Madden, would you like the services of an attorney?" asked Deputy Sheriff Kelly.

"I bet you would, you weak dick," said a casino security officer followed by a kick to Madden's gut.

"You know what, Madden? We're tired of trouble makers like you coming to our loving community and acting like badasses. You want some badass? We'll give you some badass shit," screamed Deputy Sheriff Kelly as he reached down to pull Madden up to his feet.

Madden's ripped shirt revealed an assortment of tattoos never observed before by the cluster of law enforcement officers in the room. An Indian reservation security officer physically stopped a blow from another officer before it reached Madden's head and ordered, "Hold it a minute—I said hold it!"

The blows stopped and the room became quiet as Madden was still trying to get up off the floor. He was relieved that the bashing had stopped but didn't know why. The room grew quiet with all of the law enforcement officers staring at the tattoos Madden had on his chest and arms.

The officers were huddled around Madden now pointing at the tattoos and making comments about their origins and meanings as if they were in a military museum. Most in the interrogation room had spent some time in the service or were members of the local guard or reserve unit. They knew from their own or their families' experiences what those tattoos meant. The officers began talking to each other in low voices trying to determine what to do now. They were confused and dumbstruck.

"John, I take it Madden here is some sort of hero in the Army."

"George, look at those tattoos, he's got a master parachute badge, a Ranger tab, a combat infantry badge, a pathfinder badge, an air-assault badge, a …"

"Holy shit, I dreamed about earning any one of those badges," commented another officer.

Madden was coming to his senses and barely heard the commotion and voices around him, but he did pick up on the comments on his tattoos and thought, *Ah, yes, the tattoos.* Madden remembered his wife hated them, but in many of Madden's past units and assignments, it was a rite of passage and an informal bond that had to be preserved.

The officers were still standing over Madden, "Charlie, what kind of tattoo is that on his left shoulder? Is that some sort of service badge or patch?"

Getting down on his knees to study the mysterious tattoo, Charlie determined, "Guys, you're not going to believe this shit, but this guy looks like he has a tattoo of what looks like the Air Force or Navy Cross."

All of the officers were now reflecting on what had transpired the last few hours while Madden still lay on the floor. One startled Tres Rios police officer and a casino security officer began helping Madden to his feet.

"You cocksuckers are going to pay for this shit, I promise you that," Madden spoke for the first time since the interrogation began, defiant as ever.

The damage was done; it could not be taken back. The officers were nervous and the finger pointing began. "Damn, we thought he was just some dipshit stranger causing shit over at the casino, and come to find out he's a war hero and schoolteacher to boot," stated Deputy Sheriff Kelly.

"Hey, Kelly, how did you know he's a schoolteacher?" asked Joe Stephans, a mine security officer.

"My cousin Sarah works at the casino. When she called to ask about the stranger, she told Joe the guy was a teacher," replied Kelly. "Hey, Harold, you and Charlie escort Mr. Madden to cell number twelve," he ordered.

"Okay, boss, number twelve. But what if the mayor's son comes in all doped up or liquored up. Where're we going to put him then?" asked Deputy Sheriff Chris Aponte, chief of the county jail.

"Put him in whatever's available, but Madden gets number twelve," Kelly demanded.

Cell number twelve at the Calico County Jail was considered the VIP suite reserved for prisoners who had influence in the community or money; it was a first-class jail cell, as jail cells go. Carefully laying Madden down in the cell-twelve bed, each officer felt a degree of shame for beating up a fellow serviceman and war hero who had seen his fair share of action.

All of the officers agreed they wished this incident had never happened. They only wanted to patch him up and get him back on his way like it never happened. The wheels of justice were now moving to get Madden out of Tres Rios and Calico County.

"We're screwed!" acknowledged a Tres Rios officer. "What's Billy going to say?"

Later that evening in his office, Sheriff Russ Wells, the top law enforcement officer for Calico County, was briefed by lead deputy sheriff Frank Kelly. He explained the entire course of events with the stranger named Rob Madden. Now fully aware of the incident with Billy Hemrod at the casino and the interrogation conducted by his deputies and other officers, the sheriff just gave him a puzzled look and said nothing.

That evening at the Calico County courthouse and while Madden was recovering from his interrogation session, Sheriff Wells was approaching his various outside contacts regarding the stranger. Wells's sources, both official and unofficial, came back with a large folder of information that included his military record, officially called a Department of Defense form DD-214; college transcripts; and numerous news stories on the deaths of his wife and daughters; as well as his recent retirement from the Air Force. He silently thanked his underworld contacts for their timely information.

After reading the reports, Wells was curious about this prisoner. As an Army veteran, he knew how to read a DD-214, and what he saw sent chills through his body. The official DD-214 showed Madden had more medals and citations than the form was designed to carry, including the Air Force Cross for valor. *Holy shit,* thought Wells as he continued reviewing Madden's record and learning about his many assignments around the world; many were marked as classified.

Madden was airborne qualified, proficient in both Spanish and Arabic, and retired as a senior master sergeant from the Air Force with over twenty years of service. "This is no ordinary prisoner we have here. You got to admire this guy, Madden. Why did he have to start shit with Billy?" mused the sheriff, taking off his reading glasses and pausing for a minute before finishing the reports.

He shook his head and grabbed another file entitled "Teacher." Wells was even more astonished and surprised to find that Sergeant Madden was indeed a certified teacher and reported to be a very good one. Besides earning bachelor's and master's degrees in education, he was en route to California to earn a doctorate in education at Stanford on a military scholarship.

He went on to read about the mysterious and unsolved deaths of his wife and kids and thought, *What a sad tragedy for this guy. He has gone through a lot.* Wells had lost his wife and child due to a drunk driver, and like Madden, he would never get over it.

CHAPTER

13

Later that evening while Sheriff Wells was obtaining updates and information on Madden, he made a phone call to Dr. Jim Lightfeather and asked him to attend to a newly arrived prisoner at the county jail. Hanging up the phone, Lightfeather knew what to expect because he'd been through this routine with Wells before.

"Gringo, you're lucky to be alive," muttered Lightfeather as he surveyed his new patient on the old military-style bed in the jail's private cell. Lightfeather made a quick examination and determined this prisoner, like so many others in the past, had been beaten to an almost-critical condition. He turned Madden over on his side and began checking his vitals for possible internal bleeding. The prisoner appeared to be unconscious with a possible concussion. Luckily, no bones were broken, just numerous cuts and bruises. Lightfeather set up an IV and began stitching Madden's deeper cuts and gashes.

After several minutes of work, Lightfeather noticed some unfamiliar and unusual-looking tattoos on his arms and chest. Madden was just becoming conscious as Lightfeather prepared to leave. Suddenly, Madden yelled, "Medic, get Satterwhite on a copter now—I can wait! Get me a quick pack for the stomach, Brabham needs it now. Let's move, Sarge."

Madden's eyes were open, and he recognized the dark complexion and Native American facial features of Lightfeather. For a moment Madden thought he was back in the jungles of Colombia with a military doctor, so in perfect Spanish, he asked Lightfeather about the medical care of his team. Lightfeather looked at Madden's slowly opening eyes and assuredly replied in Spanish, "Right, I understand. All are now getting medical care.

You'll be okay!" He didn't know what else to say. Satisfied with Lightfeather's response, Madden rested.

Dr. Lightfeather had cared for many of the prisoners at the Calico County Jail; some recovered, and some did not. As an aspiring young doctor, Lightfeather had the noble dream of becoming a family practitioner in the Native American tribal lands. He was identified by his teachers as a promising leader in the tribal community, one who took an interest in the welfare of his family and people.

After much work and education paid for by the United States government and the State of New Mexico, Dr. James Lightfeather graduated from the University of New Mexico School of Medicine and completed his residency at the University of Nebraska Medical Center. Due to the conditions of his grants and scholarships, he was to serve five years, "at the pleasure of the United States government."

Upon completion of his residency, he received a rather official letter from the United States Bureau of Indian Affairs stating,

"Congratulations, Dr. Lightfeather. You have
been selected by the director of medical affairs
for the U.S. Bureau of Indian Affairs to serve
as the chief physician at the Kwanki Indian
Reservation medical clinic located in Tres Rios,
Calico County, New Mexico.

Lightfeather was beyond surprised; Calico County and the Kwanki Reservation were known to be nothing but trouble. With an active uranium mine, controversial tribal lands, and located next to an Indian casino, everyone knew that bad things happened in Calico County. As the only medical doctor within a twenty-five-mile radius of the county, he would be the only physician at the clinic. Now, he was just patching up another stupid gringo who'd caused trouble at the casino, Lightfeather angrily thought. However, to Lightfeather, this new gringo was different; Lightfeather was intrigued.

Lightfeather considered himself a Native American idealist who took pride in his heritage and its way of life. He was constantly at odds with the senior tribal leaders at the Kwanki Reservation, especially over sharing the revenues from the various tribal operations on their sacred tribal lands. From the ugly uranium mine that scarred the land to skimming the casino profits, a few tribal leaders were wealthy, while the majority of the Kwanki Tribe lived near the poverty level. They eked out a living by working at the mine or washing plates at the casino.

Warned several times by the gringo mine owners and the New Jersey bosses who managed the casino, Lightfeather now kept his opinions and ideas to himself. He just wanted to fulfill his educational-loan commitments, earn valuable clinical experience, and get out of Calico County as soon as possible. Little did Lightfeather know that the gringo he was treating had the same goals and aspirations as his—getting out of Calico County.

"Well, Dr. Lightfeather, did you get our new inmate all patched up and ready for his new jail cell?" Deputy Sheriff Kelly sarcastically asked.

Lightfeather detested Kelly and it showed. "You're all truly brave men, Kelly: eight of you to beat up a handcuffed man." Lightfeather was just getting started, "Boss Hemrod would be so proud of you almost killing a man who was trying to teach his son some manners. Imagine, a stranger in the casino attempting to stop the beating of his daughter-in-law and grandchildren—what a criminal!"

Deputy Sheriff Kelly felt uncomfortable about Lightfeather's knowledge of the arrest and his mouthy opinions. Kelly wondered if it was time for Lightfeather to learn another "lesson" about his troublesome mouth. Kelly's silent stares at Lightfeather told the story. He was thinking about giving Lightfeather another "lesson" but thought it best to let it pass for now. Kelly had bigger problems and required Dr. Lightfeather's assistance.

Kelly uncharacteristically nodded his head as he stated, "Doctor, please listen to me carefully. We need you to patch up this guy, Madden, as quickly as possible. It's been determined to get him out of here and back on the road as soon as possible." Lightfeather was taken aback and shocked by Kelly's sincerity.

For the past two years as the town's only doctor, he was obligated and paid to care for troublemakers in the county jail where they would heal while awaiting a plea bargain—or serve time until a trial was scheduled. In most circumstances, the beaten prisoners were bilked or forced to pay a hefty fine by the local county attorney to close the case. The outcome of a trial, if it ever even went to court, was predetermined with a certain trip to the state penitentiary. Plea bargains were the preferred choice of justice in Calico County.

"How long do you think it'll take to get him back behind the wheel of a car?" asked Kelly.

"Listen, Kelly, I've had to attend to all of your handiwork around here, and I know that taking care of Madden and getting him on his way is not your way of doing things. Why is this gringo so different?"

Kelly wasn't prepared to explain Madden's special treatment and was getting annoyed with Lightfeather's tone. "Again, just get him what he needs, and get him up and going. Also, he'll remain here in this cell unless you hear otherwise. Lightfeather, one last thing: don't mention our conversation about Madden to anyone. As far as you know, he's just another sick prisoner requiring your care. You got that?" he said pointing his finger in Lightfeather's face. Lightfeather just stared at Kelly.

Lightfeather continued to care for and monitor the progress of gringo Madden, as he called him. Gringo Madden was certainly a mystery to both Lightfeather and a group of bad local cops. The tattoos did not mean anything to Lightfeather, but they did to several other people, including the law enforcement officers of Calico County.

CHAPTER
14

Two days after Madden's interrogation at the county jail, a large group of the local law officers met near a deserted mine trail just outside of Tres Rios to informally talk things over, as they had so many times over the past years. Officers and police cruisers from Tres Rios, Calico County, the Kwanki Reservation, and the casino were parked in various locations along the gravel road. They sat around an old wooden picnic table that was used by mine workers at one time. Much like a small police-union meeting, the officers usually convened to discuss current local affairs, gossip, and any other situations that might require informal police action. The Madden situation definitely required immediate attention.

"How'd we know this guy was some sort of war hero and schoolteacher just passing through?" stated one officer. "What was he thinking starting a fight with Billy? What a damn do-gooder. I'm sure he didn't know what he was doing, or did he?"

"Listen, we've all seen Billy rough up his wife and kids a few times, and we all wanted to do something to stop it, but this guy actually did it," explained Rich Carter, Tres Rios police officer. The other officers looked to the ground and nodded their heads in agreement.

"When the call came, we all thought it was some drunken miner or Indian who was causing trouble and started a fight at the casino. This guy just got what we usually give troublemakers, a thorough interrogation," added one of the sheriffs.

"We've reviewed the security-camera footage of the fight several times, and it's pretty obvious this guy did not start the fight with Billy. It appears he was just protecting Billy's wife and kids and then himself," Carter observed. "Something else we saw on the camera we don't normally see: this guy knew exactly what he was doing in confronting Billy. We've never seen professional fighting skills like his before—he had lots of experience in dealing with toughs like Billy. Might account for all the tattoos we found on Madden's arms and chest." The other senior officers agreed with that reasoning.

"What's the significance of the tattoos on this guy, and why'd they affect you like that? Are you all scared of a few tattoos?" a young casino security officer asked. Those who knew the significance of those tattoos shook their heads in astonishment at his comments.

"It's pretty obvious you never served a day in the military," one Tres Rios officer stated. "His tattoos are reminders of some pretty elite units this guy served with in the past. What I saw included master airborne jump wings, some markings of a Ranger battalion, some sort of Special Forces insignia, and something that looked like a Navy or Air Force Cross."

The young officer asked the significance of the Navy Cross, which only served to annoy the other men and showcase his ignorance. But then, only a special few knew the real significance of the tattoos, and those officers who did, treated them with the utmost respect.

"All right, maybe we did get a little rough with Madden, and maybe he didn't deserve it, but this is what we got." Deputy Sheriff Kelly went on, "It might be best for all if we just patched him up and got him the hell out of here as quick as his Honda will carry him. In other words, it never happened."

While the officers were discussing their options, the lights of a vehicle quickly approached amid a cloud of dust swirling around the gravel road. The officers turned to identify who was driving so fast.

"Oh shit, it's Billy," announced one officer. "What the hell's he doing up here? And how did he know we were having a talk?"

The black pickup truck came to a screeching halt a few feet from the table where the officers were mingling while drinking their coffees and cokes. Hemrod jumped out of the truck with two of his henchmen. They were obviously doped up or drunk, maybe a combination of both.

"Well, what've we got here? Calico's finest taking a long-deserved break from protecting us law-abiding citizens from the bad guys," Hemrod began insulting them.

The officers didn't speak until finally Kelly softly said, "Hello, Billy. What can we do for you?"

"What you can do for me? How can a crazy man suddenly appear at the Flying Buffalo Casino and attack me in front of my family? He even breaks my arm while I'm trying to protect my wife and kids, and now he's taking a vacation in the VIP cell at the jail. How does this happen?" Hemrod screamed.

"Okay, Billy. What do you want from us?" Sheriff Wells asked.

"You know damn well what I want. I want you fine and honest law enforcement officers to take care of this Madden SOB. That's what I want." A few seconds passed as Hemrod stared at each of the officers. He asked again, "When're you planning on taking care of him?"

Wells approached Hemrod trying to reason with him, "Listen Billy, this stranger, Madden, there's more to him than just a crazy passerby who was looking for trouble. Who in their right mind around here would have the nerve or guts to confront you and your family, especially in the casino? It just makes no sense," the sheriff explained.

"What kind of BS are you feeding me, and what the hell am I paying for around here?" Hemrod angrily replied.

That statement struck a nerve with every officer standing around the picnic table. Each resented the fact that they were constantly reminded about being owned by Hemrod's family, which meant twisting or, in most cases, overlooking the law in Calico County. The law, from the law enforcement officers to the county attorney, were all on Hemrod's payroll. They knew that as long as Hemrod was around, they would never have the opportunity to return to the right reasons for being in law enforcement.

As Hemrod's demands grew from simple security overtime at the mine to other more dangerous and unlawful tasks over the past few years, the extra money he paid them grew with the expansion of his operations. The officers enjoyed the money, but were beyond weary of the ugly arrangement. They felt stuck in Calico County for the rest of their lives as tarnished law enforcement officers. And if any of them were caught, they all faced possible prison time. Their survival depended on the unholy bonds they had with each other.

The sheriff had watched Hemrod ever since he arrived at the mine five years ago and almost felt sorry for the spoiled young man. His affluent lifestyle and endless appetite for cars, booze, drugs, and women resulted in an out-of-control boy at the age of thirty-five.

"Billy, listen to me. We've know each other since you got here, and we've always done the best we could to protect you. In many cases, you have been very generous with us." Hemrod's temper slowed with the sheriff's sincere remarks. "We saw the security-camera footage of Madden in the casino, and it was pretty clear that this guy just wanted to protect your wife and kids. Billy, you know you can get pretty rough them. He had no clue who you were. If he'd known, I'm sure he wouldn't have laid a hand on you," added the sheriff, trying to appease Hemrod. "With your okay, we'd like to let him go, like it never happened. Besides, if he stuck around here for a trial or ended up in prison, he might learn things he doesn't need to know about."

Hemrod was unusually quiet and thought about the sheriff's reasoning.

"Hey, Billy boy. Are your stooge cop friends going to take care of this SOB who busted you up? If they won't, we will," yelled one of Hemrod's gang from the cab of the pickup.

"Hey, keep your mouths shut. I'm trying to figure this out," Hemrod yelled back.

Casino security officer Becky Hawk got up from the picnic table and asked to be heard by Hemrod.

"Yea, go ahead Becky. What do you want now?"

"Let's face the facts. We have a good deal here, but lately we've been getting a lot of attention from the feds and the state police about the alleged rape of a schoolteacher over at the rural school plus several other incidents—and now the roughing up of a schoolteacher and war hero."

Billy stopped her and cried, "War hero? What the hell are you talking about? I thought you told me he was a schoolteacher."

"After questioning, or rather interrogating, him, it became obvious that he's some sort of military hero," added Hawk.

"How do you know this just by the interrogation? He's probably lying to you."

"We don't think so," Hawk explained, "his ink tells the story. He hasn't mentioned this to us and probably won't."

"Just because he's got tats don't make him no hero! Looky here, I got tattoos, and I ain't no hero."

The officers found this statement laughable and some mumbled, "For sure, Billy. You ain't no hero."

Hemrod's crew was getting impatient waiting near the truck, drinking Wild Turkey, and relieving themselves on the side of the road. "Billy boy, tell them to get off their asses and teach this guy Madden a lesson."

"Shut up while I handle this," an agitated Hemrod shouted back while emptying his own pint of Jack Daniels. Hemrod staggered to the edge of the picnic table and announced, "Okay, this is what we're gonna do. Keep Madden, or whatever his name is, in the cell until I figure out what to do with him."

"Does your daddy know what's going on here, Billy?" the frustrated sheriff asked Hemrod.

"So, you want to get my daddy involved? Better think back to the last time my daddy was involved," Hemrod reminded them in a rage, almost coming to blows with the sheriff if not for the cast on his arm.

The sheriff and other officers remembered, and it was not pretty. No, they did not want to get Billy's father involved if they could help it. Randolph Hemrod was the Chief Operating Officer of the La Mesa Uranium Mining Corporation that had financially saved Calico County by reopening the old mine that had been closed for over twenty years. The mine was successful under its new management; it earned huge profits for the stockholders and invested millions of dollars in Calico County. Mr. Hemrod's resources and influence literally owned the county—all county officials followed his wishes to the letter.

Mr. Hemrod thought it wise to assign his errant son, Billy, as the mine's chief of security. He was sure that the responsibility would do Billy good and get him away from the many bad influences in Chicago. On a few occasions and always as a last resort, the law officers of Calico County asked Mr. Hemrod to intervene in stemming Billy's bad behavior. The calls to his father were not appreciated by Billy because his father usually sided with the local law enforcement. Billy resented the officials going to his father, and he often used their mutually lucrative association to threaten them into submission.

Billy threw the empty whiskey bottle into the desert landscape and zipped up his pants after relieving himself. After trying to regain some composure, he slurred, "Again, you fine upstanding officers don't mind keeping him until I decide what to do with him."

With an acceptable performance in front of his crew, Hemrod jumped back into his pickup truck and recklessly drove down the gravel road, leaving a dust cloud behind him, while his crew drank beer in the bed of the truck. The officers did not say another word; they got into their vehicles and followed Hemrod's dust back into town.

At the same time, Dr. Jim Lightfeather was examining Madden and monitoring his vitals. He was satisfied his new patient was getting better. Madden became more alert, surveyed his new surroundings, and asked, "Doc, where am I?"

"During the night, I had you transferred from the county jail to the medical clinic here at Tres Rios. Believe me, it's a lot more comfortable than the jail, wouldn't you agree?" replied Lightfeather. "Madden, how are you feeling? I know you took a god-awful beating, but you appear to be in good shape with a few cuts and many bruises."

"Yes, it came close to being the worst I've ever had, that's for sure, Doc." Madden found it challenging to speak with stitches in his mouth.

"Mr. Madden, I hope you don't mind if I ask you a few questions, if you feel up to questions that is?" Lightfeather asked.

"Doctor, please call me Rob. And maybe I should be asking you a few questions. What the hell is going on around this place?" Madden's head was still hurting as did his best to speak. "Doctor, first, when can I get out of here? I have commitments to honor."

Lightfeather was shocked to hear the word "honor" in this environment. "Rob, are you hungry? Would you like something to eat or drink?" offered Lightfeather.

"Yes, I'd be grateful. I suspect that casino all-you-can-eat buffet kind of worked itself out of me these last couple of days," Lightfeather nodded, arranged for the meal, and then left to care for his other patients at the clinic.

In his break from making his clinic rounds, Lightfeather stopped by Madden's bed and noticed he was awake and just staring out the window. "Rob, good afternoon," he said while taking a seat next to Madden. "In the past two days, you have literally made yourself a legend in Calico County."

Madden looked at him, puzzled, and asked in a daze, "Why?"

"Why?" Lightfeather repeated. "Don't you realize what you did and who you did it to?"

"Listen, Doc. Some joker was beating up his wife in front of their kids at the casino up the road. I just wanted to stop it, and I thought I did."

"Who do you think you are, some sort of Don Quixote?" Lightfeather commented. He was amazed at anyone who would come to the defense of a woman being abused in this part of the country.

"I didn't have a choice, Doc. I had to stop it," Madden emphasized and lay back on his bed holding his throbbing head.

Lightfeather just stared at him with amazement. *Who is this guy?* he thought, *God must've sent this angel to us sinners in Calico County, an avenging angel.*

CHAPTER

"I'll be over there at two o'clock to get this Madden thing sorted out. He will pay," Hemrod yelled in his cell phone to the sheriff.

"Okay, Billy, I'll be here. But only you; I don't want any of your crew coming to the courthouse." At that, Hemrod slammed his phone on the pickup's floorboard and headed to town.

Sheriff Wells knew the upcoming meeting with Hemrod about the casino incident would be tense and heated. Hemrod was not the forgive-and-forget type of person. Wells was always cognizant of the fact that Hemrod and the local law enforcement officers had a "marriage of convenience" relationship. They hated each other, but needed one another to continue their newly acquired lifestyles. Sheriff Wells struggled with what to do about this stranger Rob Madden.

"Damn him," Wells yelled as he slammed Madden's case file on his desk.

The intercom buzzed, "Sheriff Wells, Mr. Garcia, the county attorney, is here to see you. Should I let him in?"

"Yes, please show Mr. Garcia in," Wells replied.

Raymond Garcia was the newly elected county attorney and also part of Hemrod's association with the law officers. The previous county attorney was not reelected due to the fact that his honesty and integrity affected his decision-making abilities in the courtroom. These honesty and integrity "problems" would not affect Garcia's decision making because he was too involved in the "marriage of convenience" with citizen Hemrod.

"Ah, Raymond, it's good to see you. Would you like some coffee?" Wells offered.

"Thank you, no, Russ," Garcia answered somewhat nervously.

"Billy is on his way over here, and you know what he'll want to do," Wells stated.

"You mean in regards to the casino event?" Garcia asked.

"Yes, it involves this guy Madden. What's your take on it?"

"I understand from the casino security and employees, as well as the law enforcement present, that Madden, not knowing any better, tried to protect a lady in distress and her kids from an obnoxious drunk in the dining room—Billy," Garcia recounted. "Everyone in the county would agree that Madden, besides trying to protect some innocent people, was trying to defend himself from Billy. And he appears to have done an expert job by only breaking Billy's arm," Garcia conveyed, and Wells agreed.

"Yes Raymond, I am well aware of the facts and agree with what you say. However, due to our 'circumstances,' Billy trumps everyone in the county," Wells pointed out, and Garcia understood and agreed. "If Billy presses the issue, what're you looking at for charges?" Wells asked.

"If Billy pressed it, Madden could be charged with disturbing the peace, assault and battery, etc., enough to give Judge Warren an excuse to send Madden to prison for a long time," Garcia provided.

Wells and Garcia looked at each other and shook their heads. They had never faced anything like this before: someone trying to do a good deed in such a disgusting, crooked environment. Wells wondered sadly, *How'd we let it get this far out of control?* But what he said was, "Raymond, you and I both know that Billy will want to go the maximum on this, I mean the worst punishment."

"Yes, I know."

For the next two hours, Sheriff Wells and County Attorney Garcia discussed different options to resolve this sensitive issue. Finally, they settled on a plan. Wells looked at Garcia and said, "Raymond, what do you think? Will justice be done here?"

Garcia was relieved about the decision and stated, "Yes, justice will be done. Billy's not going to like it, and Madden certainly won't like it."

"Good, I'll brief Billy this afternoon. Tomorrow you and I will have a nice chat with Mr. Madden," Wells concluded as he escorted Garcia out of the courthouse.

Garcia was departing the office of Sheriff Wells when he saw Hemrod enter the building. "Hey, Garcia, I hope you got everything fixed to take care of that asshole."

Garcia momentarily looked at Hemrod, nodded, and replied, "Yes, everything will be taken care of."

Hemrod entered the sheriff's office and began a heated rant that could be heard throughout the entire courthouse, which was not uncommon now with his visits.

"Look, Billy, your father has already approved our plan— it's a done deal." Wells announced to Hemrod.

Like a spoiled and pampered little boy, Hemrod erupted; he threatened the sheriff and the other officers and stated he would handle Madden with his own brand of justice. When Billy's father overrode his son's wishes, it always caused a scene. Slamming the door behind him and yelling a few familiar vulgarities at Wells, Billy departed the courthouse with his crew.

Shaking his head, Sheriff Wells observed Hemrod leaving the courthouse and again murmured, "How'd I ever get into this mess?"

As soon as Billy was gone, Wells began preparing for his interview with Madden the next day. He wondered how he would take the arrangement the county was about to offer him, although Madden really didn't have much of a choice. While preparing the documents and reviewing the information he had obtained on Madden, Wells looked forward to meeting with him. He thought, "Tomorrow is going to be very interesting."

"Madden, get ready to move. The sheriff wants to talk to you," shouted the shift jailer. Madden was feeling better but preferred the care at Lightfeather's clinic to the county jail, so he started to prepare himself for whatever was coming next. His mind raced back to his prisoner-of-war and interrogation training and his experiences with foreign national authorities while in the military, especially in South America.

"Any word on my request for an attorney?" Madden routinely asked the county jailer.

"Sure, Sergeant Madden, the attorney will be waiting for you at the sheriff's office," replied the jailer smugly.

Madden assumed these cops probably already had his life history in their hands. "Take the hits and keep your mouth shut, take the hits and keep your mouth shut ..." Madden repeated to himself over and over again, ingrained from his experience and training. *Oh well, let's see how this interrogation goes. Hope it's less stressful than the first one I had here,* he thought almost laughing at himself.

"Madden, out of the cell. Let's go, sheriff's waiting," the jailer ordered.

Turning Madden over to the deputy sheriff on duty, the jailer turned and said, "Madden, for your sake, I hope they just let you go." The statement surprised Madden. It was better than being beat up again.

"Please bring Mr. Madden in, Deputy Collier," Sheriff Wells instructed.

Deputy Sheriff Collier escorted Madden to a large conference room table and asked him to sit in a chair next to the sheriff at the head of the table. County Attorney Raymond Garcia sat across from Madden and directly next to Wells. The deputy left the three men alone in the room.

"Mr. Madden, I'm Sheriff Russ Wells and to my right is Mr. Raymond Garcia, the county attorney for Calico County." Madden just nodded; he could sense both men were somewhat nervous.

Wells and Garcia were noticeably concerned about Madden's terrible appearance to the point of being conciliatory. "Is there anything I can get for you? Coffee? Coke?" asked Wells.

Madden just shook his head, adding in a hoarse voice, "No, thank you."

"Mr. Madden, you're being held on a variety of charges that include assault and battery, disorderly conduct, disturbing the peace, leaving the scene of a crime, and a few others." Garcia continued, "If you go to trial, you're facing a minimum of five years in the state penitentiary."

Madden had seen this coming and asked again, "I requested an attorney. Could I please speak with an attorney?"

"Mr. Madden, please let me explain a few facts of life in Tres Rios and Calico County to you here." Madden sat motionless as Wells continued. Sitting back in his leather chair, he smiled at Madden, "I'll ensure you receive the finest attorney in this county for your defense or you can obtain your own attorney, if you like. Your call. But do you really believe an attorney is going to help you?"

Raymond Garcia was uncomfortable with where this was going, but he was in it, too—up to his neck. "Mr. Madden," Garcia said, "my experience as the county attorney has taught me that Calico County juries are averse to strangers coming into our county and starting fights with citizens in public places. If, or rather when, the jury finds you guilty, it will be my duty to recommend sentencing for you—probably a few years in the state prison."

Madden stared at Garcia in disbelief, and Wells was trying hard to keep a straight face. Madden sat emotionless trying to read the men's faces across from him while thinking, *Why are these two highly corrupt law officers reading my future? Why give me this whole song and dance?* Madden was perplexed.

"At the casino, you just happened to be at the wrong place at the wrong time. However, now, you could be at the right place at the right time for a win/win situation." Garcia advised.

"Mr. Madden," Wells quietly stated, "we know all about your Stanford scholarship, your credentials as a teacher, your Army record, and the tragic deaths of your family members."

This got Madden's attention; every ounce of him was holding back the rage he felt for the two men he now faced. "I was in the Air Force, not the Army," was Madden's only reply, fighting himself to take the hits and say no more.

"Mr. Madden, we all know what happened last week. It was a brave thing you did by trying to save a distressed woman and her children from her drunken husband." Wells continued, "The only problem is that the man you restrained and whose arm you broke is a very important person in the community. You might say that his father owns it."

"That means he owns you," Madden suddenly injected.

Wells stared at Madden and replied seriously, "Yes, Mr. Madden, he owns us, which also places us in a very difficult and delicate situation. The Hemrod family wants to ensure that you are duly punished for the assault on their son, Billy. It would be bad for business and their reputation if you were simply released with a fine," Wells informally passed this information on to Madden.

"Please forgive me if my speech is somewhat unclear, but the stitches in my mouth are gradually healing from the interrogation your brave and honest officers gave me," Madden sarcastically remarked.

"Listen, Madden, we had no idea of your intentions when you protected Billy's wife and kids. From the reports we received, we assumed you were just some stranger looking for trouble," Wells stated as he got up from the table, walked to the window, and stared out. "Yes, it was wrong to interrogate you, and you shouldn't even be here in the first place. Let's get real—trying to assist a woman and children is a decent act, but not here. As your days in the Army taught you, 'No good deed will go unpunished.'" Wells continued, "And you will be punished."

"I was in the Air Force, not the Army," Madden restated.

"I don't think it's going to make any difference in prison," Wells replied laughing.

"When does the trial begin?" Madden asked in disgust.

Sheriff Wells looked at Garcia and nodded his head. Garcia said, "Mr. Madden, if we went to trial on the charges listed, it would not last long, and you could be in the state prison within a month. However, we have an option that would spare you any prison time with no criminal record. Plus it would help out our community."

Madden was now totally puzzled as Garcia continued, "Mr. Madden, we live in a diverse community made up of whites, Latinos, blacks, Native Americans, and a few illiterate rednecks. Almost all of them are well below the poverty line." Madden listened to Garcia with no expression as he went on, "With this diverse community of citizens, we've had problems retaining qualified schoolteachers. To be blunt, and as you may be aware, such an environment doesn't attract qualified teachers."

"Mr. Garcia, after my short visit here and the fine reception I received from your community officials, I cannot understand why teachers aren't flocking to teach here," Madden voiced, shaking his head and almost laughing.

"Okay, smartass, here's the deal. All charges against you will be dropped if you volunteer to teach at the Tres Rios Rural Elementary School for one school year—starting next week." Madden was stunned by this proposal. "One year will give us enough time to recruit another teacher," Garcia added.

"Madden, we know your record and qualifications. We need you now," Wells pleaded.

"Let me get this straight," Madden said addressing Wells and Garcia professionally, "I protect a woman and kids from being beat up by her doped-up, drunken husband. I'm handcuffed and busted up by some of your law enforcement officers. And now you want me to stick around and teach school?" Madden couldn't help but laugh.

"Mr. Madden, I take it you find this offer rather amusing?" Wells responded.

"No, sir. I find your offer ludicrous—and when I say ludicrous, for your redneck population, I mean bullshit." Madden settled down and said, "I again request an attorney, and I'm prepared to go to trial."

"Suit yourself," Wells commented as he shouted for the jailer to take him back to his cell. "But, Madden, one last item I think you should know. We're planning to call Stanford University tomorrow and brief them on the many legal challenges you'll be facing here in the next few months. I hope this doesn't affect your scholarship or career in teaching."

Shit, Madden thought, *how do they know about Stanford and the scholarship, and what else do they know?*

"Madden, think about this in your cell while I get you an attorney," Garcia said to toy with him.

"What would happen to my scholarship if I did volunteer to do this community a big service by teaching here?" Madden asked, suspecting Wells and Garcia had already worked this out and had an answer.

"If you decided to volunteer for our teaching needs, we would contact Stanford University and explain our dire need for a qualified teacher—you. Also, we'd state how we specifically sought you out, and you realized the needs of this community were greater than your own personal needs, specifically the scholarship," Garcia smiling assured Madden.

"Please help me here. How can you ensure that Stanford will allow me to defer for a year?"

Garcia winked at Wells said, "You'd be surprised by the many 'friends' we have, Mr. Madden."

"Think about this in your cell, Madden, or can I call you Rob?" Wells said almost as a friend. "Jailer," Wells hit his intercom, "please escort Mr. Madden back to his cell."

Reflecting on the last few days, Madden wondered how fate, bad luck, or spiritual intervention had placed him here; maybe he was in purgatory for his past sins. He lay down on his bunk and began thinking of his beautiful and faithful wife and his two girls, so bright and pretty with their blue eyes. He wondered if they would understand his current predicament. He hoped they would accept that he did his best to protect that woman and her children as he would've protected them. The only solace Madden had was they would be proud of their father for doing what was right, not what was easy. Madden's dreams and nightmares came alive as he fell into a deep sleep on his bunk.

"Madden, get up. You have a visitor," the jailer yelled inside the cell.

"Tell Little to pop some flares for the LZ," Madden shouted as he awoke, looking somewhat surprised by his environment. The jailer just stared at him and walked away shaking his head.

"Good evening, Mr. Madden. Not sure if you remember me, I'm Doctor Lightfeather."

"Of course, Doctor," replied Madden still a little groggily from his sleep.

"I thought I'd come by and check up on my patient here. How're you feeling today?"

"Doctor, thanks for your care. I'm better, but these stitches in my mouth are awkward. Many thanks."

Doctor Lightfeather made a quick examination of Madden and asked why his blood type was tattooed on his arm. Madden explained it was necessary in his prior military life, and Lightfeather completed the exam.

"Well, Mr. Madden, it appears you heal very quickly. Are you hungry?"

"Absolutely, doctor," Madden replied, "really hungry."

From another bag, Lightfeather brought out some containers filled with tacos, enchiladas, rice, and beans. They sat together eating, and Madden definitely enjoyed Lightfeather's company. Madden's first impression of Lightfeather was that of an intelligent, hardworking doctor who wanted to practice medicine for all the right reasons.

"Tell me Doc, how'd you ever end up in Calico County?"

Lightfeather laughed, sat back, and told his story about how he was repaying the fine people of New Mexico for his medical school expenses. Lightfeather went on about his Native American heritage, family, and future aspirations.

"What about you, Rob? If half the stories I've heard are true, you're now some sort of legend by taking on Billy Hemrod in the casino." Lightfeather added, "I'm sure they want their pound of flesh for your actions. But seriously, Rob, you're lucky just to be in one piece. Why were you spared?" Lightfeather was curious.

"Bottom line," Madden thought, "is apparently the county is hard up for a seasoned schoolteacher, which is my saving grace or my back luck." What he said was, "Doc, do you know anything about the schoolteacher situation here, in particular a place called Tres Rios?"

Lightfeather was uncomfortable with that question; he might be the one person who knew it best.

"Rob, for your own sake, you don't need to know," Lightfeather's cold response caught Madden off guard.

"What's so darned sensitive or dangerous about discussing the teacher shortage here?" Madden's asked with growing curiosity.

"Rob, trust me and leave it alone." Lightfeather tried to change the subject by asking Madden about the Sheriff Wells's deal.

"Doctor Lightfeather, I've been given the option of either having a trial here in Calico County for assaulting Billy Hemrod, for which I would most likely go to the state prison for a couple of years—or I can volunteer to teach school in Tres Rios for one year, with all charges dropped, like it never happened."

"I hope you've learned your lesson about protecting ladies in distress at Indian casinos," commented Lightfeather while Madden laughed despite a few sore stitches.

"You know, Lightfeather, next time I'll just wait for him out in the parking lot and get out of town sooner. What do you think?"

"Yes, spend your time in Tres Rios purgatory and earn yourself out with good deeds. And Rob," Lightfeather recommended in a very serious tone, "if you do accept the sheriff's deal and live here in Tres Rios for the next year, for God's sake, keep what you see to yourself and don't be asking a bunch of questions. From what I know, the school you'd be assigned to has had nothing but problems for the past few years. New teachers are always coming or going for various reasons.

"The students at Tres Rios are considered the bottom of the barrel, the rejects or the misfits of the Calico County public school system." Lightfeather added, "However, the county is required to provide them with an education, something to do with the No Child Left Behind law. Are you familiar with that law?"

"Yes, I know all about that law."

Lightfeather gradually started to open up to Madden with more information. "We've seen many new teachers come to this area with the romantic notion of making a change and with a truly sincere effort to move the underprivileged forward. In the end, the teachers either got very frustrated or left and we never heard from them again."

"What a shame to place new, highly motivated teachers in such a difficult environment right out of college," said Madden, agreeing with Lightfeather. "Where exactly is this school? Nobody has mentioned its location," asked Madden.

"The school is located in an area west of town known as the Flats. It's a rather poor community of mine workers, casino help, county workers, ranch hands, and people with nowhere else to go. You can probably tell from my description what type of students you'll find at Tres Rios. You'll also receive free housing as a resident schoolteacher in the Flats." Madden received this news suspiciously. The doctor added, "It's a sight to behold, a genuine double-wide trailer in the Flats. I think it served as a whorehouse for the miners at one time."

"Thank you, Doctor Lightfeather, for caring about my quality of life. Any more good news you can pass my way?" Madden laughed with Lightfeather.

"I'll check on you tomorrow," Lightfeather stated as he was departing. "Rob, one other thing, rumor has it that you speak perfect Spanish, is this true?"

Somewhat amazed by how Lightfeather knew, he answered, *"Sí mi doctor, hablo español perfectamente. ¿Y usted?"* Madden replied.

"Bien, va a necesitarla," Lightfeather answered, *"¡Hasta manana!"*

The Roosevelt Hills Elementary School staff was shocked to hear that their favorite teacher had been detained in New Mexico for getting involved in a domestic-disturbance incident at a casino. Some were not surprised. Superintendent Tessa White had counseled Madden many times not to get involved in family issues—he certainly had enough to do as a teacher. She had warned Madden on numerous occasions that altercations with a student's parents were totally unacceptable. Even though some parents deserved a good thrashing for not caring for their children, it was not up to Rob to resolve the matter. He needed to cope with the reality that he had to work issues out through due process with the local authorities.

Funny, thought Dr. White, *Rob usually took care of business in a dark parking lot with no witnesses. Wonder why he did it in public, in a casino no less? Oh, Rob, just learn that you can't cure all of the world's ills.*

In the afternoon, White had a long conversation with Madden over the phone, and he explained everything, including the deal he'd received from the sheriff and county attorney.

"Well, Rob, you really got yourself into a mess this time. What're you going to do?"

"Tessa, I suspect I really don't have a choice but to take the deal and teach here for a year. Will you still have me back?"

Knowing Madden and his propensity to always side with the underdog, she replied, "Of course, Rob. I don't think we'll have a problem rescheduling your admission to Stanford after you complete this volunteer work." She added. "Also, the county attorney, I believe his name is Raymond Garcia, and the school superintendent for Calico County called me yesterday. I'm not sure who these people are, but they certainly knew everything about you—everything. Rob, it's up to you, but I could get you in contact with the school attorney here and possibly challenge what's happening in New Mexico."

"Tessa, I've thought a lot about that option, but Garcia and Wells made it very clear to me: either I teach or go to jail," Madden sighed. "Anyway, they could hold me up for months or years playing with the legal paperwork."

"All right, Rob. But if you need legal assistance, don't hesitate to call the school attorney or myself."

"Thanks, Tessa, for understanding, and I'll keep you posted on what happens here."

"Good luck, Rob," White said. As she hung up, she thought, *For God's sake, Rob, would you please stop playing the darn crusader?*

Madden hung up the phone and picked it up again to place the one he'd been dreading. "Mr. Garcia, good morning, this is Rob Madden."

"Good morning, Rob. What can I do for you?" asked Garcia knowing full well why Madden had called.

"I've decided to accept your generous invitation to teach school at Tres Rios," Madden remarked sarcastically.

Not surprised, Garcia smiled and replied, "Outstanding. We certainly do appreciate your assistance in our time of need. Mr. Madden, are you at the courthouse?"

Madden knew he really meant, *Are you still in jail?*

"Mr. Garcia, I was just released from my cell and I'm in the reception area collecting my belongings."

"Good, a couple things: first, we need you to visit Dr. Helen Kramer, the superintendent for Calico County public schools," Garcia directed. "I'll have all of the information about when and where to meet her prior to you leaving the courthouse. Then Sheriff Wells and I need to have a short meeting with you, a kind of 'welcome to Tres Rios orientation.'"

"In other words, I'm to receive my volunteer work dos and don'ts," Madden offered.

"Exactly, Mr. Madden, you understand completely. Hope you enjoyed your stay in the courthouse and please get over to see Dr. Kramer as soon as possible," Garcia gleefully remarked.

Madden wanted to tell Garcia where to go but decided to hold his tongue, he was in enough trouble, so he replied, "Thank you very much, Mr. Garcia. I appreciate your support." Reflecting for a minute, he thought, *Why couldn't I have been a truck driver. They would've just beaten me up, taken my money, and let me go. But, oh no, they needed a schoolteacher—lucky me.*

When Madden found the Calico County schools administrative building on Third Street, it was obvious they were waiting for him. Walking into the old hotel that had been converted into the county's administration office, he realized all eyes were on him as he approached the reception desk.

"I'm Rob Madden, here to see Dr. Kramer."

The young assistant behind the desk was visibly nervous, "Yes, sir, Mr. Madden. Dr. Kramer will be right with you, please take a seat over there."

Low hushes rushed through the building with the common theme, "He's the guy that beat up Billy."

The office area was quiet as assistants and directors stared at the new Tres Rios teacher. Madden felt the stares and the awkward quiet in a normally active and noisy work area; he was getting a small kick out of it. Reading yesterday's *New Mexico Times* for a few minutes, he was then ushered into a large working office with a huge oak desk and a conference table, both filled with stacks of folders, not uncommon for a school superintendent. Madden was asked to take a seat at an empty chair on the least-cluttered end of the conference table. He found an old copy of the *National School Board Association Magazine* and began reading it, noticing that many articles were about No Child Left Behind.

After a few minutes, the door opened and a petite, tanned, and well-groomed middle-aged woman entered the room. Madden noticed that she wore a little too much makeup to cover her wrinkles and she sported a hairdo that looked right out of 1964. "Mr. Madden, I'm Helen Kramer, superintendent of Calico

County schools. It's very nice to meet you. I've heard and read a lot about you."

Madden stood politely and put out his hand, "Thank you, and you have me at a very big disadvantage, Dr. Kramer, I don't know anything about you or your school district."

Dr. Kramer held back the laughter and said, "I'm so happy that you've volunteered to teach here this year. I'm sure the students will benefit from your credentials and experience."

Madden was laughing while thinking, *One minute I'm getting the hell beaten out of me from the local cops, the next minute praised as a community-minded schoolteacher.*

"With all due respect, Dr. Kramer, I suspect you know the whole story of why I'm here. Is that correct?"

Dr. Kramer asked Madden to take a seat as she reviewed some reports in a thick folder. Placing her reading glasses on, she said, "Let's see, Mr. Madden, the only thing I know is that you just happened to hear about our need for a rural schoolteacher, and you volunteered," as she gave a quick wink.

Madden was trying to read and understand Kramer. "Isn't that what happened, Mr. Madden?" repeated Kramer as Madden remained silent. "Mr. Madden, for your benefit, I know about Billy Hemrod and how you tried to protect his wife and children, the miscarriage of justice in your interrogation, your injuries, the deal, and most important of all, your qualifications and experiences. I also understand you were on your way to Stanford University on a full-ride Distinguished Veteran scholarship to earn a doctorate in education."

"Yes, that's all correct. May I ask how you were able to obtain my personal records?" Madden replied.

"I understand the sheriff has many informal connections among the law enforcement brethren, and you might say the sheriff and I are close friends," again Kramer winked at Madden. "I also understand you were some sort of hero in the Army."

It was becoming standard for Madden now to state, "Air Force, please, not Army."

"Whatever. Mr. Madden, would you like to see where you will be teaching next week?"

It was a beautiful summer day with blue skies, never-ending desert terrain and mountains on the horizon. As they drove down the old asphalt road known as the Flats highway, Madden sat back and somewhat enjoyed the ride.

"Mr. Madden, I suspect you've not heard much about our small community next to Tres Rios called the Flats."

"I've heard a little, none of it good," Madden replied.

As they drove through a sprawling complex of shantytown mobile homes haphazardly arranged with no order or plan, Madden realized the area was also an abandoned adobe village. In the middle of the community were a liquor store, a convenience store, and a few cantinas.

"What a crummy little community," Madden muttered.

"What was that, Mr. Madden?" asked Kramer.

"Oh, I said I can hardly wait to see the school," he replied.

At the edge of town, there it stood in all its glory; the sign above the cattle guard read, "Tres Rios Rural Elementary School."

Situated on a small hill, the school looked fairly new. However, due to neglect, it was in desperate need of repair and cleaning. Madden and Kramer walked from the small parking lot to the front door of the school where Kramer fumbled in her purse to find a key. Madden surveyed the schoolyard and noticed that the playground equipment was broken and shabby trees and bushes were almost everywhere. All types of trash littered the schoolyard, predominantly beer and soda cans and typical house waste.

Madden also noticed the unmistakable gang graffiti painted around the school building. Madden had made it a habit to take a hard look at the graffiti in the foreign countries where he'd lived or been stationed. He found it to be a good source of intelligence regarding who was trouble in the local communities. One piece of newly painted graffiti quickly caught his attention: "Madden, RIP." As Kramer finally found the keys to the large chain lock, she also noticed the graffiti mentioning Madden.

"Oh, Rob, don't pay any attention to that. I'm sure some kid did it as a joke."

"Dr. Kramer, we both know who put that there."

Madden and Kramer looked at each other for a moment. There was no winking or smiles. "Okay, Rob, here we go," she announced, finally opening the door.

It was clear to both that no one had been in the building for quite some time. Without looking and by the smell, the bathrooms needed immediate repair and a thorough cleaning. As they made their way through the building, Madden judged the school had been built with three classrooms and a common area for meals and school functions. Trash, textbooks, and old tossed assignments littered one classroom floor. The other two classrooms were used as the school depository with stacks of boxes filled with books and school equipment.

"Whoa, this place sure could use a good cleaning, wouldn't you say, Mr. Madden? Good thing you showed up when you did," said Kramer now smiling.

Giving Madden the dollar tour of the school, they arrived at the teacher's office that no one had entered since Betty Wilson left three months ago. It was locked, and again Kramer worked her purse trying to find the keys. Opening the door, the stench escaping from the small office was nauseating. After catching his breath from the smell, Madden studied the room, became serious, and said to Kramer, "There was a horrible struggle in this room—possibly a fight or a rape."

Madden was pointing out to her what appeared to be dried blood on the desk and the floor with some residue of body fluids. Kramer did not act surprised at Madden's observations.

"Mr. Madden, last year, a small boy was hurt on the playground. I suspect the teacher cared for him here."

That was the answer Madden expected from Kramer, but he thought it was really something more sinister from what he had heard about Tres Rios. The teacher's office haunted Madden, but he wasn't prepared to show it.

Returning to the main classroom, Kramer asked, "Do you have any questions?"

"Yes, ma'am. If I didn't volunteer to teach here, who would be teaching this school year?"

"Fair question, we most likely would've hired substitute teachers as we've been doing since last year."

Madden could not imagine an inexperienced teacher or even a substitute in this environment, which was unfair to the students, teachers, parents, and the community. "Would you say the elementary classrooms at your main school in Tres Rios are similar in appearance to these classrooms?" asked Madden.

With that question, Kramer asked Madden to take a seat with her at a desk in the classroom.

"Mr. Madden, I've been a teacher for over twenty years and an administrator for almost five years. I can tell you're a seasoned educator as well. As superintendent, I have to allocate our resources and teachers to where they will do the most good for the students of Calico County."

Madden listened with little emotion as she continued, "Many of our students are high achievers and motivated to go beyond the county to go to college versus the mines and casinos. So yes, Mr. Madden, for your benefit, the classrooms and facilities here are different, significantly different. Who are we to save—the children with promise and potential or the children with no future?"

Madden was surprised, although to Kramer's benefit, she was speaking the brutally honest truth. He said, "I thought it was our job to give every child a chance, a fighting chance, for a good education. Dr. Kramer, with all of the laws pertaining to equality in teaching and standardized testing, how in the hell do you get away with not caring about the children here at Tres Rios?"

An ominous smile came over Kramer's face, "Mr. Madden, I'm sure you are well aware of all of the provisions and waivers in No Child Left Behind, we certainly are. Calico County has several important waivers to the law: most of our students are impoverished, we also teach students from the tribal reservations, and many of our students require English as a second language. Summing up, you might say that redistributing the education dollars is perfectly legal and within our right; there is a waiver for everything."

Madden was floored and not prepared to ask any more questions; he was actually going to be teaching in this environment. After preaching to him about education, Kramer put on a smile and added, "How do you think we obtained your services as a schoolteacher? We waived a few rules of the law. Would you like to see where you'll be living for the next year? Oh, and I had the …" Kramer stopped and started again, "The sheriff sent a team of prisoners out here to clean your new residence."

"Thank you, Dr. Kramer. If it's as nice and luxurious as this school, I truly have something to look forward to," answered Madden cynically.

CHAPTER

Kramer drove her SUV down an old two-lane highway out of the Flats and into what looked like a mining quarry. Just over a small rise in the road, Madden viewed, for the first time, his home for the stay: a double-wide house trailer near a large parking lot.

"Dr. Kramer, how long has this trailer been the residence for the Tres Rios schoolteacher?"

"Well, you see, Rob, one time, it was a private meeting place for the county fathers. Now it's been transferred and put to better use as the teacher's residence. You know, like an incentive to attract good schoolteachers," she answered.

Madden could hardly contain himself and burst out laughing. The way he figured it, the casino ended the need for an out-of-the-way meeting place, or rather house of ill repute, for the local kingpins. After controlling his laughter, he thought, *These people really need a dose of reality. Everything they know is either a dream or a lie. Maybe at this point, it doesn't make any difference.*

"Here we are, Mr. Madden—home, sweet home," Kramer announced as she stopped in front of the trailer.

After inspecting the furnished trailer, he was thoroughly surprised at how clean and organized it was—even the furniture and bathrooms were spotless. "My God, who cleaned this place? Very good work," said an amazed Madden.

"Well, Rob, with your Army experience, I'm sure you're a stickler for order and cleanliness," said Kramer smiling and making fun of him.

"Air Force, not Army, thank you," he said under his breath.

"Oh whatever, Rob. Isn't it all about the same? Now, everything you should need should be here—from bedroom linen to a fully furnished kitchen. You should be set to move right in. So here are the keys. Enjoy!"

Madden was still pondering what this furnished and exceptionally clean trailer was doing out in the middle of an old mining quarry. He was sure there was a story, and for now, he would believe anything.

"Okay, fine," Madden replied.

Kramer and Madden were heading down the trailer steps to Kramer's SUV when she turned to him, "Rob, would you like a lift back to your Honda at the courthouse?"

Madden again came close to laughing and replied, "Do I have a choice?"

Madden was getting the feeling that Kramer was going to enjoy having him around, kind of like a trained pet to use at her disposal. "Dr. Kramer, would you mind if we dropped by the school for a few minutes? I want to set some goals and requirements with you. In other words, let's talk about what I'm going to need to do my job."

"Why of course, Rob. I think I can spare a few minutes," said Kramer, somewhat perplexed by the request. She was no longer smiling as they drove down the rural road toward the school.

Kramer's SUV entered the school compound under the late afternoon sun. The wind was sending dust particles from the direction of the mine into the Flats. Kramer and Madden headed back to the common area and sat at an empty table, both trying to read each other's mind. Each thought they were the person in charge.

"With all due respect, I understand there's a history here with an endless procession of newly assigned teachers to this school for the past few years," commented Madden.

Kramer became uncomfortable with Madden's observation and said sternly, "Please, Rob, continue."

"You and I both know that I was literally drafted, or rather shanghaied, into working as a teacher for you this year. I think it stinks, but there it is. You also know, and I don't mean to brag, but I'm a good teacher, especially with multiethnic, poverty-stricken children," Madden added.

"Like the ones here at Tres Rios?" Kramer asked.

"Maybe so, but the point is this," Madden emphasized, "I'm a professional, and yes, I know this sounds corny or trite, but I don't plan on being just another substitute teacher to help Calico County fill in that square." There was a short silence, and it was obvious Kramer was getting frustrated with Madden's attitude.

Kramer rose from her bench and stared at Madden stating firmly, "We're giving you a very nice place to live for a year, and I'm sure it beats the county jail, Rob. Also, for your benefit, we're not expecting you to work miracles here in the Flats. However, the state and feds do expect a certified teacher, and so here you are. You're only going to be here a year; why do you care what happens to this place after you leave? What does it matter to you? It's not a perfect world, especially here in Tres Rios. It can get ugly, very ugly. I recommend you just worry about teaching the students you're assigned with the resources provided you."

With that statement, Madden looked around the disorganized and dirty school interior and repeated, "With what resources, I might ask?"

Kramer slowed her voice and looked around, realizing Madden's point. With her venting finished, she asked, "Okay, Rob, what do you think you'll need to make it worth your precious time to stay here?"

Madden was prepared for the question and more than ready to answer. "First, Dr. Kramer, we need a small computer lab, preferably about ten computers with educational software and Internet access."

Kramer almost fell off her chair laughing, "Are you serious, Rob? Why would I want to invest in ten good computers for ..." Kramer's words stopped in midsentence.

"Please continue, Dr. Kramer," Madden said, knowing exactly where she was going with her sentence.

Kramer quietly gathered her thoughts, "Nice, Rob, but where am I going to get ten computers and setups for this school?"

"I understand the board of education usually authorizes such purchases," Madden sarcastically answered.

Kramer was trying to understand Madden's motives for such a request. "Mr. Madden, the Calico County school board is mostly made up of the gentlemen you met when you first arrived at Tres Rios. I believe you met them at the courthouse?"

Madden quickly got to the real point regarding the school board, "I suspect the board defers a lot of the decision making to you, Dr. Kramer. Is that correct?"

Kramer now with a large smile replied, "Why yes they do, Rob. You're very observant. I guess you learned that in the Marines."

"Air Force, thank you," Madden again replied.

Kramer was having fun always bringing up his military service—in every branch except for the Air Force. She was beginning to feel comfortable with Madden, learning quickly that he was indeed a different type of teacher—one they certainly were not accustomed to at Tres Rios. She was actually starting to respect her new teacher.

"Okay, Rob. If it'll make you happy, I'll get some computers up here and have them installed in the common area tomorrow. Is there anything else I can do that will make life better for the students in the Flats?" she jokingly asked.

"Since you asked, I do have another request that I believe you are just the person to make happen."

"Oh please, Rob. Ask away, I'm here for you," Kramer was entertained by this new teacher.

"You mentioned that the excellent maintenance and upkeep of the teacher's trailer was due to a detail of county-jail prisoners. Is that correct?"

"Yes, that's correct. They do wonderful work don't they?"

"Outstanding work," Madden noted and continued, "Given your association with the sheriff, I suspect you could use your influence for another little project for us."

"What might that be, Rob?" said Kramer, preparing for another request.

"Dr. Kramer, look around. School starts next week and look at this place."

"Yes, it does look a bit disorganized," she sheepishly stated.

"Disorganized? This place is a mess. There's dirt everywhere, and the smell from the broken bathrooms is worse than many third-world-country facilities," said Madden, now lit up.

"Okay, Rob, I get the picture. I'll talk to the sheriff tonight and see if we can get his inmates over here tomorrow to start cleaning," Kramer said to Madden, who was nodding his head in approval. "If I get the prisoners here tomorrow, can you supervise them and direct what needs to be done?"

Shocked at her quick approval, he said, "Of course I'll be here, and thank you."

"I'll have my maintenance people at the main school drop off some supplies tomorrow, such as paint, cleaning supplies, and the rest of the things you'll need. Fine with you?"

"Good idea, Dr. Kramer. Glad you thought of it," he answered.

Weighing the school-district priorities, Kramer thought, *I wonder if he really can make a difference out here?* The idea hadn't crossed her mind until now.

CHAPTER

The county bus arrived early Thursday morning to the rural school where Madden was waiting. Busy noting all of the projects that needed to be accomplished, he noticed a trail of dust following an old converted school bus (now the prison bus) that was driving up the road to the Flats. Madden was inventorying all of the tools, paints, and hardware that Dr. Kramer had delivered the previous day. It seemed she was also keeping her end of the bargain by sending the prison labor.

Madden sat back and reflected for a moment while the old smoking bus chugged up the asphalt road leading to the school. Sitting on the picnic table under a large cottonwood tree and drinking some coffee, Madden reminisced about the events of the past few years—especially with his wife and two girls—and where he was today. Madden did not like reliving those tragic days. "Oh, my dreams. What the hell happened to my great dreams?" he silently repeated. He blamed the nightmare on himself, his stupid righteous attitude of attempting to step forward and correct the ills of the world, or at least in his little sector of it. "Now, here I am in purgatory, shanghaied to teach school in this rural cesspool." The county bus was just entering the school parking lot and Madden shook his head, "Well, this certainly beats Stanford University."

"Hey, buddy, are you Madden?" the bus driver yelled. Viewing the eight prisoners in the passenger seats wearing orange jumpsuits, Madden nodded his head.

"Come on, Madden. Take your prisoners so I can get out of here," the bus driver pleaded.

"Okay, everyone, please get off the bus," Madden directed and pointing to the tree said, "We'll meet at the picnic table under that tree."

"Hey Madden, did you really take on Billy Hemrod and break his arm?" the bus driver anxiously asked.

"Heck, friend, do you think a guy like me could do anything like that?" Madden answered with a smile and a smirk on his face.

The driver laughed and yelled out, "Good luck to you, Madden. Been nice to meet you, and hope you last," as the bus left a trail of dust leading back to Tres Rios.

Madden turned his attention to the eight prisoners milling around the picnic table. He was trying to size them up to organize into work teams that could begin refurbishing the school. All were conversing loudly in Spanish, cracking jokes, and making rude comments about Madden. Unbeknownst to the prisoners, of course, Madden understood everything they said.

One prisoner laughingly pointed at Madden, gave him a hand signal, and made derogatory statements about Madden's family. Madden answered the prisoner in perfect Spanish and shot back comments about the prisoner's ancestry. The prisoners were astounded by what they heard from this gringo in their native tongue.

The first prisoner was so taken aback by Madden's quick reply that he lunged at Madden to strike him. Expecting this reaction, Madden gave him a quick blow to the stomach. The man immediately hit the ground with the wind knocked out of him. No one moved or said a word. Madden helped him up while continuing to survey the rest of them—looking for a leader.

Out of the corner of his eye, he noticed one prisoner wearing what he thought was an old, worn-out Marine utility cap with the faded, barely recognizable Marine Corps emblem. Also, Madden noticed a "Semper Fi" tattoo on the prisoner's arm that marked him as a Marine. *Very good, I have my leader,* thought Madden, now satisfied.

Approaching the former Marine, Madden bellowed, "What's your name, prisoner?"

"Mr. Madden, my name is Hank Romez, and your Spanish is very good. We did not know," he answered.

"Mr. Romez, you're now in charge of the prisoners," Madden announced. "Here's a list of the projects that need to be accomplished here at the school. You'll find all the necessary supplies stacked at the school entrance. Okay, you have the list, the supplies, and the manpower. Any questions?"

The shocked Romez professionally answered, "No, sir!"

Instinctively, Romez drew from his military past and began expertly assigning the other prisoners to details and inventorying the supplies for the projects. Romez was now encouraging his fellow prisoners to do their best or face a one-on-one with him in the back of the school.

Good progress, Madden thought, *It appears I made the right decision on this one.*

Madden stayed out of Romez's way as the prisoners put the rural school back into some semblance of order. He'd seen many older veterans like Romez around the world; they left the service for various reasons and found it hard to cope outside of it. Madden reasoned that Romez was a Native American from the local tribe who'd joined the Marines to get away and see what life was like outside the reservation. He also suspected that something happened to Romez that brought him back to the reservation: a fight over a woman, too much drinking, trouble with the law, or getting on the wrong side of a gunnery master sergeant. Could have been anything, but now he was back where he started, in jail, with little future or promise. *Heck,* Madden thought, *why am I judging anyone? I'm in jail too.*

During a break in the work, Madden commented, "You know, Romez, those tattoos of yours are going to get you in trouble."

"Or save me, sir," came Romez's reply. Madden thought about that reply for a long time.

The rural school was taking on a new look, and the prisoner team and Madden were grabbing a lot of attention from the populace of the Flats and Tres Rios. Throughout the day, groups of people came out of their small shacks, trailers, apartments, or wherever a person could find shelter, to marvel at the renewal of the rural school.

Madden didn't know it, but watching the rural school being refurbished was lifting up the townspeople. It gave them hope for the future, especially for their children. The construction sounds of hammers hitting nails, the cadence of sawing wood, and sporadic conversations in Spanish—something was stirring the energy and, above all, creating hope.

As the sun slowly went down on the desert valley to be hidden by a small mountain range in the distance, Madden was impressed with the day's outcome. The school was truly looking new again.

"Hank, have all the prisoners stop their work and secure the tools and supplies for tomorrow," Madden instructed Romez. "Also, you and the prisoners meet me down at the dry creek bed when you're through," Madden pointed to where he wanted them to meet.

"Yes, sir, boss," Romez said, not wanting to tangle with this crazy gringo.

Madden started winding down the work and cleaning up. The prisoners watched him drag a large wooden box in the direction of the creek bed while they followed at a safe distance led by Romez. In excited Spanish, they wondered what was happening and why they were being taken to the dry creek bed.

One excited prisoner cried, "He's going to kill us where nobody can see."

"You heard about what he did to Billy Hemrod, right?" another prisoner warned.

Cautiously, the prisoners climbed down the creek bed and observed Madden sitting on the side of the bank drinking a cold beer with a couple of cases at his feet. The prisoners stopped—startled to see Madden drinking a beer. Madden laughed loudly and yelled in Spanish, "Are you just going to watch me drink the beer? I can drink your share too."

The prisoners smiled with relief that Madden had not gone mad, and they ran for the cooler holding the beer. Sitting back on the side of the creek bed drinking beer and swapping stories in Spanish, the prisoners were glad to be working at the school. And they did cherish the cold beer; life was good for the time being.

The cool, dry breeze felt refreshing to Madden. The desert climate of the Southwest was nothing like that in Kuwait, Saudi Arabia, or Iraq. As the prisoners happily drank their beers and enjoyed themselves, Madden reflected on the past, present, and future and wondered where all of this was going. To himself he said, *Three years ago, I lost my wife, my daughters, and our future dreams to a terrorist explosion. Two weeks ago, I'm traveling on a highway of my dreams to Stanford University to earn a doctorate in education. Since then, I've beaten up the county's gang kingpin that resulted in my detention at the county courthouse and interrogation by the local brotherhood of "honest" cops.*

Madden laughed at himself as he pulled another beer from the case. "Then they find out I'm an experienced teacher," Madden said letting the alcohol control his lips. "Now, look at me, I got it made here," he howled, nearly in hysterics. "I volunteered to teach six grade levels in a one-room, one-teacher school in the worst part of the county with a bunch of poor, forgotten students. And now I get to clean the school with a bunch of county jail prisoners. Oh, Madden, but wait, you do get to live in a double-wide trailer parked in a stone quarry out in the middle of nowhere for a year," Madden said quite enjoying the conversation with himself.

"Hey, boss, you okay?" yelled one of the prisoners to Madden in Spanish.

"*Amigo*, I still can't believe my luck that we're all here together drinking beers in a dry creek bed."

"Yea, boss, we're pretty lucky today, but what about tomorrow?" replied the prisoner. Madden was thinking the same thing.

"Let's go, I don't have all day," yelled the prison bus driver at the prisoners who were heading back to the school. Madden walked along with them. "What the hell is this? Have you scum been drinking, and where in the devil did you get the beer?" the driver screamed at the first prisoner to get on the bus. The prisoner looked at the driver and shrugged his shoulders. Madden was just approaching the bus when he heard the commotion from the bus driver.

"Driver, I don't like drinking alone. The prisoners here are the only ones who will socialize with me." Madden stared at the driver adding, "You understand why, don't you?"

The prisoners were now all seated, still laughing and talking about their crazy day with the new schoolteacher. Madden pulled a six-pack of beer out of the crate, placed a towel around it, and handed it to the bus driver. The surprised driver lowered his voice, gratefully took the six-pack, and hid it in an empty cargo holder. Smiling at Madden, the driver nodded his head, "Yes, Mr. Madden, I understand, and see ya tomorrow morning."

At that, Madden shook his hand and again thanked the prisoners for their work. Watching the bus make its way back to the county road and Tres Rios, Madden heard the prisoners laughing and singing. Madden suspected there hadn't been much singing or laughing in the Flats for a very long time.

In the setting and after years of neglect, the face of the school shone like a beacon with its new paint and clean grounds. It looked to Madden like Hank had installed outdoor lights around the school and it did add to the brilliance of their work. How and where Hank got the lights, Madden never knew and never asked.

Walking to his Honda Element for the drive back to his trailer, Madden's sixth sense indicated someone was watching him. *Oh well,* he thought, *maybe it's nothing. Most of the Flats are probably admiring the progress here.*

From the nearby hill next to a mesa, a couple sets of eyes were focused on binoculars watching Madden. "Why's he doing this?" came a voice from behind binoculars.

Hemrod was also watching from the bed of his pickup truck and without thinking said, "Just another stupid-ass do-gooder."

Returning to his trailer home, Madden found the interior spotless and furnished with everything from towels to soap. He was tired and a little too relaxed from the six-pack he'd consumed earlier. Then he noticed the delicious aroma of Southwestern food filling the trailer. Looking in the kitchen, he found a variety of different foods on the stove, warm and ready to eat. "What the heck is this," Madden commented as he admired and inspected this treasure trove of black beans, tortillas, enchiladas, and a fresh garden salad in the refrigerator. It also contained cold beer, Diet Cokes, and a cornucopia of foods including cold cuts, pasta salads, and fresh fruit.

Overjoyed at the remarkable feast, he couldn't help but wonder, *Why would anyone do this for me?* A nice, clean residence, excellent food, and, of course, cold beer—Madden thought this would be great until he got back on the road to Stanford. But who was doing all of it? He'd make his inquiries to Dr. Kramer and Sheriff Wells in the morning, but for now, he wasn't going to ask any questions and just enjoy the fruits of being an interim teacher at this rural school.

CHAPTER

20

"Madden, do you want your prisoners this morning or what?" yelled the prison bus driver early the next morning.

Madden came from inside the school and again greeted his "county staff," as he liked to call them. The reception was quite a bit different from the previous day. Ol' Hank led the prisoners out of the bus and was greeted by Madden motioning the prisoners inside the school. The prisoners were still, however, wondering what that crazy gringo was up to now.

In the small common area/cafeteria renovated by the prisoners just yesterday, Madden had arranged some burritos and eggs for the group's breakfast. They couldn't have been any more surprised than if Madden had given them beer for breakfast. Of course, that wouldn't have been bad either, they thought.

"Okay, Hank. We have a long day ahead of us—get them going."

His Marine Corps experience was gradually coming back to Romez over the past two days. "Yes, sir. Okay, Pedro, Juanito, start cleaning the classroom. Hernando, begin …" as Hank ordered them around.

Madden again thanked his lucky stars for the prisoners' help and ol' Hank's leadership. As the prison team continued their tasks, Madden began working on the year's lesson plans at a desk. The prisoners renovated every inch of the school, from bathrooms to the playground. The only area intentionally left alone and locked was the head teacher's office.

Madden had purposely kept the prisoners from cleaning that room because he wanted to investigate it for himself. He could sense that most of the residents of the Flats and Tres Rios knew what happened in the small teacher's office, and he'd heard many different reasons for its condition. Madden had a good idea what really occurred there, and he was going to try to confirm it. He kept his inquiry to himself, though, especially from the prisoners. He knew that many local parties would not appreciate him opening past wounds that might also implicate them or reveal their incompetence.

Madden finally reentered the teacher's office cautiously and slowly. The sickening smell was a horrible reminder of what must have happened there a few months earlier. Madden wanted to get a picture of whose caked blood was on the teacher's desk and how what looked like dried human fluid, possibly semen, was also present on the desk and floor.

After a few minutes of slowly moving around the room and viewing things from different angles, it came to him that he'd seen ugly sites like this before—in Colombia, Peru, Iraq, and now New Mexico. Experience had taught him that this was no student who received first aid for a playground accident, and it surely wasn't the place some county employee used to clean a wound. As much as Madden was trying to exclude the worst possibilities of this gruesome site, it became ever more obvious that this was a site of a rape or some sort of personal violation.

"But who or why?" he murmured to himself. "Come on, Madden. This isn't your affair. Clean up this mess and get the school going."

If the attack was as savage as he envisioned, and if there were any students who might have witnessed the senseless and ugly cruelty, disposing of the desk might prevent the evoking of memories past. He felt it was the only thing he could do. He'd have Hank and the prisoners burn the desk at the end of the day, prior to their afternoon siesta, of course.

Madden found an old oak executive desk hidden behind some heavy truck parts in the back of the county storage shed next to the school. It appeared the desk was being used by the workers as a lunch/card table. He was sure the county workers really didn't want to share their personal free-time activities while on the county time.

"Surely, they wouldn't miss this table. Just trying to help the county with its labor productivity," Madden reasoned. So he and a prisoner moved the heavy oak desk into the teacher's office and removed the old one outside to be burned. He noticed the prisoner was a little nervous about being in the office and no less nervous about moving the blood-stained desk outside.

"*¡Dio Mio, que horrible!*" the prisoner shuddered.

After watching the prisoner's reaction, Madden suspected he knew what had happened, possibly from rumors or gossip in the county jail. *No,* Madden thought, *I'm keeping the prisoners out of this. It could get ugly, and there's no point in dragging them into it.*

Madden's training and experience helped him to gradually structure the school in the best way he could for the students and parents alike. School was scheduled to begin in three days, and Madden thought they were about as ready as they would ever be. The prisoners were working on the last of the projects. They took pride in their accomplishments, and the local people verbally thanked them. Lastly, on a four-by-six-foot piece of plywood, Madden painted in large letters, "My goal is to provide the students at the Tres Rios Rural Elementary School with the best education possible."

Madden had completed his lesson plans, which were the most challenging he had ever written or imagined. *How in the world am I to seriously build lesson plans for children from grades one to six in a rural school where they've gone through teachers like popcorn? There's no continuity at all,* Madden continued venting to himself, *God only knows what kind of achievement levels they're on.* Madden had no doubt that student achievement was going to be the least of his worries for now, however. He suspected student discipline and respect were going to be his biggest challenges.

Using a combination of experiences from the military and the classroom, he knew he needed to turn the students into one large learning unit with the older students taking the lead with the younger students. He felt it was the only way to get immediate results. As for the troublemakers and bullies, he could easily identify them on the first day. They would either be reformed or immediately processed out of school. He didn't have time or the resources to play the No Child Left Behind game that had paralyzed so many schools.

Besides getting the children off on the right foot, he needed to engage the parents so they would support his goals and standards for the year. He realized it was unheard of in the Flats, but he was going to hold the parent, guardian, uncle, aunt, or foster parent responsible, just like the student, for the student's education.

Yeah right, Madden laughed at himself for having such a noble and politically incorrect idea, but he would give it his best. Putting the finishing touches on his plans and schedules, he included nothing but math and English and, when time permits, computer lab work.

Regardless, my number-one priority has to be providing the students a safe physical environment that is an emotionally stable place to learn. Tres Rios just may be their only place in the world to learn, grow, and develop hope, he thought. The only thing Madden looked forward to, aside from the day he could finally leave Tres Rios, was returning to his trailer residence for a wonderful meal. To whoever was doing the cooking for him, he was grateful.

Unbeknownst to Madden, the local law enforcement officers and their police union had commissioned Señora Ramona Arroyo, a local café owner's wife in the Flats, to deliver evening meals and beverages to Madden's trailer every day— except for the weekends. The officers hoped this was one way they could make his life more comfortable in Tres Rios and it did help to ease their guilt. Madden just assumed the school district had arranged for his meals and would have never suspected it was his former interrogators.

The prisoners were finishing some trim work when Hank ran into the school looking for Madden. "Mr. Madden, Mr. Madden," Hank yelled while searching for him.

"Yes, yes, Hank! I'm in here. What's going on?"

"Billy Hemrod is coming up the road with his crew."

Madden was getting the feeling that people were afraid of Hemrod and his ways. "Understood, and thanks for the heads-up, Hank. Why don't you and your men go to the creek bed until he leaves."

Hank almost asked Madden if he needed any help with Billy and his friends, but he wasn't that crazy. In a moment, the prisoners were on their way to the creek all wondering if this would be the last of this crazy gringo, Madden. They all took viewing positions on the sandy bank.

Madden saw the pickup getting closer with its plume of dust leaving a hazy cloud. He thought it best to keep his trusty 9mm service pistol hidden in the back of his pants, as he had so many times in the past. Madden sat at the picnic table under the large cottonwood tree reading an education magazine while Billy Hemrod and his friends were speeding straight for the school. Madden was just getting into reading an article on managing problem children when the truck carrying six dirty and drunk men in their late twenties and early thirties came to a screeching halt in the middle of the parking lot.

Looking up from his reading, "Good afternoon, fellows, school doesn't start until tomorrow. I bet you just want to get a good head start on your lessons," Madden cracked wise to Hemrod.

"Well, aren't we the funny man?" Hemrod shouted back to Madden.

The other men got out of the pickup bed and slowly worked their way to the school entrance, while smoking and drinking from half-pint bottles from their jeans pockets. Madden remained cool and unfazed. Realizing the chance of a fight was high, he sized them up, because he needed to know who was carrying guns, knives, and other weapons.

"You know, Madden, that was a pretty stupid thing you did in the casino a while back, very stupid," sneered Billy.

"You know, Mr. Hemrod, I've been thinking about that incident and you're completely correct. That was a stupid thing I did," Madden acknowledged while Hemrod nodded his head, acting as if he truly received an apology from his enemy.

"I should've broken your other arm to make sure you truly remembered it." Madden added, "Now, Billy, if I may call you Billy, what brings you and your friends out here to this center of higher ..." Before Madden could finish his sentence, two of Hemrod's goons grabbed him from behind and held him down on the playground. They easily found his gun and threw it to Billy.

"Well, Madden, I don't think you'll be needing this any time soon," Hemrod croaked as he hurled the weapon out into the dusty playground. "Now, we're going to have a little payback time. Do you know how payback time works, Mr. Madden? Or is it Sergeant Madden?"

Knowing he was in an unexpected jam that he'd stupidly set up for himself, Madden noticed one of Hemrod's crew pulling out a baseball bat from the bed of the pickup and handing it to Hemrod.

"Hey, Madden, how's it gonna feel starting school tomorrow with a broken arm? Enjoy this, you asshole do-gooder," Hemrod yelled as four of his crew held Madden in a position where he had an easy shot at breaking Madden's arm with the bat.

Madden was preparing for the incoming blow when all of a sudden he heard the horn blowing on Hemrod's pickup truck and saw someone driving it down the road, honking the horn, and revving the engine. Everyone was stunned by the scene, including the men holding Madden, giving him the opportunity to break free in the confusion and level the thug holding the bat.

"Shit, it's the truck. Who's driving my truck?" Hemrod cried, while his crew flailed around trying to figure out what to do in their liquored state of mind. Madden loved seeing a bunch of drunk and doped-up men, all out of shape, running after a pickup truck on the loose screaming, "Shit, it's the truck!"

Whoever hijacked the truck was certainly making a show of it with lots of horn blowing and engine revving; the noise could be heard throughout the surrounding community. Madden was laughing hard while watching Billy and his "keystone cops" run after the truck. Eventually they all stopped, bent over attempting to catch their breath and, in a couple cases, throwing up.

The truck was observed loudly leaving the Flats and creating a magnificent dust-and-sand trail down the county highway. After gaining his composure while still bending over to catch his breath, Billy could make out Madden laughing hysterically in front of the school.

"You'll pay for this, Madden. We'll be back," yelled Hemrod as he gave Madden the finger. Hemrod and his crew shuffled back to the road to hitch a ride to Tres Rios and find the asshole who "borrowed" his truck.

Who in the hell was driving the truck? Madden pondered with relief. *Whoever it was, I certainly owe him my health.* Madden dusted himself off and attempted to retrieve his pistol. The prisoners also had a good idea where the pistol landed and were on their way to help find it. Hank found it lodged under a bush and handed it back to Madden.

"Sergeant Madden, you were lucky today, but what about tomorrow?" asked a worried Hank.

"Well, that won't happen again. How stupid of me to play games with those jokers," Madden remarked and stopped and looked the prisoners. "Any idea who might've taken the truck? I was thinking maybe one of you did this brave act—no?" Prisoner Raul came forward and said he saw someone come out of nowhere with black coveralls and a black mask, run for the cab of the truck, and start it.

Hank spoke for them all, "Hey, boss, we may be stupid prisoners, but we aren't crazy."

"I understand," Madden grinned, "crazy like me." The prisoners just smiled, relieved that Hemrod didn't see them.

It was becoming a common occurrence as binoculars were again trained on Madden and his group of prisoners from atop the mesa and small hill.

Elsewhere, a mad and frustrated Sheriff Wells yelled, "Listen, Billy, and you listen to me good!" at the little gathering by the side of the road. Wells had had his fill of Hemrod after hearing about his incident earlier that day with Madden. "We made a deal with this guy Madden, and he appears to be sticking to his word." Wells added, "In fact, he's going above and beyond what we expect from him." Pointing his finger at Hemrod, Wells shouted, "Billy, as long as I'm sheriff, you and your crew will have nothing to do with Madden, nothing. Do you understand?"

The other law enforcement officers of Calico County were present and backed Wells's decision. "Billy, Wells is right. We made a deal with this guy," Deputy Sheriff Kelly affirmed.

"Maybe you assholes made a deal with him, but I'll be damned if I did," said Billy raising his fist and finishing a pint of Jack Daniels from his back pocket. "Well, well," he slurred, "the mighty brave and honest law officers of Calico County seem to have forgotten a few facts of life."

The officers knew where Hemrod was going with this outburst. "Wait a minute, fine and loyal law officers, who beat the hell out of this guy when he had the misfortune of tangling with me. Who's been getting nice little second paychecks from yours truly for 'additional security' at the mine—let's not call it payoffs or bribes because it might give people the wrong idea, right?" Hemrod continued, "And why would I have to pay our loyal and just public officials for additional services? Can anyone help me with this one?" Hemrod went on while his crew were happy to see the police, sheriff, and deputies remain quiet, knowing what was at stake.

"Sheriff Wells, Billy, I'd like to propose a solution to the situation we're in," said Deputy Sheriff Ellis, emphasizing the "we're in." Hemrod and Wells agreed to hear Ellis out. "As it stands now, this Madden guy poses no threat to any one of us. It appears he'd just as soon leave and forget about Tres Rios," Ellis summarized and went on. "Yes, we were wrong to interrogate him so hard, no doubt. However, think about it. If any of us went to a strange place like Tres Rios and saw a guy beating up his wife, girlfriend, whatever, I truly believe we'd act the same way— including you, Billy."

Hemrod was taken aback by what sounded to him like a compliment while Ellis continued, "Billy, we have a good thing going here. Please think about the consequences if something happens to that schoolteacher."

This comment prompted Wells to say, "It's a fact that Madden is some sort of war hero who spent a lot of time with Special Forces, Air Force, whatever. My point is if something happens to him here in Tres Rios, don't you think his old buddies will take it personally and come looking around here to see what happened?" Hemrod started to envision his worst nightmare: outside toughs coming and asking questions about the volunteer schoolteacher. "And these outsiders just might bring their friends, the feds. If that happens, we all go down," Wells emphasized.

It was obvious to the officers that Hemrod was thinking this over. His silence was always a good sign.

"Billy, would you like to teach school at the Flats for even a day? Can you think of any worse hell than to teach at that school and live in the Flats?" Ellis questioned Hemrod.

After a minute Hemrod replied, "Okay, we'll leave him alone until he leaves, as long as he doesn't interfere with our operation. Can you straight and honest public servants make sure Madden doesn't get too smart about mine security?" All nodded yes, returned to their patrol cars, and headed back to town on the gravel county road.

PART THREE

CHAPTER

"Bong, bong, bong," the school bell rang loudly across the Flats as the little community was awakening for the first day of school. Everyone, from the local bartender to the large immigrant families, was waiting with great anticipation for what this day would bring.

For days now, they had watched the local rural school evolve from a dusty, dirty, forgotten memorial to everything that was bad in Flats to a small beacon of hope for a community that had nearly given it up. This day might possibly mean a new start and something to look forward to—a future for the left-behind, impoverished children of the Flats. Like it or not, the gringo savior Madden was on a journey that would change the lives of all the people in the Flats, but no one knew it—yet.

Families, guardians, parents, friends, and relatives were all preparing their children for the first day of school. They hoped it would be different and would last, not a temporary success like so many others. As the ragtag bunch of students headed up the dirty gravel road leading to the school, they also thought, "Maybe, just maybe, this time will be different."

Madden continued to ring the bell and look at his watch. "Well it's time to start a new school year, God help us," he murmured as he said a small prayer and headed to the front yard of the school. He attached the flags of the United States and New Mexico to the newly refurbished flagpole and raised the colors in the blue, clear New Mexico sky.

As the students arrived, he personally greeted each one with a short handshake and asked their names. Most of the incoming students were somewhat intimidated by meeting Madden in person. Some were scared after what they'd heard from their parents and friends about his fight with Hemrod. Madden continued to welcome the people waiting in line to greet him.

My God, Madden thought, *most of these kids are wearing rags and look like they haven't bathed in days. And God only knows if they had anything to eat this morning.* He didn't want the children to know how he felt about his sad observations, but he knew he had to correct these problems soon. After volunteer teaching rural students in South America while in the Air Force, he felt confident he could fix these problems. Madden realized that his first order of business was to convey to the students that they would be safe and healthy at the school and could expect a supportive, learning environment from him as their teacher.

"Good morning, students. Welcome to our first day of school, I'm glad you're here. My name is Mr. Rob Madden, and I will be your primary teacher this school year." The classroom was beginning to fill with the normal chatter of children excited and anxious about their first day of school. "Please, students, take your seats and we'll get started," he instructed. The students stopped what they were doing and stared at their new teacher. Madden was facing children of every size, age, intellect, personality, race, and religion—all in this melting pot called a classroom.

"Before we begin with introducing ourselves, I'd like to set a few rules for our classroom that will also be on the bulletin board located there. First, when you show up for class, you will be on time and ready to begin your lessons."

Madden immediately spotted a potential problem in the back of the classroom, one of the six older students. Madden stopped discussing his ground rules and focused his attention on the older student. "Excuse me, you in the back, what's your name please?" he asked. All six of the older students were now laughing and making faces at the rest of the class.

"Again, you please," pointing his finger at the student, "what's your name?"

"Ain't none of your fuckin' business, Rob," the boy sneered.

"I don't allow disrespect or bad language in the classroom. Again, what's your name?"

"Yeah, who is going to stop me, Rob?' replied the older student who then pulled a switchblade knife from his back pocket. The other students remained completely quiet.

Watching the student pull the knife and open the blade, Madden announced, "Besides language in the classroom and disrespect, I do not allow any weapons. So please give me the knife and tell me your name."

"Why don't you just come and get it, Rob?" the student yelled.

Madden stared at the student for a few seconds and headed directly toward the boy so quickly it frightened some of the others. Seeing the teacher charge him caused the student to panic and begin yelling, "You can't touch me. I'm a student, and it's against the law."

Madden took the knife away from the troublemaker and manhandled him to the front door of the school while the confused boy attempted to fight his way out of Madden's grasp.

"You two," Madden said looking at two startled boys, "please open the door for me." The small boys looked at Madden without really understanding him. Madden saw the perplexed faces and realized they had no idea what he just said.

"¡Por favor, abren las puertas—ahora!" Madden said in Spanish.

The brothers understood, nodded to Madden, and immediately opened the two large front doors. Madden forcefully exited the school with the older student who was still screaming obscenities at Madden. After reaching the bottom of the front steps, Madden threw the older student to the ground and quickly ran back inside the classroom. He then picked up a desk, exited the front door, and threw it on the ground next to the dazed student.

The boy, realizing what had just happened, wasn't used to such treatment by a teacher and pulled another knife out of his pocket. Madden instinctively grabbed that knife and slammed it against the student's side. The knife fell to the ground where Madden stepped on it and broke it to pieces.

Looking at the now-crying boy on the ground, Madden came very close to him and in a very calm voice said, "I can't afford to have students who don't want to learn and prevent the others who do. Also, don't ever bring a weapon to school or threaten me again, or I'll have you shipped to the county juvenile detention center. When you straighten up your act and learn some manners, you can return to the classroom. At that time, bring your desk in, place it in the back of the classroom, and live by our school rules."

Madden was heading back into the classroom when the crying student shouted, "Teacher, my name is Ben Davis. You'll pay for what you did to me today." Madden ignored him and went back into the classroom.

"What do we do?" one student cried. "I don't know what kind of teacher this guy is. He can't be treating us like this, can he?"

"Well, maybe Ben got what he deserved," observed Alan Moore. The majority of the students were glad Ben was out of the classroom. He and his pals had bullied them enough the last few years. The other teachers had tried being nice to Ben, but that had only made him worse.

The emotional chatter in both English and Spanish went on until Madden returned to the classroom to dead silence. The older friends of Ben Davis were now motionless wondering if they too were in line for a taste of the new rural-school discipline.

"Again, good morning, students, I apologize for the interruption. Now let's get back to our school rules and introductions …" continued Madden.

After his class of thirty-four students had the opportunity to give their names, ages, and grade levels, he had memorized their names and sensed who spoke English and Spanish. About two-thirds of the class spoke English, or at least had a good working knowledge of it, the rest were fluent in Spanish. *Okay,* he thought, *maybe it'll work with this ratio; might even be beneficial for the class. But shit, teaching first graders with sixth graders in one classroom? That's back in the Stone Age.*

"Students, could I have your attention please?" Madden announced to the students after all of the rules and the first day formalities had been completed. "Your attention, please. *¡Los estudiantes, Yo necesito su atencion, por favor!*" the students stopped their chatter and focused on Madden, knowing what could happen if they didn't.

Just prior to breaking for lunch, the students understood Madden was different and he appeared to care about them. Just learning each of their names in a short time demonstrated he cared about them as people. From their faces, he could see they had little hope in their lives—only the day-to-day survival in the Flats. Politicians had created No Child Left Behind to save the inner-city youth, but Madden realized he would spend the next year teaching the children who were intentionally "left behind."

"I'm a teacher and I believe a pretty good one," Madden said, talking slowly to ensure all of the students understood what he was saying. "My purpose, or goal, is to be the best teacher possible for each of you this school year," he continued while staring at each student as he spoke. "I expect each of you to also do the best you can."

All the students were nodding their heads. At the blackboard, Madden picked up a piece of chalk and wrote

Goals:

Learn English Grammar

Learn Mathematics

Learn Computers

"Please write these down in your notebooks and take them home to show your parents and guardians. Older students, please assist the younger students in writing this down."

After a few minutes of sharing notebook paper and different versions of the goals, Madden asked to see everyone's papers. It was obvious that there were some older students who did a good job of helping the younger students, while others were on the same level as the younger students; this bothered Madden greatly.

"Let me explain why we're going to concentrate on learning only English, grammar, mathematics, and computers."

One of the older students in the back of the class yelled out, "Are you going to be teaching us all this stuff yourself, teacher?"

Madden stopped, looked at the student for a moment and commented, "Your name's Will Terrell, isn't it?"

The student was surprised Madden remembered his name, "Yeah, that's right."

Still staring at the student, he said, "From now on, Will, when asking a question, please raise your hand and stand."

"Well okay, Mr. Rob." With his hand raised, the boy again asked the question about who was going to be teaching all this stuff now.

Madden was about to split a gut laughing on the inside, and thought, *Poor Terrell, he could use some lessons in manners.* Aloud, he asked, "Mr. Terrell, what do you mean by 'this stuff'?"

Terrell, still standing with his hand up, was trying hard to follow Madden's instructions. "Well er, um, like grammar, 'rithmetic, and computers?"

"For the benefit of the class, Mr. Terrell has asked a very good question. You can drop your hand now, son, and take your seat," Madden instructed. Terrell took his seat and felt relieved he wasn't thrown out of class like Ben.

"Class, the simple answer to Mr. Terrell's question is that I'm not going to be teaching all of our lessons, but some of you are." The younger students didn't understand what Madden was talking about, but the older ones did. Madden announced to the apprehensive students, "Listen closely, I want you all to understand," and while smiling he continued, "that each of you has different talents and skills given to you by God. Some of you are stronger in some things than others."

Juanito Gomez suddenly blurted out in broken English, "Math—I can know good."

Madden was surprised to hear this comment and thought about it for a moment, "Juanito, I'm sure you are and I expect you to assist your other classmates to be better. The older students will share teaching responsibilities with me," Madden explained while the five oldest students wondered what he meant by 'sharing teacher responsibilities.'"

Unlike Madden's goals, the older students' goals were to have a few smokes, come up with some money for a can of beer or two, and just get out of school. Helping Madden to teach school was definitely not in their plans. Knowing how the school went through teachers at an unprecedented rate, they simply smiled and nodded their heads.

The likelihood of Madden not lasting more than a few weeks at the school was high. Then they started wondering what the next teacher at Tres Rios would be like. But they did know there was something different about Mr. Madden, and they sure didn't want to cross him. They certainly couldn't understand that Madden was preparing his students to lead.

"How many of you would like to learn more about computers and the Internet?" Madden asked. This question received the attention of the entire class, and they knew Madden wasn't bluffing after seeing the new computers that had just arrived in the old storage room. "And if given the opportunity, is there anyone here who'd like to learn more about computers and possibly teach others how to use them?" Madden asked and noted that everyone in the class was staring now at Alan Moore.

Madden thought Moore must be the class geek, and he sure looked the part. He was often teased about his weight by the other students and with his thick glasses, he did definitely fit the role of the class dork. However, Alan Moore loved computers and was known around the Flats as the smart kid you went to for computer help or advice.

They all wanted to learn more about computers; their simple desire was to find all the wonderful websites, games, music, and other goodies that they'd heard were waiting for them. All they needed was a computer with Internet access and someone to unlock the door. The other schools around the Flats had modern computer labs for the students to use and on which to do their homework. Tres Rios Rural Elementary School had a couple of old PCs that were considered ancient by modern standards and no Internet access. Now, ten brand-new computers were hooked up and ready for student use. *Yes, this teacher's different,* they thought.

"Okay, good. Who wants to volunteer to take the extra time to learn these computers and be ready to teach the rest of the class?"

"Mr. Madden," Alan nervously announced, "I would like …" the bespectacled Alan Moore spoke up to volunteer to teach the other students.

Madden stopped Alan and said, "Mr. Moore, from now on, please stand when you address the class and me. Do you understand, Mr. Moore?"

"Ah, sure. Yes, sir, Mr. Madden." Alan rose from his desk and announced to Madden and the rest of the class, "I can teach computers."

The other students who usually made fun or teased Alan were quiet and showed some respect for him. Madden was now viewing Alan Moore's performance and sincerity as a minor miracle. *God, I hope you are good at this computer stuff,* Madden thought to himself.

With a little more confidence and swagger, Moore continued by asking, "Mr. Madden, if you'll allow me to spend my recesses working computers …"

Madden stopped Alan again and very kindly announced, "Alan, I need for you to be at recess with your other team members."

"Other team members?" the students whispered among themselves.

In broken English, Manuel Cortez asked, "*Qué es* team?"

"Mr. Cortez, good question. We're going to play soccer every afternoon, and everyone plays. Also Mr. Cortez, a team is also called *un equipo,* okay?"

Pedro Gomez sat at a little desk thinking about what he'd just heard about teams and now soccer surprisingly voiced in Spanish, "But the big kids will kill us. How will it be fair?" Pedro nervously looked around and then took his seat.

"Another good question. Thank you, Mr. Gomez." Madden explained, "The teams will be divided fairly with each team having both older and younger students. Don't worry, it'll be fun, and the teams will be equal in size and number of students." Looking at the students in the back of the classroom, he nodded and smiled, saying, "The older students will be the team leaders."

The older students didn't know whether to laugh this off or take Madden seriously. They presumed he was serious. Nobody ever expected much of the children of the Flats, but these forgotten students were now going to be instructors and team leaders. It was a culture shock for all of them.

"We can't be leaders or teachers; we're only here because we got to be here," Jesse Walker instinctively said. The other students voiced their support for Jesse and endorsed the same sentiments. Most of the older students worked odd jobs around the Flats to support their families or their own teenage lifestyles. School to most was an unappreciated nuisance and requirement imposed on them by their parents and the state.

"What's school going to do for me?" was a common question asked daily by the children of Tres Rios Rural Elementary School. Madden thought they had every right in the world to ask that question. Most knew their fate was waiting tables at the casino, working at the mine or for the county, and in many cases ending up in the New Mexico State prison system.

CHAPTER

Noon arrived, and Madden announced it was time for lunch and recess, "May I have your attention, everyone, let's all grab our lunches and find a place to sit." Like so many activities at Tres Rios, he didn't have a clue about how lunch or recess worked here, not a clue. He had assumed that the students sat down with their friends at a picnic table to eat whatever they had in their sack lunches, and recess followed, the typical American public school activities.

But when all of the students looked at Madden as if he was from a different planet, he realized lunch wasn't a formal function, or a function at all, at Tres Rios. "Oh my God, don't tell me, these kids don't eat lunch here—what other surprises will I find at this dysfunctional school?" Madden mumbled to himself while still smiling to the students. *"Bueno, mis estudiantes es la hora del almuerzo."* Again, in English he announced, "Students, it is time to eat your lunches."

Some students had bags that resembled a lunch, but most had nothing. *Shit,* Madden thought to himself. In all of his detailed planning for the school schedule, he completely overlooked lunch or assumed the lunch situation was standard. From teaching impoverished students around the world in small villages in South America and at a low-income school in the United States, he knew the schools all had some sort of lunch program, except for the Tres Rios Rural Elementary School.

Hurriedly and vigorously trying to correct this rare oversight, and as usual showing no panic, Madden immediately came up with a plan. No time to call the main office and ask, "What in the hell is going on here? How long has it been since the students ate a meal here, you uncaring administrators?"

So he changed gears and said, "Students, hold off on going to lunch for now. Please follow Alan to the computer room; he's going to start now with some computer basics." Alan, a little surprised and unprepared for such a duty, answered positively, "Why, yes, sir, Mr. Rob." Madden looked at Alan for a moment and nodded his approval as the small troop of school students followed Alan to the computers.

"Hold up, Brian," Madden spotted the young student going in with the others. Brian Thompson looked around and was surprised to see Madden pointing at him to come over near him.

"Yea, Mr. Rob?" Brian replied wondering what kind of trouble he was in and hoping he wasn't being thrown out of school like Ben.

Pulling two twenty-dollar bills out of his wallet, Madden bent down and handed Brian the bills. Brian was somewhat uneasy and confused. "Brian, it looks like you can run pretty fast—can you?"

"Yes, sir, Mr. Rob. I can run pretty good."

"Great, Brian. Take this money and run down to that local store and café and see if you can buy enough chicken and potatoes for our lunch—everyone's lunch. If they don't have chicken, get whatever the place will sell you in the way of lunch food." With a large smile on his face and a confident demeanor, Madden asked if Brian could carry lunch for everyone at the school. "Brian, we're depending on you, and thank you!"

Brian nodded his head, awkwardly pocketed the forty dollars, and ran out of the school as though he was on a mission from God.

"God, I hope he comes back," mumbled Madden to himself as he headed into the computer room where he was surprised to see Alan busily sharing his basic computer skills with the remaining thirty-one students. Madden thought he had seen it all, but here was this class geek, teased and bullied by many, but now leading and motivating the entire class. He was showing the others how to navigate the Internet on a computer—from cartoons, courses in Spanish, and websites on repairing/rebuilding pickup trucks.

The students were actually engaging with Alan. Even the older students were working on the computers and asking Alan for assistance, which he was more than happy to give.

Madden encouraged Alan to continue his tutoring until Brian returned with lunch. As he would never have suspected, this day was a new beginning for the Tres Rios Rural Elementary School and its newest teachers, Alan Moore and Rob Madden.

Out of the teacher's office window, Madden observed an antique, banged-up Chevy pickup approaching the school. Still gazing out the window with a bit of curiosity, he thought, *Who and what now?*

The pickup stopped and young Brian jumped out of the cab and retrieved two large boxes from the truck bed. Seeing Brian and a stranger carrying the boxes toward the front of the school, Madden opened the door as Brian flew in with an assortment of Mexican foods. "I couldn't find chicken, but Señor Arroyo said we could have the leftover tacos and burritos from his café," Brian hurriedly explained.

Since his arrival in Tres Rios, Madden was understandably suspicious of unfamiliar men approaching him. His impression was they all wanted to fight him, harm him, or make a deal with him. Arroyo was admiring the newly refurbished building. Showing his front gold teeth in a big smile, he asked in broken English, "Where *usted necesita*, you want *el* food, Sergeant Madden?"

Making a quick assessment of Arroyo, he said, "Please call me Rob. And your name, sir?"

"I am Ramos Arroyo, the owner and manager of the *Perdido Mundo Tienda Café y Cantina.*"

Madden remembered passing the establishment numerous times on his way to and from the school—always plenty of cars in front of the store/café. It certainly appeared to be the area watering hole for the locals to sing, dance, drink, and eat. Knowing his propensity for finding trouble in local establishments, Madden thought it best to pass it by.

"Thank you very much, Señor Arroyo, and to you, Brian. Great job and much appreciated." Brian stood between Madden and Arroyo smiling as though he'd just made the deal of the century. "Señor Arroyo, would you care to stay with us and share your generous lunch with the students?"

"No, *amigo*. I *doy* gave Brian a ride, then his hands had much full, but I *necesito* to return to business. *También*, me give *opportunidad* to see the school new." Arroyo's eyes were roaming the school with a hint of appreciation for what he observed.

"*Amigo*, Rob," smelling slightly of tequila, Arroyo motioned to Madden, pulled two twenty-dollar bills from his denim jacket pocket, and placed them in Madden's hand. "*Tienen* lunch *para* me as *un celebración* of the new school," Mr. Arroyo gleefully said as he headed back to his pickup truck. "*Adios amigo, y buena suerte.*"

"*Equalmente!*" Madden replied.

Rolling down the window of the cab of his truck, Arroyo yelled out, "Rob, *por favor*, come *a mi café* any times. *Yo entiendo usted habla español, que bueno y adiós.*" Grateful for the offer, Madden waved and nodded as the truck turned on the county road heading for Arroyo's cantina. Madden suspected, like most of the residents in the local community, that his life story was known by both those who cared and didn't care. In fact, some residents were even betting on Madden's future at Tres Rios; many thought he'd never last the year.

"Okay, Brian, let's get everyone fed," Madden said while Brian nodded his head in approval. "Could I have your attention please? Brian will be laying out your lunches in the activity room. Please take what you need and enjoy the lunch, courtesy of Señor Arroyo."

All of the students knew Señor Arroyo and his reputation around Tres Rios, which didn't usually include kindness and generosity. Running a cantina and café was most likely a front for other activities. Madden did not care or want to know—if he was a friend of the Tres Rios school, that was good enough for him.

"My God, when was the last time you all ate?" Madden commented as he watched the students wolf down all of the tacos and burritos as if they had not eaten for a week. *Maybe they hadn't* he thought. This was another thorny issue Madden had to work out with the county school superintendent. While the students were gathering in their prospective little groups, Madden stepped outside to make a call to Dr. Kramer about the lack of food and student meals. Madden had a gut feeling that the school district was pocketing the federal funds that should have gone to feeding the students at the rural school.

"Good afternoon, Mr. Madden. How'd it go this morning at Tres Rios? I'm sure all is going well for you and your students," Kramer sarcastically mused. "Oh, by the way, Rob, is there something in your personality that prompts citizens to pull knives on you?" she asked referring to the morning incident with Ben Davis. Word traveled fast around Tres Rios.

"Dr. Kramer, it's obvious you have completely ignored, overlooked, or taken advantage of the educational environment here at this rural school. And right now, I'll start with lunches for the students."

"What about the lunches?" Dr. Kramer naïvely asked.

"You know darn well what I'm talking about!" Madden was beside himself. "Federal law directs free or reduced-cost breakfasts and lunches to kids below the poverty line. I have a bunch of students here that wouldn't even register on that line. Why haven't you provided their lunches?" Madden already knew the answer; it was all dollars and cents. Either the superintendent was pocketing the money by producing false invoices or spreading the windfall to her premier schools in the district.

"Mr. Madden, I'm shocked that no meals are being served there!" Kramer replied as Madden gave her points for theatrics. "I'll look into this and get meals out there immediately. Is there anything else?" she asked. Though disappointed that Madden would take the meal situation so seriously, Kramer was about to get a quick lesson on just how committed Madden was to his assignment.

"Dr. Kramer, since I have you on the line, could you provide me with the past standardized test scores for the rural school?" Knowing the nature of the school, Madden suspected there was no history of standardized test scores because tests were probably never given. There was a long pause on the line while Madden waited for a reply.

"Unfortunately, Rob, all of the standardized test results for the rural school were lost in a fire we had at one of the district's depositories last year." The answer sounded too prepared, too practiced.

"Well, I'm prepared to begin standardized testing this afternoon. Any objections, Dr. Kramer?"

"Why no, Rob. Good idea to start the school year with basic testing," she said trying to sound genuinely concerned. "And please provide us with the test results. We'll find a safer place to store them in the future."

Madden tried to hold back his anger, "Does it make any difference, Dr. Kramer? Have you ever once reviewed and acted upon any test results here?"

"Rob," she said in a patronizing voice, "of course all of our students are important. We just lost or misplaced their scores."

"Wait a minute, you just said they were destroyed in a fire."

"Of course, I just misspoke," she said followed by another a long pause. "You're correct, they were destroyed in the fire. I'm so very sorry, so much happens around here, wouldn't you say, Rob?"

Madden was getting tired of listening to her excuses and lies. He was getting nowhere fast in this discussion. Madden calmed himself down and focused on the most important issue right now: meals for his students.

"Dr. Kramer, why don't you and I get to more pressing needs like feeding the students here at Tres Rios. Exactly when will the meals arrive?"

"Why Rob, you certainly are rushing things. It's going to take me some time to get this organized and approved by the school board." Madden could only imagine who was on the school board, probably Billy Hemrod and his thugs.

"Okay, do whatever you have to do, but I'll have someone there at your office at 0630 hours to pick up the meals for the day. Is that all right with you?"

Dr. Kramer was about to burst out laughing at the notion of transporting meals from the school district to Tres Rios. "And who will be transporting the meals? You?"

"No, I figure if Sheriff Wells would allow one of his prisoners to have a work-release pass, it might solve both of our problems."

Kramer listened and said, "Go on, Rob. What else?"

"There's a prisoner who helped restore the school when the sheriff authorized it. He's an older man named Hank, very dependable." Rob continued, "I'll get Hank a vehicle and he can transport meals from your central facility to Tres Rios daily and even serve the food to the students."

After a few moments of silence, Kramer slowly voiced, "All right, Rob. I'll talk to the sheriff and see if we can get Hank on this task. You will provide the transportation, right?"

"Yes, if needed, he can use my Honda; at least someone would be putting it to good use," Rob laughed.

"All right, Rob. We'll start this tomorrow morning. Have Hank at the district's central kitchen at six in the morning, and I'll have the staff load him up with the meals." Dr. Kramer began to realize the potential problems she could have by not accounting for the government funds for meals that were being diverted to other school activities. Maybe Madden was correct to push the issue.

"Rob, good luck on your testing today. Please don't expect much."

"After what I've seen, these kids are lucky just to have a building to come to—not a school, but a building."

"Let me know how the meal situation works out tomorrow," Kramer said and then hung up, just a little frustrated over what had transpired over the past few years at Tres Rios—maybe even with some remorse.

Sitting on the picnic bench under the cottonwood tree holding his cell phone, Madden stared out at the incredible beauty of the New Mexico high terrain. For a moment, he thought about his wife and daughters—how wonderful it would have been to share this view with them. Mesmerized by the quiet beauty, his reality suddenly returned.

"*¿Señor Rob, querrías comer con nuestros?*" Out of nowhere, a young Hispanic girl with a dripping burrito in hand, came looking for Madden outside the school. Smiling at the young child, he was thinking this little girl was about the same age as one of his daughters.

"Thank you, Claudia, can you also say that in English?" asked Madden.

"I try. Mr. Rob, will you like to eat lunch with us?" repeated Claudia. The sincere, innocent smile came very close to releasing Madden's deep-seated sadness. Madden got up from the picnic table and held little Claudia's hand while they walked back to the school entrance.

"Thank you, Claudia, for reminding me about lunch. Let's see what we can learn today. What do you think?" With a big grin, the child looked at Madden with big brown eyes, nodded her head, and smiled. Madden fought back his tears.

The standardized tests conducted by Madden that first day showed some of the lowest scores ever recorded. Sadly, the older fifth- and sixth-grade students were only at the second- or third-grade level of education. Madden expected no more since he was starting from scratch with lesson plans for thirty-two elementary school students who had been forgotten about and neglected for years.

Madden's new campaign would begin the next day with teaching the basics in reading, writing, mathematics, and computer skills, such as keyboarding. He felt the only saving grace was that the education here couldn't get any worse. Hopefully, he could make some positive contributions. On his way home, he made a quick stop at the county jail to meet with Hank and coordinate his meal-delivery services for the upcoming year.

Not wanting any trouble with Madden, the deputy sheriff and jailer were ready. "Rob, hello. Understand you need some assistance at the school. How can we help?" they asked.

Madden was relieved by their willingness to help given his experiences there. "Fellows, this is what we'll need from your prisoner, Hank Romez …" Madden went on to explain Hank's new role as the meal courier and server for the school.

They all agreed the task would be good for ol' Hank, and they would see if they could get one of the impounded cars at the county lot for his duties. With the sheriff's blessing, and as Dr. Kramer promised, Hank was formally assigned as the Tres Rios Rural Elementary School Meal Coordinator. Madden counted his blessings in getting meals to the school and for finding Hank.

Upon learning of the decision to let a prisoner work around young students, some county school officials and board members were nervous and concerned. They could be held liable in the event there were any problems with Hank and the children. When Madden heard their concerns, he became hysterical and said that the legacy of neglecting the Flats children was criminal. Hiring a reformed criminal to help the school meet acceptable standards just might be the right direction. And no one cared more about that school than Hank Romez.

The deputy sheriff walked Madden back to his car and said, "Rob, we can't undo what happened to you here, but we'll do the best we can to give you some cover while you're working at the school." The deputy put out his hand. Madden was caught off guard by what appeared to be a sincere gesture.

He shook the deputy's hand and gave a guarded smile, "Thanks, Deputy. As you well know, I'll need all the help I can get. Also, if you get wind of any more concerns about Hank, please tell them that I'll crack Hank's skull open if he ever gets out of line."

The deputy grinned and replied, "Madden, most people around here would believe it."

CHAPTER

As the sun rose on a cool late-September morning, a line of young people were on their routine trek to the school. Some parents dropped their children off at the gate, while most walked from their various homes in the Flats or were driven to school in an assortment of pickup trucks and even tractors. The daily school routine started well. The school bell began to ring exactly at 0700 hours as Madden pulled the bell's old but functional ropes and raised the flags on the flagpole. While securing the flagpole rope, Madden noticed a beat-up, dilapidated police cruiser making a dust trail toward the Flats and the school.

Smiling and shaking his head, Madden thought it looked just like the police car Jake and Elwood Blues drove in *The Blues Brothers* movie. Given its noise and ugly appearance, even by Tres Rios standards, who would drive such a car? He was greatly relieved to see Hank's weathered face and Marine Corps cap in the rolled-down window as the car entered the school parking lot.

"Hey, boss, good morning. What do you think?" Hank always greeted Madden with a big grin on his face.

"Hank, where in the heck did you get that? Oh, don't tell me, from the county auction lot?"

"Yea, boss, not sure what's going on, but the sheriff himself gave me the car for the meal trips," said Hank acting as if he were driving a Cadillac, proud of his new wheels.

"Okay, Hank. Go ahead and set up the meals in the break room and begin serving as soon as you can, okay?

Hank retrieved the many bags and boxes of breakfast items, carried them into the break room, organized the meals on a central table, and started a serving line. The students quickly devoured their "free or reduced-cost" meals. For most of the students, the school meals were a blessing and their only real food for the day. Watching them and their obvious appreciation for the food, Madden realized that he'd never thought a balanced meal would become an incentive to go to school and learn.

"Hey, boss, looks like they haven't eaten in a while. What do you think?" Hank commented as he cleared away the tables and gathered the trash.

"I've never seen anything like it. Keep it up, Hank. Do whatever you need to do to keep this running. Any problems picking up the meals at the central kitchen?"

"No, boss, no problems." Shaking his head and gesturing with his hands, he said, "But you should've seen the strange looks I got from the kitchen staff as I loaded the car. Wonder why?" Both Hank and Madden let out a chuckle.

"Okay, Hank, good job. Let me get started teaching school, and we'll see you again at noon."

"*Adiós, jefe.*" Hank took the trash out to his retired police cruiser and headed back to town. For a few moments, Madden eyed the god-awful-ugly police cruiser leaving a dust trail with its loud, worn-out exhaust vibrating the whole area. Heading back into the classroom to get into the challenges he knew he would be facing, he stopped by the lone picnic table under the cottonwood tree and said a short prayer for his small family in heaven, asking for guidance and endurance in the coming weeks ahead. Amen.

"Come on, Tres Rios students, let's finish up your breakfast and have some fun learning," Madden announced as the students began to stream back to their assigned desks. Observing the ragtag children he now was responsible for, he could sense the students appreciated coming to school, even if it was just to get a square meal in the morning. On each desk was a nametag with the name of the student assigned to that desk.

"Hey, Mr. Madden, What's this? We like sittin' in the back, and you got us sittin' up front. What gives?" voiced a frustrated and confused older, sixth-grade student, Robert Duncan.

"Mr. Duncan, I asked the class yesterday to stand when speaking. Please stand up and ask your question," Madden said looking at Duncan sternly.

"Yea, er, yes, Mr. Madden," said Duncan standing now. "How come we can't sit where we want? You got all of us older kids sitting up front with the young ones behind us. What's going on here?"

The rest of the students were mingling around searching for their new desk locations saying things like, "Why can't I sit where I've always sat?" or "I don't want to sit here, I want to sit next to Juanita, James, Hernandez, Mary ..."

"Okay, class. Find your newly assigned seats and I will explain why we have to make a seating change." Madden knew this was a shock for his class, especially on the second day of school, because no previous teacher had probably ever assigned seats. It was going to be tough for the first few weeks, but after that, Madden was sure they would not want to give up their new seats for anything.

"Class, as you can see, the older students are now sitting up front with the younger ones behind them. The reason is simple. The older students are going to assist me with teaching and taking care of the younger students, functioning as team leaders," Madden announced as groans and muttered disapprovals filled the classroom.

Hector Rodriguez awkwardly stood up and all eyes turned toward him. In part English and part Spanish, Rodriguez asked how he could possibly teach anyone else. "Señor Madden, ah, why Mr. Madden, I no have time *para* me *y* you would like me others to *enseñar,* teach *además?*"

"Mr. Rodriguez has brought up a very good question. Thank you, Hector. You may take your seat. If I could please have the older students look behind themselves." The older students turned and looked down the rows of desks at the staring students facing them. "You older students are now looking at the students you're responsible for: they're right behind you."

Full pandemonium would have erupted in the classroom had it not been for their fear of Madden. He slowly eyed each of the older students and advised, "You're leaders now. Watch after your people and take care of them—and also trust me, because I'll take care of you."

Silence now filled the classroom with Ken Arlen slowing raising his hand; the entire class was still panicky over the seat changes and older student leadership. "Yes, Mr. Arlen, question?"

Ken Arlen stood up and asked, "Mr. Madden, you said you'd take care of us if we did this leadership thing with the young ones. What's in it for the leaders?"

"A fair question, Mr. Arlen." Madden continued, "As the class leaders, I expect you to take care of the people in your team, and in return, I will personally hold self-defense classes for the leaders in the afternoons. In other words, you'll be able to better protect yourselves." This statement quickly got the older students' attention.

Both Hank and Dr. Lightfeather had told Madden about the particular challenges and problems the Tres Rios students faced in the community. For years, the students at Tres Rios were considered third-class outcasts and were constantly harassed by the students from the premier county schools. The local toughs from the schools were known for getting the best of the Tres Rios students in fights and confrontations.

The opportunity and chance to stand up against their nemeses sparked hope in the older students, and Madden had known this from day one. Besides giving the older students an equal footing, providing an equal playing field against their richly advantaged peers, it could provide a little discipline—sorely needed.

"Yes, Carlos, you have a question?"

"Yes, Rob. Sorry, I mean, Mr. Madden, so the deal is if we look after our assigned kids, you'll teach us judo and karate?" he said while raising his fist and slamming it on his desk like the boy in *The Karate Kid*. Madden was chuckling as Carlos was now shouting with pain from his not-so-glamorous karate chop.

"Carlos, please don't do that again. Yes, I'll teach each of you how to defend yourselves," said Madden emphasizing the words "defend yourselves." He walked from behind his desk and approached the older students now seated in the front. "Leaders, do we have a deal?" he asked.

Noticing the leaders were looking at each other with some apprehension, Madden recommended that they meet for five minutes in the backyard of the school and discuss it among themselves. The leaders got up from their desks and regrouped in the schoolyard. The new leaders gathered in an informal circle to discuss the situation. Madden knew that the actions these students took today would set the tone and direction for the rest of the year. Madden sensed the leaders were beginning to like being leaders.

After a few minutes, the small group came back and agreed to his proposal. "We'll look after the younger students the best we know how as long as you teach us to fight, er, I mean self-defense," voiced Carlos nervously.

Madden nodded his head in approval and shook each leader's hand, saying, "It's a deal then, and we'll start self-defense classes this afternoon—for leaders only." For the first time, the student leaders felt special and they greatly liked that feeling.

Madden knew he was going to catch grief from Dr. Kramer and the rest of the Calico County School District for teaching self-defense, but Madden reasoned, *What're they going to do, fire me?*

In an unbelievable few days, Tres Rios students were being fed two meals a day on the government's dime, leaders were created to care for the younger students, and the older students were learning self-defense martial arts. In both his military and public teaching careers, Madden had never started a school year quite like this one. He knew that creating a safe environment where the students looked forward to school and where they did not dare miss a day was key in achieving his next goal: instilling motivation in the class.

Now recognized as leaders, the older students showed behaviors he never dreamed possible: their confidence, pride, and morale were obviously boosted—a stroke of genius or just plain luck he wondered. "Damn, Madden, you're good!" he chuckled to himself, "Remember this and use it down the road in the next rural school where you're forced to teach."

As Madden's time passed in Tres Rios, so did the nonstop activity at the uranium mine. The mine operated 24/7 with the constant traffic and rumble of heavy diesel trucks moving in and out of the mine's security checkpoint. The trucks checked in empty and left loaded with uranium ore to be processed at a uranium mill in South Texas. Madden was uncertain about how a doped-up, spoiled rich kid and his crew of goons would be motivated or capable enough to provide security and safety for the mine.

As Madden viewed the mine from a nearby highway, he saw that the trucks appeared to be inspected and processed by Billy's crew prior to leaving the security checkpoint—twenty-four hours a day. Just as long as Billy and his thugs stayed away from the school, whatever else they did was unimportant to Madden. However, things just didn't add up. Madden thought, *Leave it alone and don't get involved,* as he drove down the barren, two-lane desert highway.

Up the steep canyon gravel road, perched on a small stone outcrop was a set of high-power binoculars still monitoring both Madden and the daily operations at the uranium mine. Any unexpected passersby would believe the observer was some drunk old-timer looking for lost treasure, which was the desired impression.

After five months of teaching, motivating, and guiding his students, Madden had developed a routine. The students and teacher were becoming more comfortable with one another and their new spirit of achievement. Tres Rios did have potential, and the parents and students finally felt it.

The county school district officials were also noticing the positive changes but were somewhat bewildered by the increasing progress—how would the school's success affect the other Calico County schools? Although, they reasoned, Madden's instruction in self-defense and martial arts was having an impact on the community, maybe it actually balanced the scale of achievement between the other schools and Tres Rios. After a few weeks, students and teacher were gradually trusting and respecting each other—Tres Rios students felt safe with a teacher who didn't mind taking on Billy Hemrod and his crew. No one else would, including the local law enforcement.

CHAPTER

Coming with their parents, guardians, and older siblings, new students were trickling to the school from all over the county. Madden welcomed everyone to the Tres Rios Rural Elementary School, which, by January, had thirty-nine students. The newly enrolled students were at the same or lower levels of education and achievement as their peers. He warned the new students and their parents that his school policies and rules would be enforced; otherwise, the students would be asked to leave.

Madden knew he had no other option and did not have time for disciplinary actions. Either the rules were followed or the students left the school. Several parents of the new students met with Madden after school one day to voice their concerns. Madden was direct about the necessity of having the parents and guardians become partners in their children's education.

"Señor Madden, thank you for taking the time to speak with my family about our children. I understand you are different," José Alvarez conveyed to Madden in his office with all five of the Alvarez family members.

"Señor Alvarez, you are very welcome, sir. Rest assured, your son and daughter will receive the best education I can provide, but also I need your help."

"How can I be of any assistance?" a surprised José questioned.

"Sir, simply this. Please understand that we have limited resources here at Tres Rios, I mean the equipment and books for student use." Madden continued, "I expect all of my students to work with their parents at home, especially with their English-language skills." Madden saw that Alvarez spoke adequate English but knew that Spanish was most likely the language spoken in the family environment.

"Señor Madden, according to many students, I hear you speak Spanish very well, and I'm sure this will help Anna and Pepe," said José trying to put the responsibility on Madden.

"Yes, I'm blessed to speak fluent Spanish, and you are correct, I do use it occasionally to help those who don't speak English well. But for your children and my other students in the class to succeed, they must learn English," explained Madden again trying to get the point across. "Please, I encourage you to practice with them at home."

Nodding his head in approval, Señor Alvarez commented, "Yes, you're right, of course. I promise that my family will begin using English more in our home." He then conveyed to his family members that from now on, they would work at speaking only English the best they could at home. Discussions broke out in Spanish, but by the end of the meeting, the family agreed to work at speaking only English—for the childrens' future.

With a huge smile, Madden shook José's hand and walked him and the family out to the old Ford pickup parked in the school lot. "One last thing, Señor Madden," said José while holding Madden's arm prior to climbing into the truck. "You're gaining the reputation as a possible godsend or savior for our children."

Madden sarcastically thought to himself, *Right, truly a godsend and only God knows why.*

"Thank you, José, and where did you hear this?"

"Your *amigo,* Doctor Lightfeather, he's a godsend also. Señor Madden, the whole county knows why you're here, and our church believes you were sent to us for the purpose of helping our children," Jose sincerely expressed his belief. The whole family in the back of the truck and the cab smiled and nodded their heads in agreement with a departing, "*Vaya con Dios,*" or go with God.

"Thanks, and please help me help your children," Madden shouted as the pickup left the parking lot. He was getting a kick out of being a godsend and wondered if they knew the choice he was given—either several years in the state prison or teaching school for a year at Tres Rios. Well at least he's a godsend and not number 45725421 in the New Mexico penal system.

After the Alvarez family's visit, Madden had time to consider many of the other meetings he'd had with parents, relatives, guardians, and other caregivers about their students. More and more parental involvement was taking up Madden's teaching time. But the one common thread throughout all of the parent interviews was their newly founded hope for their children's future.

Madden thought long and hard about hope. Something had struck him—an idea, a solution to a problem. Searching his small personal library, he found what he had been looking for—a book titled *Making Hope Happen* by Dr. Shane J. Lopez, senior scientist at Gallup. Madden knew that hope was one of the most potent predictors of children's success in school because it expressed the ideas and energy for the future. He had audited the course Hope and Student Achievement during his graduate school studies and was definitely reaching back for that information.

"This is what I have been missing," Madden shouted out with excitement as if he had won the lottery. Quickly scanning the sections of the book, he found the research that showed "children can create more hope with the use of simple strategies and the support of a caring adult." Bingo, Madden thought.

Pushing aside the student assignments to be graded and the reports required from the county school office, Madden grabbed a legal pad and began writing checklist items for how to instill hope in both his students and their parents. In addition to speaking English at home and assisting with homework, the parents and guardians needed to talk with their children about their futures. Their children's goals had to be a regular topic of discussion.

Although he realized that most of the parents and guardians were lucky just to get a meal on the table at night, asking for their involvement in helping their children achieve goals might be a stretch. Madden felt it was important enough to make the attempt, though. He wanted to create a classroom environment where his students were more concerned with learning and mastering new skills than with just obtaining good grades.

Most importantly, and Madden already knew this, his students had various challenges and barriers that were preventing their academic growth and setting goals for the future. He was most excited about starting two ideas immediately: helping the students to set goals by building on their strengths and past performance and leading the students in finding different routes by using their inherent strengths to break through any barriers that present themselves.

The hope concepts were understandable on the academic level, but applying the principles to a poverty-stricken, rural school was overwhelming. Hope was growing at Tres Rios. But it was clear that maybe a little too much hope was not good for everyone else in the county. The possible competition of a rising Tres Rios that shared district resources might be perceived as a threat to the other Calico County schools.

Madden had some concerns about the mental states of several students—in particular, Ramon Rodriguez, who was a lonely, quiet eight-year-old still in the first grade. Ramon's uncle acted as his sole guardian and had once mentioned to Madden that Ramon sometimes screamed in the middle of the night with unknown nightmares for the last eight months. Madden also noticed that Ramon had a difficult time concentrating and often attempted to hide in the school building during recess.

"Class, good job on the grammar lesson," Madden announced one day. "Keep it up, and tomorrow we'll put your future goals on paper. Now class, I want you all to know that if you ever need to talk to me about any problems here at school or at home, you are welcome to see me in my office any time after school. As you know, I usually stay late. Come on by and if you feel more comfortable, bring your family or friends." Madden was discreetly focusing his statement on Ramon and any other students in need. "Okay? Now let's get your mathematics book and look at the exercises in chapter five with …"

Later that day, Madden was in his daily routine of grading papers and preparing tomorrow's lesson plan when he heard a soft knock on his door. Taking off his reading classes, Madden looked down and saw Ramon Rodriguez standing in the doorway looking a little frightened

"Ramon, come on in. Good to see you, how are your lessons going?" Madden sensed there were serious problems with the child—almost to the point of being shocked into silence and withdrawal by something horrible. Madden remembered that he had needed time to heal after experiencing his own past traumas. Nightmares and screams in the night were not uncommon for men like him who had seen too much. But for a child of Ramon's age to have such occurrences, it was too much to handle. Madden had been through it too and saw it in others.

"Mr. Madden, can I talk to you? I saw something. I think I saw something really bad," Ramon whispered.

Madden got up from his desk chair and asked Ramon to set next to him on a visitor's chair. Sitting next to him, Madden patiently and slowly explained that he wanted to help him. "Ramon, I'm so glad you came to see me. You can trust me, I'm your teacher."

"I know, Mr. Madden, I know," said Ramon, now crying.

"It's okay, Bud. I cry a lot myself, gosh do I ever," Madden honestly replied.

"You do, Mr. Madden? But you're a tough guy and a teacher," asked a surprised Ramon.

"Ramon, I'm just like everyone else. Sometimes I get sad and cry. I believe it's even good to cry at times." Madden added, "Sometimes when I think of my family, I have bad dreams and I cry. Ramon, what did you see that makes you cry or makes you sad?" Madden queried Ramon to try to find out his problem.

"Can I trust you and you'll tell no one else?" Ramon asked looking directly at Madden with wet eyes and trembling lips.

"Yes, no one else will know."

"I truly liked Ms. Wilson, but I couldn't help her, I couldn't help her," Ramon sobbed while looking down at the floor.

Allowing Ramon to regain his composure, he patiently said, "Please, Ramon, tell me why you couldn't help Ms. Wilson—now Ms. Wilson was your teacher here last year, is this correct?"

Ramon nodded his head, "I really liked Ms. Wilson, but they shouldn't have done it."

"It's okay. Tell me what you saw, Ramon?" Madden was getting a good idea about where Ramon's story was going and it might answer the questions he had when he first arrived at the school.

"I hid over there," he said, pointing to the old wooden storage locker across from the teacher's office. "Billy Hemrod grabbed Ms. Wilson and forced her into that office," Ramon continued to tell Madden all that he saw from his hiding place.

Madden was enraged by what he heard from Ramon, but not wanting to show it, Madden was supportive and patiently listened to the story. From what he gathered, the previous Tres Rios schoolteacher, Ms. Betty Wilson, was brutally raped by Billy Hemrod in her office, and poor Ramon witnessed the entire scene.

"You did the right thing by staying where you were," Madden reassured Ramon. "There was nothing you could have done to stop it or help Ms. Wilson then. Nothing." Madden suspected that Ms. Wilson most likely filed rape charges against Hemrod and nothing was done by local law enforcement—no surprise to Madden. Ms. Wilson left the school and was never heard from again. Madden asked, "Did you tell anyone about what you saw happen to Ms. Wilson?"

Obviously feeling better about talking his ordeal over with Madden, he said, "No, I was too scared to tell anyone. I really liked Ms. Wilson."

"Okay, Ramon, this situation is now my responsibility, and I will take care of it. You did the right thing by telling me, and I know there was nothing you could've done to help Ms. Wilson at the time. But you have helped her now by telling me," explained Madden while nodding his head. "Now Ramon, this is very important. Do not talk to anyone right now about what happened to Ms. Wilson. I'll take care of it, all right?"

Madden was thinking about the repercussions and the consequences if word got out there was a bona fide witness to

Hemrod's rape of Ms. Wilson. Madden believed Ramon's life would be in danger if Hemrod learned he saw the crime.

"Okay, Mr. Madden, I won't tell anyone."

Walking Ramon to the school front door, Madden promised, "Don't worry Ramon, I'll take care of Billy Hemrod." And Ramon knew he would.

After Ramon left his office, Madden was helping the Gomez brothers with some grammar assignments when they heard strange noises coming from the classroom. The brothers were surprised and shrugged their shoulders. "Wait here," Madden instructed, "I'm going to check this out. I'll be right back; just continue reviewing the assignment."

Arriving in the main classroom, Madden saw Ben Davis bringing his desk from the storage room back into the classroom. Noticing Madden and feeling awkward and ashamed, Davis asked, "Mr. Madden, where can I put my desk?"

"Ben, please put your desk back next to the last row of desks, there on the right." After placing his desk in the area designated by Madden, Ben asked Madden if he could be admitted back to the school.

"Okay, Ben," said Madden much relieved he was back, "let me get your books and assignments. Start looking over the first two assignments while I finish my work with the Gomez brothers. I'll be with you soon."

"*¿Qué es esto?*" asked one of the brothers of Ben Davis at his desk in back of the classroom. Davis just looked up from his workbook, smiled, and waved to them.

"Ben, come on back to the office," Madden ordered.

"Yes, sir," Davis replied, carrying his new stack of books and assignments.

Davis expected, and knew he deserved, a chewing out from the teacher. Instead, Madden sat him down and began working with him to catch up on his past assignments. This lasted until the early evening. After just his few hours with Davis, Madden was convinced he was a smart and capable student who would eventually be a good leader. Nothing was mentioned about his conduct the first day of class.

CHAPTER

25

"Juan Carlos, please ring the bell, let's get this cold February morning going," Madden said patting him on the back—and off went Juan Carlos. After the morning ritual of prayer, the Pledge of Allegiance, breakfast, and roll call, Madden asked the student leaders for their reports. The reports normally included absent members, problems, or just need-to-know information.

Juan Carlos gave his report first. "Mr. Rob, Susan Williams called me to say she was sick today. We checked her trailer on the way to school but no one answered."

"Very good, Juan Carlos. Thank you and the class for checking on her. Anything else?" Madden's sixth sense told him something was amiss just by the children's squirmy behavior. They knew something but remained quiet. "Okay, maybe I should stop in after school to check up on her also. Is that a good idea Juan Carlos?" Juan Carlos just looked away from Madden without answering.

"Okay, leaders, takeover and get your students ready for some multiplication problems." Madden marveled that his leaders relished their new stations in life and took their responsibilities seriously.

"Juan Carlos, could I see you for a minute please?" Madden asked him right before he left school for the day.

"Yes, Mr. Rob," he answered somewhat startled at the prospect of Madden wanting to talk with him.

Sitting down with Juan Carlos in the now-empty classroom, Madden asked, "Juan, you know Susan Williams pretty well—you're friends, right?"

"Yes, sir. I live kinda near her in the trailer park, and we play together in the small park."

"I'm worried about Susan," Madden probed. "Is there anything I can do to help her? She appears tired and sick most of the time. Is she treated well by her family?"

Nervously looking around to ensure no one was listening, he said, "Mr. Rob, she lives with her stepfather, and he doesn't treat her very nice."

"What exactly do you mean by 'not very nice,' Juan?"

Juan Carlos explained Susan Williams's problems in the best way a ten-year-old possibly could.

After listening to Juan Carlos describe Susan's situation for nearly fifteen minutes, Madden knew exactly what was occurring in the Williams trailer. Trying to hold back his emotions and temper, Madden did not want to explode in front of the boy. Juan Carlos might not understand the reasons for many of Susan Williams's problems, but Madden did. Calming down he said rationally, "Juan, this is very important. I want you to do Susan and me a very big favor this afternoon."

"Sure, Mr. Rob, what can I do?"

"I want you to go to Susan's trailer on your way home and get her to play outside with you. Then I want you to take Susan to your house to stay with your family for the night. I'll come by and explain why to your parents; they'll understand." Madden thought they probably already understood but did not want to cause more problems in the community.

"Okay, Mr. Rob, I'll go by Susan's house now."

"Do it quickly, Juan," Madden emphasized as Juan Carlos raced out of the schoolyard on his mission. "All right," Madden angrily said to himself, "I'm going to have a little parent/teacher conference with Mr. Williams this afternoon." Madden hated nothing more on this earth than child molesters and pedophiles, and he would make sure their ungodly behavior didn't touch the young people he was responsible for.

Madden got into his Element and headed for trailer #56 in the Pine Ridge Trailer Park. Number 56 was situated on large junkyard and trash depository. A week's worth of food cans, beer cans, old magazines, and even a couple of old broken toilets surrounded the trailer. The smell was nauseating. Madden was amazed anyone could live here, especially a child.

Madden knocked on the door, saying, "Mr. Williams, I'm Rob Madden, Susan's teacher at Tres Rios, and I'd like to talk to you." Madden heard a blaring television and what sounded like rap music in the trailer.

"What do you want, asshole? I have the graveyard shift tonight at the mine, so buzz off," came the reply from Williams.

"Mr. Williams, it's important that I speak with you about Susan. Please take the time."

"Listen, Madden, I have a gun. And if you don't leave now, I'm going to call the sheriff," Williams yelled from within the trailer.

"Better yet, Mr. Williams," replied Madden, "how about you and I talk to the sheriff together?"

There was silence in the trailer with the television and the stereo now turned off. Suddenly the door opened and the stench from the inside of the trailer was sickening, even for Madden. There stood a paunchy, middle-aged man with long hair and a scraggly beard, smelling of hard liquor and possibly on drugs—Madden could not be certain.

"Let go of me, you son of a bitch," Williams cried as Madden kicked the door open and grabbed Williams by the shoulder straps of his soiled overalls. Madden swung Williams out of the trailer and into some rotting garbage pails. Lifting him up, and still clutching the shoulder straps, Madden slapped him against the side of the trailer. Williams was in a state of panic and looking for anyone to get this wild man off him.

"Two things I hate most in life are child molesters and pedophiles. Are you one of those kinds of slime, Mr. Williams?"

"No, no, Madden, you've got it all wrong."

"I don't think so," said Madden as he shoved Williams to the front of his car.

"Listen, mister, listen!" Williams pleaded, "You're right, I do need help. I know, I'll talk to the county tomorrow about help."

"Not to worry, Williams. I'm going to get you some counseling this afternoon—one on one," Madden replied still holding Williams. Manhandling Williams to the front of his Honda Element, Madden tied him on top of the hood of his vehicle with rope. The entire time, Williams screamed for help and begged Madden to let him go.

In the late afternoon, the trailer park neighbors were looking out of their windows at the strange sight of their problem neighbor being tied to the hood of a car. The neighbors were glad to see him go, and one yelled to Madden, "Please, take him away and don't bring him back!"

While tying the last knot to hold Williams, Madden just looked at the neighbor and grinned. "Mr. Williams and I are going to have a little parent/teacher talk down the road," Madden said to a group of curious neighbors. "Please relay this to the sheriff when he arrives." Madden pulled out of the trailer park with Williams tied to the hood as if he were carrying a deer he had just shot. Williams could be heard screaming as Madden headed down the county road.

Traveling down the county road, Madden's car passed Sheriff Wells's patrol car. Both the sheriff and his deputy were responding to a disturbance call at the trailer park when they noticed Williams tied to the hood of Madden's car.

"Isn't that nice, Rob's making friends with Jesse Williams," the sheriff said sarcastically to his passenger. Both men knew Madden was taking care of a long-rumored problem in the community, one the sheriff knew he should have investigated earlier.

"Are you going to turn around and pull Madden over?" asked the deputy.

Pausing for a moment, a smiling Wells replied, "No, to me it appears that Madden and Williams are just fooling around. I don't see any reason to spoil their fun." They continued on to the trailer park.

The next day, Susan Williams was placed in a local foster home for abused children with the assistance of Dr. Lightfeather and Dr. Kramer. Lightfeather was shocked at the physical and emotional condition of Susan Williams—the young child had clearly been repeatedly molested and abused by her stepfather. For his part, Williams immediately left the county after Madden's "counseling" with two missing fingers and a permanent stain on his chest that read, "I Molest Children."

CHAPTER

26

"Brothers, God is great, I've located him!" yelled an excited Sahim Abdul to the others in the small and cluttered apartment located just outside the campus of the University of Michigan–Dearborn near Detroit. The brown-colored apartment in Dearborn was in a typical student apartment building, just a short walk to the university, and the perfect location for a foreign terrorist sleeper cell to blend in with the local environment.

Hurriedly, the other three men ran to the computer screen to see what was causing all the commotion, each one squeezing in on the screen trying to get an idea what this meant. Pushing the others aside, Humza Aldawasari stared at the screen and couldn't believe what he saw.

As the low voices spoke Arabic in the background, Aldawasari yelled, "Silence." Nothing else was heard except for the low hum of the computer fan. "Brothers, we have found him. This is a great joy, a great joy!" he repeated. Aldawasari rose from the computer and went over to a messy book cabinet looking for the road map of the United States. Opening the torn and dirty atlas, Aldawasari began turning the pages looking for something. Kareem Zohody, the most recent addition to the cell, asked why everyone was so excited about finding one person on the Internet.

"Humza's brother, Anwar, was killed by a drone strike while meeting with al-Qaeda leaders in Yemen in 2004," said Abdul while frowning and shaking his head. "He had arranged for a hawk hunt with a member of the AUR royal family, and they were meeting at a small airport near our training camp at Al Mukalla. They were all killed."

"What does this infidel on the Internet have to do with the assassination of Anwar Aldawasari?" asked Zohody while rubbing his long black beard.

"No news or information about the assassinations was ever released. From what we understood, the royal family was compromised and embarrassed that a prince would associate with Anwar Aldawasari, whom they considered a terrorist. The United States was also surprised to learn that, besides killing Anwar Aldawasari, the CIA spy team had also killed a member of the AUR royal family. It was agreed by both the United States and AUR to officially say that an aircraft accident took their lives. An aircraft accident," he repeated.

"Why didn't al-Qaeda leadership make a public announcement about the assassinations?" Abdul asked.

"Sahim Abdul, have you not been paying attention to your instructions and the manuals you've been studying? We never acknowledge the death of one of our members, never!"

"So why is this man on the Internet so important?" he asked again.

"He is the only person we found linked to this crime. According to our sources, the United States blamed an overzealous military sergeant for acting on his own in ordering the CIA drone strikes. The Great Satan explained to the AUR royal family that they were going to punish the person responsible, a Sergeant Rob Madden with the CIA. Our sources say this Sergeant Madden only got a meaningless slap on the hand for his barbaric actions, and the royal family was too embarrassed and ashamed to ask for anything more."

"What happened to this Madden? Did he go to some military prison?"

"No, we understand Madden was secretly placed in a CIA training base in Florida to teach other infidels how to assassinate our leadership and brothers," explained Aldawasari.

After spending several minutes searching the Internet for the exact whereabouts of Rob Madden, a triumphant cry came from Humza at the workstation, "We've found him and his days are numbered. Where is this place called New Mexico? We must leave immediately to settle this terrible act with Madden."

"My brother, Humza, you were only recently released from Guantanamo by the American government after more than five years. Do you believe it wise to be chasing after one person so far away just for personal revenge? We have a mission here to recruit other Muslims to join the jihad and raise money for our groups in other countries," Assim Maghed, the Detroit cell leader, sternly stated. "You also know the FBI is probably tracking your movements. The chance of failure is too great, and what purpose would it serve to kill just one American? Also, my brother, you are well aware that Madden's wife and children were killed almost three years ago by unknown assassins. How much further do you want to avenge your brother's death at the risk of all our lives?' questioned Maghed.

"Assim Maghed, you miserable coward, I suspect it was our brothers in Florida who avenged Anwar's death with Madden's family. However, Rob Madden is going to be next. I go with or without you," Aldawasari announced while staring at each person in the small apartment.

"If you go, you will go without authorization from our masters and with no resources," voiced Maghed. He added, "Is this man worth your life and possibly our own?" The question remained unanswered.

"I'm leaving in a few days for this place called New Mexico. Who's going with me?" Aldawasari asked. Finding the exact location of Rob Madden in Tres Rios, New Mexico, was as simple as hitting the "Find" button on a search engine.

Two FBI communications technicians with the Joint Counter Terrorism Assessment Team located in Virginia had been monitoring and recording the conversations of Aldawasari and his other sleeper-cell networks for the past year. After analyzing the recent conversations, the senior monitor lead contacted FBI Senior Special Agent Jay Tarver. "Sir, this is Scott Peterson, senior monitor lead, we've just picked up an intercept of interest. It could be time sensitive."

"Thanks, Scott, I'll be right down," replied Tarver. After reviewing the sleeper-cell update and the status of Aldawasari, Tarver began the normal protocol of notifying the other appropriate federal agencies about new information and preparing possible action plans. "Thank God for the Patriot Act," voiced Tarver as he walked through the center. Everyone in earshot nodded their heads in agreement.

"Without it," he thought, "there's no way on God's green earth we would be able to track terrorists, drug traffickers, and organized crime members."

In room 3G12 of the J. Edgar Hoover Justice Building in Washington, D.C., Senior Special Agent Tarver exclaimed, "Well, looky here. Guess who's on the move to New Mexico? Aldawasari and his merry band." Jay Tarver was sitting in the secure briefing room at the Terrorist Threat Integration Center receiving information about the sudden emergence of a sleeper cell near Detroit of which Humza Aldawasari was a member.

Agent Charlie Seale briefed, "So, let's review what we know. Aldawasari was recently released from Guantanamo Bay on a pardon by the president of the United States and is sent back to Yemen to be held by the Yemen government. He easily escapes detention there and joins a terrorist sleeper cell in Germany. Not long after that, he shows up in the outskirts of Detroit—new person, new identity papers, etc."

Seale continued, "Until now, there's been no operations or activities by this cell, just a bunch of talk. They continue to receive funding from sympathetic charities in the Arab world, though. Now, all of a sudden, Aldawasari wakes up and wants to travel to New Mexico to finish some old business with some guy named Madden; believe his name is Rob Madden."

Tarver was perplexed by this information, and asked, "Why would Aldawasari, who knows we are actively tracking his whereabouts, drive like mad to get to New Mexico to settle an old score—it just doesn't figure."

"I just pulled up Rob Madden's bio and fact sheet. You fellows are not going to believe this," announced Agent Mark

McDermott. "Do you remember that 'aircraft accident' in 2004 that occurred in Yemen? The one that killed the number-three terrorist on the A-list, Anwar Aldawasari? Well, it was Madden who literally pulled the trigger on the drone strike that killed him, and that dead terrorist is Humza Aldawasari's brother. Madden was an Air Force combat controller attached to a CIA Special Operations team in Yemen tracking down high-priority terrorist targets with armed drones. According to the official report, Madden exceeded his authority and executed the strike without State or DOD approval. He was denied a promotion and later retired after twenty years of service."

"This is really interesting," added Seale. "Madden's last assignment was training the Colombian military and DEA agents in special tactics against the FARC in Colombia. By the insistence of the Colombian government, he was awarded the Air Force Cross for valor against hostile forces." All was quiet in the center as agents and technicians were impressed by Madden's bravery.

"Okay, can I have your attention please?" Tarver asked. "It's pretty obvious Aldawasari is traveling to New Mexico to seek revenge against Madden for killing his brother. Mark and Charlie, you know what to do. Let's get some agents working this in New Mexico and please keep me posted on any further developments. Let's have another briefing today at 1600 hours with any updates." Tarver added, "And get on the horn with the DEA. Brief them on this situation; there may be more to this than we currently know. Any questions?"

"Yes, sir, one," Seale asked, "what's Madden doing in New Mexico?"

"This gets more bizarre every minute," replied McDermott, "but he's teaching at some rural school in a backwater called Tres Rios."

"What in the hell's he doing there?"

"Sir, just received an update from our friend, Carlos Aponte at DEA. He stated that they have two agents currently working a case in that area, but he wouldn't elaborate further."

"Okay, Charlie, brief DEA on everything we know thus far about Aldawasari, and ask if they have any further information on Madden," Tarver directed. "We may need their help when Aldawasari arrives."

CHAPTER

27

"Now leaders, use his momentum to your advantage. When an attacker comes at you, don't try to ..." Madden's phone rang in mid-sentence. "Hold on gang, I'll be right back." Dressed in his usual gray warm-up suit with tennis shoes, Madden headed over to the picnic table under the cottonwood tree, his favorite meeting place for working on school issues.

"Good afternoon, Rob, I trust you are well," Dr. Kramer politely stated.

"Yes, thank you, Dr. Kramer and how may I be of service to fine Calico County School District today?" Madden replied, amused at himself with the surface niceties between superintendent and teacher.

"Rob, for your benefit, I'm sending out a textbook vendor who I'd like you to meet. Could you review some of his books to see if they'd be of any use to you at Tres Rios?"

"Dr. Kramer, I do appreciate this offer, but we have plenty of math, reading, and spelling books. However, we sure could use more computer training books and software. Can he help us out with that?"

"We'll see," Kramer replied and added, "Listen, Rob, we've been working with this vendor from Albuquerque for a while, and we have a very good relationship with them, so please just give him a few minutes of your time this afternoon."

"Okay, Dr. Kramer. I'll look over what he has, but please tell him I'd be more interested in beginning-level computer instruction books and software for elementary students."

"He'll be at your school in about thirty minutes—please be nice to him," requested Kramer.

"All right, Dr. Kramer, send him over. Between tutoring this afternoon and parent conferences tonight, I'll be more than happy to speak with him," Madden replied sarcastically and hung up. What he thought was, *I bet Calico County's probably getting some huge kickbacks and stuffing somebody's pockets with school-funding money.*

Madden and the leaders were just finishing their afternoon self-defense class when a nondescript Ford SUV with a Northern New Mexico Publishing sign on its side rolled into the school parking lot. Wrapping up the class, the leaders picked up their backpacks and headed home. *What a waste of my time,* Madden thought while heading to the SUV to politely welcome the man to Tres Rios.

Watching the salesman get out of his SUV, Madden was not surprised at all by his appearance. He wore Coke bottles for glasses and his hair was trimmed but heavily greased back. He had on a cheap black suit that was obviously too small for a rather large man, and the pants were so short, he was ready for a flood. However, Madden sensed this man was in extremely good shape, possibly even a prior military type.

Extending his hand, he said, "Good afternoon, sir. I'm Rob Madden, the teacher here at Tres Rios. I understand Dr. Kramer sent you out so I can review some textbooks."

"Yes, Rob. I'm Steve Webb," he said slipping Madden his business card. "So nice to meet you and thank you for taking the time. I understand from Dr. Kramer that you've been very busy and have worked miracles here at Tres Rios."

"Listen Steve, I'm ..." Madden quickly interrupted.

Webb politely asked, "Rob, is there a quiet place we can talk?" Webb acted as if he had been through this routine before.

"Sure, Steve. Let's walk over to that picnic table under the cottonwood tree, good place to talk. Can I get you something to drink—water, coffee, Coke?" Madden offered as both men sat down opposite one another with the cool, dry wind blowing the leaves of the cottonwood.

"No, thank you," Webb said, adding, "What a peaceful meeting place."

Opening a rather large professional-looking carrying case, Webb pulled out a few books and laid them on the wooden picnic table, clumsily attempting to arrange them for Madden's review. He sat back watching Madden from his Coke-bottle glasses and talked about the advantages of using his company's books. He recommended one book in particular, *Entry-Level Computer Magic for Young People*. Madden was interested in the book, thinking about its potential usefulness in the computer lab.

Still sitting back and smiling with an odd grin, Webb told Madden to read the introduction. Madden opened the book to the introduction page and there appeared a message aimed directly at him. Webb very softly said, "Rob, highly recommend you read the entire introduction—it may prove interesting to you."

Amazed that the publisher would go this extra mile for the customer, Madden read:

"Mr. Madden, while reading the following message, act as if this is your typical textbook-vendor meeting with a teacher. There are elements watching our meeting right now. After leaving, I am sure that I will be stopped by the local law enforcement to investigate my meeting with you.

Government agencies have been monitoring local activities for various drug-smuggling and lab-production operations, including one at the uranium mine. We are aware of this operation's leadership and those directly and indirectly involved, which includes the county law enforcement agencies.

Also, we are totally aware of your situation and how you came about teaching at Tres Rios. It is common knowledge that Mr. William Hemrod will do whatever possible to have you killed before your departure from the area. In the past, he has made numerous individuals who knew too much disappear."

Working hard to keep his composure and truly absorb what he was reading, Madden smiled and returned to the page. Webb also smiled and stated, "Please, Rob, continue reading. You just might be able to use this book."

> "Government agencies are preparing a major
> operation to correct and resolve the situation
> here soon. Possible assistance and expertise
> from you would be greatly appreciated when
> the execution date is authorized. We know of
> your background and skills; plus you are in the
> perfect position within the community."

"Rob, you may want to read the last paragraph very closely, it will be important to you in the near future," Webb recommended as Madden continued playing the role of a customer.

> "We will be contacting you when necessary by
> various simple means. We recommend that you
> follow any guidance you receive to the letter—no
> deviations. Frankly, your life depends on it.
>
> We understand this is the last month of
> your obligation to teach at Tres Rios prior to
> departing for Stanford University. Continue with
> your normal lifestyle and duties at Tres Rios,
> and do not act differently in the community
> after reading this message. Contact will be made
> with you later. Only contact me using the phone
> numbers printed on my business card in an
> emergency or if you are in imminent danger."

Finished reading the message, Madden politely handed the book back to Webb and asked if there were any other books in which he might be interested. Webb grabbed a few more for Madden's review but none had personal messages.

"Steve, I certainly appreciate your time, but please tell Dr. Kramer I didn't see any books we could use here. Thank you for your visit out here though."

As Webb awkwardly placed the books back into his travel case, Madden tried to get a good read on Steve Webb. The vendor put the Coke bottles he called glasses back on and walked to his vehicle knowing that unseen binoculars were focused on him.

He sure did play his part well, Madden thought to himself while carrying the sample textbooks into his office. He was sure Webb did not create this charade just to warn him about Billy—there was something big going on here. Having spent years abroad working various assignments with Special Forces, CIA, DEA, and the FBI, Madden could tell this man was a skilled operator, someone you would normally avoid.

Driving the dusty gravel road back to Grants, the vendor began analyzing and recollecting Madden's reaction and statements. Madden would eventually have to know about the terrorist cell coming after him; they were close and getting closer. Webb noted in his log, "No use playing our hand too early with Madden. Just in time will be fine."

Getting close to the Interstate and as predicted, Webb was pulled over by a Calico County deputy sheriff and searched on suspicion. After searching the vehicle and confirming his identity, he was released and headed back to Albuquerque where the publisher was located. He knew there would be many inquiries from various sources to confirm his identity, and it would all appear legitimate.

Back at the picnic table, Madden stared at the calm beauty of New Mexico's high desert while reflecting on what he just encountered with the "textbook vendor." He knew there was something strange about Billy and his crew working security at the uranium mine while acting like a bunch of doped-up, wild badasses. Also, he recalled the warning by Dr. Lightfeather: don't ask any questions. After reviewing the personal message from Agent Webb, Madden was sure of two things: Billy was producing and distributing drugs from inside the mine perimeter, and the DEA/FBI were going to make an imminent bust.

If/when the feds sought him out for assistance and cooperation, what would they require from him? Madden's only thoughts were completing the school year on a high note, loading up his car, and getting on the road to Stanford. *Now this.*

Getting up from the picnic table and heading back to his school office to finish grading papers and work on a lesson plan, Madden was bothered by what the vendor did not tell him. Besides Billy, the mine, and drugs, the vendor had another reason to warn Madden, but what was it? It was now obvious to Madden, there was a potential threat coming his way, but from where?

He had pissed off people all over the globe, including his own military leadership, but now he was just a simple rural schoolteacher—with an edge. Madden knew full well that it was against the law to have a weapon in a school, but under the circumstances, he had no choice. And who was going to enforce that law in this lawless environment anyway? He checked his 9mm service handgun and held it more closely. *If shit does hit, better make sure that it's far away from the school,* he thought. *It's time to make plans.*

CHAPTER

"Good morning, everyone, and please take your assigned seats. What an opportunity—we may never have a chance like this again," announced Senior Special Agent Jim Stock to the cadre of FBI and DEA agents and technicians gathered in a classified-operations briefing room at the FBI Engineering Research Facility in Quantico, Virginia. The facility is the center for the FBI's tactical operations for deploying agents to ad hoc assignments in the field.

Stock continued, "For those unfamiliar with this facility, it is a tactical operation that monitors terrorists and collects data while they're in the planning phases of an operation. Usually, they tend to be rather disorganized and careless during the planning phases; however, they do show an uncanny zeal for completing their assigned missions. Special Agent Tarver, would you please brief us on New Mexico Rain, operations plan 12-0010-087?"

"Yes, sir," Tarver acknowledged as he moved the laser pointer on the briefing screen. "Operation New Mexico Rain is a joint task force with leads from the FBI and DEA. Both have significant interests in the successful completion of this operation, as I'll explain. Next slide please." Tarver continued, "The FBI's interest and participation in the joint operation centers around a known terrorist named Humza Aldawasari, who was recently released from Guantanamo on a presidential pardon. Humza was deported to a government prison in Yemen where he escaped, or was probably let go, and ended up back at his old training camp in southern Yemen. He later traveled to Germany for a new start." Looks of disgust and surprise were evident among the audience.

"Aldawasari arrived back in the United States through his travels in the Middle East and Europe using false passports and ended up joining a terrorist sleeper cell near Detroit, Michigan. Through our various networks and wiretaps, we've found that Aldawasari's primary goal is to settle a score with a retired Air Force sergeant who was supposedly responsible for the drone attack that killed his brother, Anwar Aldawasari."

Just the mention of Anwar Aldawasari piqued everyone's interest and attention. Tarver went on, "We have very good intel that Aldawasari's planning a trip to New Mexico to seek revenge for his brother's death. He's operating on his own and has been advised by his leaders in Yemen not to make the trip. He ignored directions to 'sit tight' for further instructions. Aldawasari has three other cell members with him, and we can only guess they went along with his plan due to his unique reputation in al-Qaeda as a well-known 'persuasive' personality."

"Jay, would you please provide us with the target's name and any other details that would benefit the working group?" interjected Stock.

"Humza Aldawasari is seeking to kill a rural schoolteacher in Tres Rios, New Mexico, by the name of Rob Madden. At the time of his brother Anwar's death, Senior Master Sergeant Madden was on a Special Operations CIA drone team in Yemen targeting the bad guys. Again, the information I'm providing is highly sensitive and classified top secret," Tarver emphasized. "Unfortunately for Madden, he was reprimanded by the military for exceeding his orders and taking action on his own. He was the only member identified as taking part in the operation. Hence, Aldawasari is released and it's payback time for Madden.

"One last important point, but I'm not sure if it links to our operation," added Tarver. "Three years ago, Madden's wife and two daughters were killed when a terrorist placed a bomb next to their vehicle and detonated it near their home in Florida while Madden was deployed to Colombia."

"If al-Qaeda was responsible for these murders three years ago, why would Aldawasari risk imprisonment again for the remote chance of killing Madden?" Agent Stack asked.

"I understand this investigation is ongoing and extremely sensitive—the department in charge is being very tight lipped about any updates or information," Tarver answered without really answering anything.

"With that update, we will continue with the planning and execution of New Mexico Rain," directed Stock. "Again, thank you, Jay, for the overview." Stock added, "The FBI is monitoring the progress of Aldawasari and will take appropriate steps to intercept him prior to reaching Madden. For now, we're allowing Aldawasari a free ride to New Mexico. But we, along with the DEA, have a special reception planned for his arrival. Now, to describe the second phase of operation New Mexico Rain, I'd like to introduce DEA Senior Special Agent Carl Brown."

"Thank you, Jim, and we're all looking forward to the successful execution of this operation with the FBI. I see some of our CIA colleagues here, welcome," said Brown. "As incredible as this sounds, DEA has been monitoring a large drug operation located, in of all places, a uranium mine in Calico County near Tres Rios. We currently have two undercover agents in the area providing updates, surveillance, and intelligence. With the FBI's help, one of our agents has discreetly made contact with Madden acting as a textbook salesman and advising him of the upcoming bust. No mention was made of the terrorist's plans, though," Brown briefed.

He then asked for the next slide showing an aerial view of the uranium mine layout and its facilities. After pointing out the buildings in the mine's security perimeter, Brown focused the audience's attention on a small cluster of utility sheds located next to an unused mineshaft on the side of a cliff. "This is our area of concern and target for the operation," Brown emphasized.

"Carl, for the benefit of the new team members, would you please explain how this drug operation and distribution works," Stock asked.

"Certainly, but first allow me to provide you with a bit of history on how this drug activity found itself in a uranium mine in the middle of New Mexico. An official for the mine's parent company in Chicago thought it would be a good idea to put his troubled and wild son in charge of mine security. This official believed the responsibility would do his son good and get him away from the bad element in the Chicago area. The son, William Hemrod, just took his 'bad-element' gang with him to New Mexico—where he immediately found that as head of security, he had the run of the mine and surrounding area. Hemrod found an abandoned complex of buildings next to an old mineshaft and designated this area as 'security headquarters' and the checkpoint for all trucks departing the mine with their loads of uranium ore."

Brown continued, "Each truck departing the mine receives a thorough inspection to the point where drivers sometimes complain about how long the inspections take, so the process appeared legitimate and routine. There's a special waiting area, a small lounge, where the truckers can drink coffee and watch television or movies while their loaded trucks are inspected and they're authorized to depart for the mill in Texas. However, before the trucks depart the mine, containers of various drugs produced at the mine are attached to the under rigging of the trailers. Hemrod set up lab facilities to manufacture drugs that include methamphetamine, Ecstasy, GHB, and the date-rape drug Ketamine. No one sees it or suspects it, not even the drivers. The drugs are removed by a distributor at the truckers' favorite truck stop hundreds of miles from the mine.

"William Hemrod and his 'employees' have made a small fortune from this operation, for which they also had to buy off the local law enforcement agencies, politicians, and city administrators to look the other way. There's no doubt, they all know what's happening at the mine. We can't expect any support or assistance from the local residents either; they're terrified of Hemrod and his group," Brown explained, "and with the increase in local revenues from the mine's operation, no one is interested in causing trouble for the mine's owners, especially the owner's son. Everyone looks the other way—to line their own pockets and for their personal safety."

"Carl, would you please clarify a couple points for us?" asked Stock.

"Be glad to, and I think I know what you're going to ask. Please proceed," answered Brown.

"First, with all of the information you already possess, why hasn't your team already shut Hemrod down and made the arrests?" Stock knew the answer but was asking for the benefit of the other agents and technicians.

"Fair question," replied Brown. "Every day we gain more information on the network involved in the distribution of these drugs. And frankly, it's surprising how wide this network reaches. Hemrod's activities at the uranium mine are just one aspect of the entire operation. When we execute, all of the search warrants and arrests happen at the same time—we don't want anything left to chance." Brown concluded, "My biggest concern is that Hemrod may get wind of the bust and shut down his operation before we can obtain the search warrants and make the arrests. That is my biggest worry."

The briefings continued throughout the morning with joint contingency cells working together creating a draft schedule and plan for operation New Mexico Rain. At noon, Jim Stock asked Carl Brown and CIA liaison Vernon Tobey to meet with him in the ultra-secure Secured Compartmentalized Information Facility (SCIF) located in the basement of the FBI Engineering Research Facility.

Stock thought it imperative to have a meeting about classified information there with only the three of them—no phones, no computers, only the three federal agents. After the formalities and security checklists were completed for opening the SCIF, Stock, Brown, and Tobey sat around a large wooden conference table. The security guards departed and secured the heavy metal door.

"Thanks, Carl and Vernon, for meeting with me here. I have something I'd like to run by you and see what you think regarding New Mexico Rain," Stock said, feeling a little more comfortable speaking in private. "We know that Aldawasari and his cell will be in New Mexico soon looking for Madden, and we could stop him in his tracks before he leaves Michigan. But we're not, because if we stopped him, it would jeopardize our year of surveillance work.

"Also, some lawyer from one of their terrorist-backed charitable organizations would hound us for infringing on the rights of his client and the Attorney General's office would make things right for Aldawasari with an apology. We have seen this happen way too often—not this time," Stock emphasized. "Aldawasari is going to have a clean shot to New Mexico." Stock thought for a second and added, "In fact, we're going to allow him every opportunity to meet with Madden."

"What in the blue blazes are you thinking?" Tobey questioned. "Why would you allow Aldawasari access to Madden?" Brown looked at Stock for a minute and smiled, for he suspected what Stock was thinking. Tobey was still confused about this decision.

"Through various clandestine 'contacts,' Aldawasari will be advised that Rob Madden is working with William Hemrod at the uranium mine security complex as an advisor." Complete silence engulfed the SCIF as Tobey and Brown again were completely caught off guard by Stock's statement. "So when Aldawasari shows up at Tres Rios looking for Madden, our undercover agents will make sure he's directed to the uranium mine's security complex. He will be told that Madden can usually be found working there with Billy Hemrod." Tobey and Brown were now beginning to see where Stock was going with this plan.

"Jim, quick question. Since Madden arrived at Tres Rios, has there been any association between him and Hemrod?" Tobey asked, since Brown knew the true story.

"Jim, may I answer that question?" Brown commented, "I have two agents in the town who've told me that on Madden's first day in town, he got into a fight with Hemrod. Madden apparently tried to restrain a liquored-up Hemrod and keep him from beating up his wife and kids. Madden took a gun and a knife from Hemrod and broke his arm. Hemrod has a reputation as a pretty decent street fighter, but he was no match for Madden. Frankly, I don't know who hates Madden more: Aldawasari or William Hemrod," pondered Brown.

Stock sat back in the leather conference chair, smiling and gathering in all that Brown relayed. "Interesting, both men have scores to settle with Madden—one a known international terrorist and the other a high-level dope producer and distributor. This guy Madden can piss off the wrong people, that's for sure," Stock observed.

"In this situation, it may be the right people," noted Brown.

"Are you thinking of using Madden as bait to catch both Aldawasari and Hemrod?" asked Tobey.

"No, not catch them," Stock replied, "but bring them together in the same place—the security complex at the mine."

"Carl, we need your expertise with these drug depots, meth labs, and whatever. I've heard that in many cases the producer will set up a doomsday or fail-safe system to be used in the event the feds get too close or if a rival distributor wants to take over. Is that true?"

"Yes, that's the typical scenario. After what I've seen and heard about this facility, I'd bet Hemrod has tons of explosives planted around various sheds and the mineshaft. Common practice would be to set up a switch box with a timer linked to an explosive detonator. This would be networked to the strategically placed explosives and ready to be set off in the event his cover's been compromised." Brown added, "Hemrod would most likely know that, by setting up the fail-safe, the meth lab would be destroyed with all evidence gone or buried under heaps of rock. And most important of all, it would appear to be a mine accident with mine explosives as the cause."

"Meaning, Hemrod and his gang could set up business in another location. Is this how you see it, Carl?" Tobey asked.

"Yes, I'm afraid so," Brown confirmed. "Listen fellows, I have an idea where we can possibly kill two birds with one stone. Here's my plan …"

CHAPTER

"Leaders, get your people ready for the Pledge of Allegiance. Juan Carlos, please lead us in the pledge," Madden directed after breakfast. He felt there was something different about his class today—a true change or maturity. He could not put his finger on it, but progress had been incredible in the last few months and now it was evident on a wonderful May day with a cool breeze and blue skies.

"Now let's pull out your spelling books and see what we have for today's assignment." With the normal buzz of activity, the school had its rhythm with a newfound enthusiasm, energy, and hope. In the middle of a spelling test, Madden noticed Hank tapping on the window.

"William, take over and work with Ben, I'll be right back," he said. Madden knew Hank would only interrupt him for an emergency or time-sensitive issue. Quickly moving outside, he asked, "Hank, what is it?

"Hey, boss, not sure if you know it, but Dr. Kramer is on her way here with a carload of people."

"Okay, and thanks, Hank. Would you please take a quick look around the school just to make sure everything's in order. I have no clue what she wants."

"Right, boss," Hank acknowledged and began policing the school property.

Looking down the gravel road, he saw the dust of Dr. Kramer's Ford SUV on its way to the school. "Maybe she's coming here to formally fire me," Madden mused to himself, "but probably no such luck." To Hank, he said, "Since this appears to be a surprise visit, I best get back into the classroom." Hank nodded his head and made sure the bathrooms were presentable.

Seeing the SUV park in front of the school, Madden noticed that Dr. Kramer was with some distinguished-looking people simply by the clothes they wore. All were in quality suits, had leather briefcases, and wore some special state lapel pins.

"Class, my I have your attention, we have visitors, William take charge of the class. Leaders, continue working with your teams. I'll be right back," instructed Madden. This had been the standard protocol since Madden's arrival, and it came as second nature to the students.

"Dr. Kramer, good morning, ma'am, and welcome to Tres Rios. Always a pleasure to have you visit," he said obsequiously. Dr. Kramer was used to this polite BS from Madden, and she was sure he did not mean any of it, but was playing the political game.

"Good morning, Rob. I hope we're not interrupting your class," Dr. Kramer stated, caring little if she disturbed his classroom or not. She was escorting some high-level state education officials, so she also played the political game. "Rob, I'd like to introduce you to the New Mexico Commissioner for Education, Dr. Cristobel Lopez."

"My pleasure, Dr. Lopez, and welcome to Tres Rios," Madden said.

"Thank you, Rob, my pleasure also. I've been wanting to meet you for some time. You have quite a, uh, reputation in this area, and we're glad you're here," Lopez warmly stated while trying to put the best possible spin on the reason Madden was at Tres Rios. "Rob, I'd like you to meet the Deputy Commissioner Dr. Barbara Marquez and the Calico County school board president, Peter Moralez."

"Dr. Marquez and Mr. Moralez, pleasure to meet you and welcome. To what do we owe the honor of your presence today?" Madden inquired hoping for the golden ticket to leave this area before "things started happening."

"Rob, I have some good news for you and your students. Tres Rios has showed the most academic improvement out of all the rural elementary schools in the state." The commissioner continued, "We have an award here to present to you and your students."

Madden didn't believe for one second that Tres Rios earned any type of merit or achievement award, but suspected this was just an excuse to make the community feel good about the progress at Tres Rios and give the state representatives a tour of the school they had heard much about over the past year.

"Yes, sir. Please excuse me, and I'll get the students ready for the presentation. Just give me a moment." Madden hurriedly instructed the students to stand by their desks for a special presentation.

The visitors noticed this and Marquez commented with respect, "That's what happens when you bring in these retired military people as teachers—everyone's standing at attention."

"Hank," Madden shouted out the front door, "would you please come in for a presentation?"

"Students, thank you for your attention," Madden started, "this morning we're honored to have some special visitors with us. Doctor Lopez?"

"Thank you, Rob, and please, please take your seats," Lopez looked out and surveying the audience, she saw a wide variety of sizes, races, and ages. He was stunned at the diversity but more so with the discipline for a mixed-level elementary school. "Children, the State of New Mexico has found that you and your school have the best learning record in the state for rural schools. You must be very proud of your hard work …," the commissioner went on with his standard, canned speech to elementary schoolchildren about achieving, the importance of education, and so forth.

Madden sat in the back listening, proud of his students and that this school was making a difference in their lives. Madden reflected on the road he and his students started last year.

"Now children, I'd like to present an award to your teacher. Mr. Madden, would you please step up to receive this award?" asked Dr. Lopez.

As Madden made his way to the front, Dr. Marquez was busily taking pictures of the whole event. "Thank you, Dr. Lopez, but I'd like all of the student leaders to come forward and accept this award as representatives of the school. Leaders, come on up now," he instructed. As Madden moved to the back, the seven leaders took their positions in front of the class to accept the award as a group. Hank placed a nail near the bulletin board for the award to be seen by all. There was an awkward silence from the leaders and students.

"Mr. Madden, with your permission and to celebrate this event, we brought some cake and ice cream donated by the New Mexico State School Board."

"Speaking for the class, thank you. Hank would you please assist in setting up the lunchroom with the cake and ice cream?" Hank gave Madden a quick, informal salute and was off carrying the boxes in from the SUV.

"What a nice celebration and many, many thanks," Madden commented to the visitors.

"Rob, could we please have a word with you outside?" Dr. Kramer asked quietly.

"Sure, follow me," Rob advised as they reconvened at Madden's favorite meeting place, the old wooden picnic table under the cottonwood tree. Hank appeared out of nowhere with cups of coffee for the visitors. They thanked Hank in unison for his kindness, and he returned to the lunchroom to assist with the celebration.

"Rob, your tenure will be ending this month, and I'm sure you are looking forward to getting on the road to Stanford and completing your doctorate," Dr. Kramer knew she was preaching to the choir. "You truly were a godsend to this school and community as evidenced by today's events. I appreciate your efforts through some trying and challenging times," she said putting a positive spin on the real circumstances of Madden's "volunteering" to teach at Tres Rios.

Madden just nodded and smiled and thought to himself, *Bullshit*.

"Rob, I'm totally aware of the conditions that brought you here," stated Lopez as he winked and smiled at Madden. "Apparently, there were misunderstandings from the beginning, but we're pleased it all worked out well, especially for these students. I suspect you'll be on your way to Stanford at the end of the term. I personally spoke with Stanford's dean of the education department and they're anxious to get you started immediately," Lopez added.

Madden sat idle, just nodding and smiling. The visitors knew there was no way they could make up for the injustices tossed to Madden from the beginning. There truly was nothing else to say.

"Do you have anything to add?" asked Lopez.

"Yes, sir, I do. As you stated, I'm scheduled to depart at the end of this month," Madden repeated. "I request that this departure date not be announced or posted until absolutely necessary. I want the students to press hard until the very end with no distractions." Madden emphasized to the visitors, "I don't want them thinking that I will slack off or go easy just because I'm leaving. Please give me the opportunity to tell them exactly when I'll be leaving."

The visitors looked at each other and all agreed, "Okay, Rob, that's fine," said Lopez.

"There's another issue we'd like to discuss with you that will affect the future of Tres Rios," Kramer commented. "Rob, you've accomplished so much here by getting more children back in the classroom, bringing the community together, and bringing order to a bad situation. Truthfully, I believed it was hopeless here. We couldn't possibly invest our resources in a school with no promise of achievement," Kramer emotionally pointed out.

Dr. Lopez, Dr. Marquez, and Mr. Moralez were listening intently to Dr. Kramer as she continued, "Well, Rob, you certainly opened our eyes, and I'm sorry I didn't do this sooner. With now more than fifty students and the significant increase in student retention and performance, the board of education has voted to fund construction for three additional classrooms and three additional teachers and teaching assistants," Kramer explained, leaving Madden speechless.

Moralez added, "We plan to have the changes completed by the next school year. However, we'll have mobile classrooms in place while construction is taking place on the building. Also, Rob, the board voted on a very nice severance package for you as a measure of gratitude for your accomplishments here at Tres Rios," Moralez said while handing Madden an official-looking envelope.

"What do you think, Rob?" asked Lopez.

"Yes, we've certainly come a long way," Madden replied, "and many, many thanks, Dr. Kramer and Mr. Moralez for your efforts on behalf of the students here. Dr. Lopez, pleasure to meet you, and I greatly appreciate your presentation to our students." Madden for the first time, in a long time, was close to emotional tears when hearing the good news.

All began getting up from the picnic table and walking back to Dr. Kramer's SUV while making small talk. "Rob, could I have a quick word with you?" Dr. Lopez asked as he began leading Madden away from the others. When they reached the middle of the soccer field, Dr. Lopez turned and asked, "Rob, I understood you unfortunately got involved in a situation that you were not aware of and those circumstances brought you here. May I recommend that you finish the work you started here and happily move on to California," Lopez stated.

"Dr. Lopez, I don't understand your point, what are you getting at?" Madden asked.

"You might have some sort of grudge or want retribution against some of the community leaders in Calico County for their previous mistakes to include Mr. William Hemrod." Lopez continued, "Also, it might serve you well to leave in a good light with no trouble at the end of your stay here at Tres Rios. Oh, one other thing, Rob, I would like to report to the administration at Stanford University that you performed brilliantly here in Calico County—on the day you depart. Rob, I am sure your departure from Tres Rios will be without incident," Lopez emphasized.

"Thank you Dr. Lopez, I appreciate your advice and concern," Madden stated while accompanying Lopez back to the SUV.

At this point, he suspected Lopez was wired with a listening device and had an "association" with Hemrod. There was no doubt in Madden's mind—Lopez was also on the Hemrod payroll.

The visitors departed, waving as they were leaving the school parking lot. Madden paused for a moment and reflected, "What did he mean 'without incident'?"

"Hank, how's it going?" Madden asked, "Did the kids get enough to eat, and did you get some?"

"Sure, boss, it went well," replied Hank.

"Okay, great, now let's get back to completing this term."

"Hey, boss, how many more days you got here?"

After his private conversation with Dr. Lopez, Madden answered, "Too many."

CHAPTER
30

On a busy Monday morning at the National Counter Terrorism Center, the GPS tracking technician announced, "Aldawasari is on the move, and it appears he and his three buddies are heading for New Mexico. Looks like the GPS and beacon are operating well—no problems."

"Thank you, ladies and gentlemen," announced Agent Stock. "Please continue monitoring and advise me of any changes or if you receive any new information. I'll be down in the security communications conference room if you need me," he said while leaving in a hurry.

Following the normal procedure for initiating a top-secret conference call with the DEA and CIA joint team members, agents Carl Brown and Vernon Tobey signed in on the conference.

"Good morning, Carl and Vernon. How are you reading me?" asked Stock.

"Jim, loud and clear," replied Brown and Tobey.

"We're tracking Aldawasari with his cell on their way to New Mexico—all of our monitoring systems are working normally," Stock briefed.

"When do you estimate that he'll reach Tres Rios and the mine?" asked Brown.

"We estimate he should be at Tres Rios probably around late evening on Thursday, 24 May," replied Stock.

"That gives us just over three days to prepare for his arrival—does that check with you, Jim?" Tobey asked.

"Yes, it does."

"Carl, would you please brief your agent in Albuquerque on Aldawasari's ETA and ensure that when he does arrive he's provided adequate directions to Madden's new 'office' at the uranium mine?" asked Stock.

"Sure, Jim. I'll get a hold of our book vendor and have him lead Aldawasari straight into the security complex of the mine," a smiling Brown replied.

"Carl, how in the heck are you going to be able to guide a known terrorist and his friends straight into the security complex of a uranium mine?" asked Tobey while scratching his head in doubt.

"Vernon, our agent in Albuquerque is a pretty ingenious fellow—he'll know exactly how to lead them to Madden and the mine," Brown confidently announced. "Jim, can you provide me with all of the details on what Aldawasari is driving: make, model, tag numbers, etc.?" asked Brown.

"It's on the way. Also, I'll put him in contact with the tracking center," added Stock, "so we'll know where Aldawasari is at all times to a gnat's ass. Now, all we need is Madden's cooperation."

At the same time in Tres Rios, Madden routinely announced, "Leaders, break into your study-period groups, and I'll be around to check on your progress and answer any questions." The small groups gathered at various locations around the school to do homework or be tutored by other students or Madden himself.

"Well, here we go, must be lunchtime," said Madden, realizing he had lost track of time as he watched Hank pull up with his daily load of school lunches. Hank routinely carried the boxes of lunches into the small utility room where students took their places in line and waited to be served. The students found their friends and made the most of the lunch and short break. In his office, Madden ate a chili-mac sandwich and potato chips.

Hank knocked on the office door and said, "Hey, boss, good afternoon. How's it going?"

"Hank, couldn't be better. The countdown is ten days and I'll be leaving this all to you." In Madden's view, Hank was just as big of a part of resurrecting Tres Rios as he was. He was grateful that Dr. Kramer and Sheriff Wells had approved Hank's early release and given him the position as the school's full-time facility manager. He knew how much Hank loved being the facility manager, especially given the future growth of the school.

"Oh, boss, one other thing," Hank added as he pulled out a small box from the larger boxes holding the lunches and handed it to Madden. He looked at the small package addressed to the Headmaster of Tres Rios Rural Elementary School with a return address of the Northern New Mexico Publishing Company.

Trying to keep his cool without showing that anything was out of the normal, Madden asked Hank, "How'd you come by this package, Hank?"

"I was at the central kitchen picking up the lunches when a custodian asked me to give this to you," Hank said, assuming there was nothing suspicious about the request.

"Okay, thanks, Hank. Just another textbook vendor trying to sell us stuff," Madden replied as he placed the small box in his backpack. Only ten more days," Madden commented. Not showing his apprehension or concern in front of Hank, Madden was not looking forward to opening the contents of the box—his new textbook vendor friend, Steve Webb, wanted something.

That evening in his trailer, Madden stared at the package and thought, *Shit, just leave me alone and let me leave in peace,* Madden vented alone, "*Dios Mio,* why me and why now? I've already paid my dues." Alone, Madden pulled out a kitchen knife and opened the small box, which was professionally and securely wrapped. Inside was a small cell phone with a note on Northern New Mexico Publishing Company letterhead. Taking out his reading classes from his briefcase, Madden read the following:

> Mr. Madden, Great to have made your
> acquaintance last week, and thank you for the
> time you spent reviewing our line. I hope you
> found it useful. Highly recommend you contact
> me as soon as possible via the enclosed cell
> phone; the number is preloaded. I hope to hear
> from you this evening. Find a quiet place to call
> from, I don't want to disturb your evening.
> Sincerely,
> Steve Webb, Lead Customer Service Representative
> Northern New Mexico Publishing Company

Being cognizant that his trailer was wired and possibly even had a hidden camera monitor, Madden nonchalantly placed the cell phone on the kitchen table and made a comment for his trailer's bugs: "Those damn book vendors, we don't need anything, and I wish they'd stop bothering me."

After grading countless exams and reading papers, Madden decided to take a break and his nightly walk, always enjoying the quiet beauty of New Mexico's landscape. Grabbing the cell phone and placing it in his pocket, Madden sensed his upcoming conversation with the book vendor would be eventful. He dreaded making the call. Finding a seat in an old, handmade wooden camp chair, he sat admiring the countless stars on such a clear night, again reflecting on the past and hoping his conversation with Webb would be short and sweet.

"Good evening, Mr. Webb, this is Rob Madden," he said in a professional voice. "Greatly appreciate your note and the gift of the cell phone. What can I do for you?"

"Hello, Rob. Thanks for your quick response," Webb replied. "And for your information, the phone you're speaking on is impossible to monitor, so I can speak bluntly and to the point."

"Go ahead."

"Humza Aldawasari, the brother of Anwar Aldawasari, was recently released from Guantanamo and found himself in a terrorist sleeper cell in Michigan. Aldawasari is determined to settle the score with you for the death of his brother. We estimate that he'll be in New Mexico by late evening on Thursday, 24 May."

"This is incredible. He's the worst of the lot, and he was let go?" Madden thundered.

"Listen, Rob, we don't have the time to discuss why he was released, but he's on his way to find you and attempt to kill you." Webb asked, "Do you understand?"

There was silence on both ends of the line. Shifting to his old Air Force combat-controller mentality, Madden started planning. He asked Webb, "Is there a plan to intercept and detain him?"

"Rob, listen carefully. We're going to let Aldawasari come all the way to Tres Rios and the mine. In fact, we are going to guide Aldawasari and his cell directly to you and your friends."

"Let me get his straight, you're going to actually help Aldawasari find me?" sounding upset and shocked, adding, "Well this is just great. Do you want me to have dinner ready for him too when he shows up?"

Webb made a slight giggle on hearing this remark, and Madden sensed there was something more to this operation. "Steve, you said he was coming to me and 'my friends.' Exactly who are these friends?" he asked, nervous about the safety of his students, their parents, and other close friends he made during the past year. There's no way he would ever allow them to be targets. "Steve, again, who are 'my friends'?"

"Rob, I know this is going to be difficult for you to understand right now, but Aldawasari will be told that William Hemrod and his crew are your friends. In fact, Aldawasari will be led to believe that you and Hemrod are close friends and that you work part-time for him at the mine," Webb explained.

"Listen, pal, and listen good," Madden said, having enough this scenario, "I've been through a hell of a lot here. I have less than ten days to go until I can get on the road and out of here. Nothing is going to stop me from leaving. You got that, Webb?"

"Nothing but Aldawasari," Webb quickly replied. "Now, Rob, listen to reason, if we hadn't been monitoring Aldawasari, your life really would be in danger. We have the ability to control his actions and lead him right where we want him to go—straight to you and Hemrod."

Madden gathered his thoughts and asked, "Why tie me with Billy Hemrod? The whole county knows he hates my guts and would go to any length to hurt me. How am I supposed to be a friend and associate of his?"

"Rob, our superiors from different agencies think we'll never have an opportunity like this again. You just happen to be in the middle of a perfect storm."

"What in God's name opportunity are you talking about? What opportunity and for what purpose?"

"The team feels that there is a real chance of taking down Aldawasari and Hemrod at the same time with your cooperation. Rob, in simple terms, you're the bait bringing Aldawasari into the trap—with Hemrod and his people there to greet them. You'll bring them all together, Rob, and we'll do the rest," Webb repeated.

"Where and how am I expected to bring them together?" Madden asked, now resigned to the fact that he was involved with no way out.

"We'd like you to have a friendly visit with your new buddy Hemrod at his mine security facility on the evening of Thursday, 24 May," advised Webb.

Madden and Webb continued their discussions into the night with DEA agent McCord also monitoring the conversation. McCord's participation was purposely kept from Madden. DEA leadership thought it prudent that Madden not know McCord was working undercover in the casino. A slight glance or stare at each other might blow her cover, and for now, Madden didn't need to know McCord would be a major player in the upcoming operation.

After the conversation, a concerned McCord asked, "Steve, I notice you didn't mention the rest of the plan and its possible risks to Rob. Any reason why?"

"I understand you were part of his Air Force training team in Colombia a few years back," replied Webb.

"Yes, I spent the better part of three months with his team and the Colombian military and police chasing FARC terrorists and drug organizations. He's an exceptional trainer and leader," McCord added, worried for her friend.

"Understand he is very good with explosives," Webb commented and left it at that. He counted on Madden meeting Hemrod and his crew at the mine's security facility on the appointed date and time.

CHAPTER

31

The FBI surveillance and tracking center now put Aldawasari's arrival in Calico County very close to its original Thursday evening estimate. Madden called the mine on Tuesday evening, "Hello, is this the mine security office?"

"Yes, this is security," came the reply, "who are you and what do you want?"

"This is Rob Madden, teacher at Tres Rios Rural Elementary School," Madden replied. "I'd like to speak with Mr. Hemrod, if possible." Madden felt like a fool and stooge making this kowtowing call to Hemrod.

"Oh, Madden, what the hell do you want? We're pretty busy here."

"If it's not too much trouble, I'd like to speak with Hemrod," Madden patiently asked again.

"Just a second, asshole. Let me see if he wants to talk to you."

A few minutes went by before a voice on the other end of the phone responded, "Madden, this is Billy, what the hell do you want? Another ass whipping before you leave town?"

"Listen, Billy, I know we've had some misunderstandings this past year, for which I am truly sorry, but I would like to part with no hard feelings. The past is the past," Madden patronized Hemrod with what he thought was some pretty fine acting. "Thought I'd swing by your office Thursday night with a couple cases of beer for you and your crew—just a parting gift for all that we've been through together. Will that work for you?" said Madden now feeling stupid and silly with his fake sincerity.

"Okay, Madden, I'll be here with my guys and we'll have a beer in your honor as you ride out of town," Hemrod said, looking at his crew smiling and making a fist. "I'll have one of my crew pick you up at the mine entrance at seven sharp on

Thursday night. And don't forget the beer, asshole," Hemrod slammed the phone down and began laughing with his crew. "So Madden wants a little going-away party with us? We'll give him one to remember," Hemrod announced.

"Hey, Billy, Madden doesn't seem like the type of guy to forgive and forget," one of Hemrod's crew mentioned. "What's he up to?"

"We'll I'll tell you what I'm up to," said a grinning Hemrod. "Rob Madden's going to get a good ol' fashion going-away gift from me, and we're getting a few beers from him. Does it get any better? Hey, Pete, pick up Madden Thursday night at the entrance and make sure you frisk him down good. We can't afford to have any troublemakers at the lab, oh, I mean security office," Hemrod yelled out to his crew and laughed. "Also, make sure the whole crew is here to witness Madden's goodbye to Tres Rios. Now let's get back to the lab, we've got shipments to get out. When's the next truck due in?" Hemrod asked preparing for his next delivery.

Steve Webb, undercover DEA agent and Madden's textbook-vendor contact, had been monitoring the exact progress of Aldawasari with the FBI tracking center for the past few days. From wired cell-phone conversations, the terrorist cell should arrive in Tres Rios on the evening of the target date. Their mode of travel was renting different cars from every major city en route to New Mexico with the latest rental in Denver, Colorado. Terrorist cells usually had a naturalized U.S. citizen as the designated driver, one who would not attract any attention renting cars or motel rooms. The driver was a member of Aldawasari's cell but could pass as a clean-cut, Middle Eastern college student in contrast to the group he was driving to New Mexico.

All of the travel information was being passed to DEA and the FBI on an hourly basis. Webb learned the name of the driver was Robert Case, with credit cards and a driver's license adding to his legitimacy. The car-rental companies were asked to flag the name Robert Case and provide any information on the cars he rented, personal descriptions of the passengers, and anything out of the ordinary.

Western Car Rental at the Denver International Airport reported renting a black Chevrolet SUV to a Robert Case, who had three other passengers of Middle Eastern descent. The Western customer service representative reported the three passengers had beards and appeared to be rather dirty, as if they had not taken showers in some time. However, the driver, Robert Case, also of Middle Eastern descent, looked presentable with clean clothes and had a friendly disposition. An FBI agent was able to plant a small GPS tracker and voice monitor in the rented vehicle just prior to Robert Case picking up the car.

Speaking with the FBI control center and his own DEA director, Carl Brown, Webb updated the team, "Yes, sir, FBI has done a great job with tracking. I'll be ready to take over once he gets to Tres Rios."

"Steve, we've gone over your proposed plan for assisting Aldawasari to Madden. Any last-minute concerns? It's coming fast," Brown commented.

"I'll pull the same stunt we used last year in Virginia against the Savannah drug kingpins." Webb added, "Worked pretty good there; let's see if it works in New Mexico."

"Okay, Steve. Good luck and please keep us advised, especially with any deviations. We have Madden and his new friends scheduled to meet at the appointed time and designated place. Yes, Madden is proving to be excellent bait."

"That's for sure," replied Webb, "better put on my costume for Aldawasari's arrival."

On the afternoon of Thursday, 24 May, a black Chevrolet SUV pulled up to the Flying Buffalo Casino truck stop's gas pumps. Robert Case exited the car and began to refuel it while nervously surveying the rows of semitrailers and diesel trucks. Tourists came and went from the restaurant and gift shop, but mostly to the bathrooms. While Case was filling the SUV and continually looking around, the three passengers left the car for the bathrooms and travel store.

Before departing Dearborn, they'd found a map with directions to the Tres Rios Rural Elementary School and Madden's nearby trailer from their research and other sleeper-cell assistance. Upon returning to the SUV, the driver and passengers began reviewing the map and locations to determine the best route for finding Madden. The consensus among the cell was to locate Madden's trailer and take care of him that evening. They would wait at the rest stop until dark, then make their move.

"Hey, fellows, how y'all doin'? You from out of town?" asked an approaching mechanic who seemed to be repairing a gas pump. "Darn thing's been giving me problems all day. Did you guys have any problems with it?"

"No, sir, no problems," replied Case while the passengers looked the other way in silence.

"Good. Well, y'all take care and welcome to Calico County; have a nice day," the mechanic warmly bid farewell.

Aldawasari looked at Case and gave him a slight nod of the head and pointed to the mechanic. "Excuse me, sir," Case said to the mechanic, "We're new here and would like your help with some directions."

"Sure, buddy, lived here most of my life, except for some time in prison." The mechanic went on, "Sorry, sometimes I just keep babbling. Now where do you need to go?"

"Sir, we're schoolteachers from Denver and we're looking for a well-known grammar-school teacher here in New Mexico; his name's Rob Madden." Case announced, "We hear he's very good and we'd like to meet him and learn from him."

"Sure, buddy. Everyone around here knows Rob Madden. He's that crazy schoolteacher over at Tres Rios. I've heard some stories about that school and his ways of teachin'," the mechanic stated. "A lot of folks come through here lookin' for him, so he must be doin' something right," the mechanic mentioned while monitoring the other gas pumps.

"We thank you very much for your help," replied Case while Aldawasari and the cell listened intensely.

"Not a problem. The best way to talk with Madden is to meet him with his pal, Billy Hemrod, at the uranium mine just outside Tres Rios. Yep, that's best place to find him," the mechanic recommended while cleaning a day's worth of grease and grime off his hands and face. "Y'all didn't hear it from me, but folks around these parts are convinced that Billy Hemrod and Rob Madden are runnin' some sort of antiterrorist training center at the mine for the government—in the security facility right inside the mine area. Can you imagine that, a government training center here in Calico County? Wonder who they have in that facility? Yeah, knowin' how rumors get started around here, they probably have some UFOs in there too."

The mechanic and Case laughed at this, but the passengers remained silent, not knowing what the stranger meant by UFO. "Well, we're all schoolteachers who want to meet Madden as fellow teachers," Case emphasized, "but you're saying, sir, that Madden is more than a schoolteacher?"

Shaking his head, he thought for a minute, and said, "There's lots of legends and stories around this county, but the latest is that Madden came here as a schoolteacher, but is really working for the government with Billy Hemrod at that CIA training center inside the mine security building."

Out of the truck-repair bay, a large grease-covered man in overalls came out and yelled at the mechanic, "Buzz, I don't pay you to stand around talkin' to tourists all day. Get back here, you've got some bearings need to be repacked on this truck."

"Yea, Frank, I'm coming," replied the mechanic. "Nice meetin' you folks. Hope you have a good talk with Madden." The mechanic, looking around again, approached Case, and whispered, "You're not going to believe this, but the scuttlebutt has it that Madden and Hemrod have a couple known terrorists in the mine security facility that they routinely interrogate, if you catch my drift."

Case tried to act as if this meant nothing and just looked at the mechanic grinning while the intensity inside the SUV was obvious from the passengers. Walking toward the truck-stop repair bay, the mechanic waved, "Have a good trip, and hope you get that chance to talk with Madden. He's a hoot."

The mechanic watched the SUV leave the truck stop and was relieved the encounter worked so well—pretty convincing he thought. Other undercover agents would ensure Aldawasari and his cell made it to the mine's security complex that night.

So, I was three feet from one of the top terrorist leaders in the world, Steve Webb thought. *I should've put a 9mm slug in his brain and prevented the deaths of hundreds of innocent people. Almost sorry we've got to save him for later tonight.*

The black Chevrolet SUV stopped at a secluded picnic area a few miles down from the truck stop. Case sat outside on a concrete picnic bench reading the paper like other tourists and travelers, while inside the SUV, Aldawasari and his cell planned their meeting with Madden and Hemrod. Besides seeking revenge against Madden, the possibility of freeing their own brothers from the mine was too much of a temptation for the terrorists. Plans were proceeding for tonight; there was a lot to plan.

CHAPTER

"Good afternoon, Sheriff Wells, I trust you're doing well. Do you have a minute?"

"Rob, good to hear from you. Are you nearly packed up and ready to move on?" Wells sincerely asked. He was somewhat pleased to receive a phone call from Madden.

"Yes, sir. Just taking care of some last-minute details before taking off and just wanted to know if you and Dr. Kramer might be available for one last lunch next week."

"Good idea, Rob. We'll look forward to it and will see you then," Wells added.

"Sheriff, one last item I'd like to pass on," Madden said and then paused for effect. "I know there's been some misunderstandings with a few community leaders since my arrival, and I'd like to make things right before I leave."

"Rob, I believe that's a nice and generous gesture on your part—good for you," Wells said, wondering what had gotten into Madden: forgive and forget?

"I've decided to bury the hatchet with Billy and his bunch," explained Madden. "I've been invited to have a few beers with him and his associates tonight at the mine's security complex. I can't see any reason why not, can you?"

"Rob, do you really think that's a good idea? You're just a few days from leaving for good and with an outstanding performance record. Do you really want to do this?" emphasized a worried Wells.

"I'll be fine, Sheriff, but thanks for your advice."

Madden agreed with the sheriff wholeheartedly. The meeting with Hemrod and crew at the mine was stupid and made no sense at all. However, it's not as if he had a choice. Madden suspected the sheriff knew of the meeting prior to

Madden's call anyway. Madden was just covering himself in case the "goodwill meeting" turned ugly. In fact, Madden told others, including Dr. Kramer and County Attorney Raymond Garcia of his intended meeting with Hemrod. Both thought he was crazy for attempting a reconciliation now. But Madden knew he was just covering his ass.

Completing his final lesson plans and building some continuity for the new teacher's school year, Madden nervously awaited the time to depart for the mine. He understood that, regardless of what happened, it would be dangerous. Getting ready to leave his trailer with the two cases of beer he'd promised Hemrod, Madden had no electronic devices, guns, knives, or any type of weapon. Knowing he would be frisked, there was no reason to create suspicion with any weapons.

Madden drew up a chair in his kitchen and prayed to the Almighty for strength and guidance in his upcoming mission with a special prayer for his deceased wife and the two little girls who were his world, the only loves of his life. "Oh, Jesus," he ended, "hear my prayers. Amen!" Regaining his composure, he mentally prepared himself and thought, "Let's go do God's work tonight."

Carrying the two cases of beer to his Honda Element, Madden behaved normally with his radio typically blaring out the open windows as he headed for the mine entrance. There was no doubt in his mind that binoculars were trained on his every move from afar. On a small outcropping of rock overlooking an old mining trail next to an unused dirt road, two figures were observing the quarry below.

"Aldawasari, there goes Madden!" announced Abdul excitedly.

"Yes, brother, I see him. Where do you think he's going?"

"According to our pictures and the maps, he's heading to the mine entrance." Abdul and Aldawasari still eyed their binoculars while the two other cell members made a final equipment check.

"We should've taken care of Madden when he was in his trailer. It was a sure kill; why are we waiting?" a frustrated and tired Zohody asked. Aldawasari was also tired and would have liked nothing more than to have settled the score with Madden at his trailer house and departed immediately.

"Brother, you're not alone in your thinking, but if there's a chance that mouthy mechanic at the truck stop is right, we could possibly free imprisoned brothers and settle with infidels Madden and Hemrod at the same time," Aldawasari explained, second guessing himself. "If it's the will of Allah that one of us is captured, you know what to do. Immediately ask for an attorney, talk of being an oppressed people, and like me, you'll be back at Guantanamo Bay or a posh U.S. civilian courtroom." They nervously laughed at his comments. Then Aldawasari and his group packed up their SUV and headed for the staging position near a desolate spot along the mine's fence line.

"Good job, Aldawasari," Special Agent Webb commented from his binoculars not far from the terrorist's SUV.

"Come on, Madden, grab the beer and get in the truck. We don't have all night, asshole," one of Hemrod's crew greeted Madden as he parked his Element in the mine's visitors parking lot.

Madden picked up the two cases from the trunk, calmly carried them, and placed them in the bed of the pickup truck. Out of one side of a case of beer, Madden quickly slipped his 9mm Beretta 92SF pistol under the passenger seat of the cab.

"Wait a minute. Out of the truck, Madden. I need to search you," ordered Pete the driver.

Madden followed his instructions and from the stench of liquor on Pete's breath, he'd obviously started drinking early. After Madden's clean frisk, he and the driver were heading on a hard gravel road toward the security facility.

"Well, Madden, this was awfully nice of you to arrange this little meeting with us and Billy. Sure, we'll have a going-away beer with ya," Pete said laughing while finishing off a pint of Jack Daniels and throwing the empty bottle on the side of the road.

"Thanks for the lift and you're right, we've been through a lot together this past year," Madden replied as he thoroughly inspected the interior of the truck, especially noting the keys to the ignition. He might need it later if he survived the meeting.

Looking at Madden, Pete thought for a minute and said, "You know, Madden, you certainly have shit for brains if you thought you could best Billy's crew."

"So, are you one of the mine's security specialists?" Madden attempted to work some pleasantries on his drunk driver.

"Yeah, I'm a security specialist," he laughed. "You know how much money we make out here, Madden? A ton—enough to buy your sorry ass."

"I didn't realize security at a uranium mine paid that much," said Madden looking sincere.

Pulling out another fifth of Jack from the glove compartment, Pete added, "Let's just say we've got a high-paying hobby out here, kinda like part-time jobs."

Madden just nodded his head and listened to Pete's opinions on the world according to Hemrod. As the pickup approached the lighted security complex, Madden concentrated on the layout of the various small structures and their close proximity to a mineshaft on the side of the bluff. The complex was well lit.

"There it is, Billy's office over there on the right," Pete pointed out. "I'm sure he'll have some sort of VIP reception for you, schoolteacher hero." Stopping in front of the office building, he announced, "Hey, listen up everybody, I got the schoolteacher here. Teacher, pick up the beer and bring it in the office." At that, Hemrod and eight of his thugs emerged from his office, all apparently drunk and anxious to say goodbye to their nemesis.

"Hello, Billy. Thanks for the opportunity to say *adiós* before I leave next week," Madden said while handling the cases of beer.

Hemrod's crew slowly surrounded Madden while lighting cigarettes and taking drinks from their bottles, all laughing and joking. "Hey, schoolteacher, give me some of that beer you brought us," Hemrod said as he grabbed the cases from Madden and threw them on the ground, smashing the cases with his boot, beer splashing everywhere.

"Well, enjoy your beer," commented Madden with grave doubts about his safety on this visit.

"That's right, Madden. Enjoy your beer, asshole." Hemrod suddenly kicked Madden in the groin so hard he fell to the ground in extreme pain.

"Pick him up, pick him up, we've just started with our schoolteacher," Hemrod hollered while throwing punches at a dazed and restrained Madden. "Good thing you're not a lady schoolteacher, Madden, or we'd be havin' a much different goodbye party."

Madden was now pushed around by the others including what appeared to be a female crew member with punk hair, who yelled, "Screw with us, schoolteacher, and this is what you'll get." A hard right from the woman sent him to the ground again. Madden heard more yelling followed by someone relieving himself on him.

"Everyone, stand now where you are!" came the command in heavily accented English followed by a crescendo of AK-47 rounds lighting the night air.

Hemrod and his crew diverted their attention from Madden to the four masked men holding assault rifles pointed at them.

"Ah shit," Hemrod shouted thinking the gunmen were from a rival drug operation attempting to shut him down or take over his business. The others stood pleading for their lives, all wanting to make a deal.

"Shut up, all of you, and move over there," directed Aldawasari to the lighted entrance of the mine. With what he had observed before surrounding Hemrod and his crew, Aldawasari was totally convinced this was a CIA training center and a secret terrorist detention facility. After watching Madden's brutal "interrogation" by Hemrod's crew, Aldawasari was enraged by what he had observed. Speaking in Arabic to the other three cell members, he said, "Brothers, we will do great work tonight. There is no doubt this is the CIA prison and interrogation center as we thought."

Hemrod's goons were now shaking and quickly sobering up but could not understand what was being said. Madden was attempting to get up from the ground when he heard Aldawasari and his cell speaking in Arabic. Fluent in Arabic, Madden gathered that, for some reason, Aldawasari believed this was a CIA detention and training center. More surprising to Madden was that Aldawasari thought Madden was a prisoner being brutally interrogated.

Standing now and looking worked over, Madden spoke to Aldawasari in Arabic, "Brothers, brothers, you have saved me from these bastards of the Great Satan, you have saved me."

"Yes, brother," Aldawasari stated, "we have come for you. Are there others beside you at this camp?"

"Yes, oh great one. Three are being held in the mine, and all are alive," Madden relayed convincingly.

Hemrod and his crew were silent and terrified. They had no clue that Madden spoke Arabic and no idea what he was saying to the terrorist. The crew realized the gravity of the situation and frantically called on Madden to help them.

"First, brother, identify Rob Madden to me—I understand he is here," Aldawasari instructed Madden in Arabic.

"Great one, Rob Madden is there," he said pointing directly at Hemrod, who only knew that he was being singled out by Madden for some reason. The butt of an AK-47 was thrown at Hemrod's gut as he went down crying and weeping.

"Allāhu Akbar," (God is great), yelled Aldawasari while grabbing Hemrod by the belt and dragging him behind the security office.

"Madden, Madden help me, tell them who I am. I have plenty of money!" Hemrod begged as he was pulled behind the building by Aldawasari. The begging and screaming continued until three pistol shots were heard and Aldawasari appeared alone and splattered with blood.

CHAPTER

33

Hemrod's crew was now a slobbering bunch of crying misfits, offering anything to save themselves from certain execution and pleading for Madden to intercede.

"Shut up all of you," an enraged Aldawasari ordered in English. "Brother, are you able to walk and bring us to the other prisoners?" Aldawasari asked, certain he would be hailed a great hero for freeing imprisoned brothers and destroying a CIA training facility.

"Yes, great one," Madden replied, "they're all in holding cells next to the interrogation room in the mineshaft. Let's release our brothers and place these CIA pigs in the cells."

Aldawasari nodded to Madden and, for a moment, thought he recognized him from somewhere but quickly dismissed it. While Aldawasari's men rounded up Hemrod's thugs and pushed them to the mine entrance, the sobbing and crying continued as they were pushed and prodded along by the terrorists.

Taking Madden aside, Aldawasari asked, "Brother, who are you and where did you come from?"

"Oh great one, thank *Allah* you are here to save us," Madden cried with emotion. "I'm Kurt Wessen from Germany. From the start, I trained and worked at various training camps with Abu Musab al Zarqawi in Afghanistan. I was arrested by the CIA in Hamburg while teaching engineering at the Technical University of Hamburg with other brothers in my cell. Thank you for rescuing us. Oh great one, we've been to several of these CIA interrogation camps and are ready to go back to our homelands and continue our work," stated Madden convincingly.

Madden had fought the terrorists in many locations across the world and had to work his overstressed mind to come up with a believable and plausible cover for Aldawasari. Madden knew he could come up with a better story if given more time, but this would have to work for now.

Seeming convinced of Madden's terrorist identity, Aldawasari hugged him and said, "Come, let us free our brothers and punish the remaining CIA scum."

Walking with Aldawasari to the entrance of the mine where Hemrod's closely guarded crew waited, Madden stopped. "Brother, I forgot to inform you that the keys to the cells are located in that security office," Madden said pointing to the office.

"Retrieve the keys then and hurry back. There is much to do," ordered Aldawasari in Arabic.

Madden hurriedly stumbled to the security office and immediately turned on the lights to show he was there. Satisfied he made it to the office, Aldawasari picked up his AK-47 and went over to Hemrod's men gathered under the watchful eyes of Aldawasari's cell. A nervous and excited Kareem Zohody said in Arabic, "Brother, we need to speak with you now. Something is wrong here."

"Yes, what is it? We have work to do when our brother returns with the keys to the torture cells."

"That is the problem. After interrogating some of this scum and looking in the building, there are no fellow prisoners here, and the mine appears to be filled with laboratory equipment," explained Zohody.

"What about our brother we just freed? He is on his way back with the keys!" Aldawasari screamed and began kicking one of Hemrod's crew. "Where are the other prisoners?"

"Brother, this lying scum here," Zohody grabbed Pete and forced him up, "says it is a big mistake. He says this is not a CIA antiterrorist training center but a laboratory for making illegal drugs."

Now standing up and trembling, Pete said, "There ain't no terrorists here. We're just runnin' a part-time drug lab while working security for the mine. Nothing more. The person you shot was Billy Hemrod, the mine owner's son and my boss." Trying to get some composure, he asked, "What're you gonna do with the rest of us?"

Pointing his AK-47 at the shaking man, Aldawasari shouted, "Then who is the man you and your team were interrogating?" Slapping Pete, he repeated, "Tell me now, who is that man?"

"Sir, that's Rob Madden, the local schoolteacher," came the reply. "He was causin' us a lot of problems in town, so we were just givin' him some payback tonight."

At that moment, the sound of a pickup truck being started was heard in the security office parking lot.

"Madden, that is Madden?" Aldawasari screamed, "Kill him! Kill him now!"

Ignoring their prisoners, the cell members began firing their weapons at the departing pickup truck while shouting and screaming in Arabic at each other. While the terrorists were running after Madden in mass confusion and firing their weapons in all directions, Hemrod's remaining crew saw the opportunity to find their own weapons.

"Holy shit," Madden yelled as he navigated the truck out of the parking lot with no headlights.

Suddenly, tracer bullets were slamming into the truck and flying by Madden with their red tails streaking past the desert floor. Getting on the main gravel road to the mine's main entrance, he heard and felt the pinging of bullets hitting the truck. The windshields were shattered and part of the bed was in shreds, but the truck kept going.

After a few seconds, the tracers and gunfire at the truck had ceased, followed by what Madden thought was a large firefight within the security compound and mine itself. The noise of the firefight was deafening, and it looked like fireworks in the distance. Viewing the scene in the rearview mirror, he thought, *Whoa, either Aldawasari and his cell are executing Hemrod's crew or they got a hold of their own weapons.* Madden did not wait to find out.

"Come on, baby, you can make it," a scared Madden shouted at the truck while searching under the cab's seat for the pistol he hid on the way in. Finally, he found the trusty 9mm under an assortment of cigarette packs and empty whiskey bottles.

Madden then looked up to see black smoke billowing out of the engine compartment with visible tongues of flames. The truck simply died and became a huge flare burning on the gravel road between the security office and the mine entrance.

Grabbing his pistol, Madden jumped out of the truck and ran down the road in the near-perfect illumination of the burning truck. Running for his life and now quite terrified, he could have sworn he heard a female voice screaming, "Friendly, Rob Madden, friendly. Danger close!" The voice was getting closer and sounding louder, "Friendly. Rob, friendly. DEA, Stay where you are. I'm coming to you."

Unsure whether this was a trick, he instinctively prepared his 9mm and was distracted by what sounded like a motorcycle starting a few yards from the road. Silhouetted against the burning truck, he saw the image of an approaching motorcycle with the driver wearing a black jumpsuit and ski mask.

Still pointing his pistol at the bike's driver, a female with nothing but urgency in her voice screamed, "Get on, Rob. Now. DEA!" Hurriedly placing the 9mm in his belt, he barely got himself on the passenger seat while the female voice behind the mask continued to yell, "Get on, damn it and hurry up, Madden."

Madden was barely able to hold himself on the bike, but he noticed the driver wore night-vision goggles. Riding now a little more securely, he saw the security office firefight continue to light up the clear night sky and heard the ongoing noise of bullets and tracers. The pickup's gasoline tank had since exploded, adding another source of light. The barren, dusty dirt terrain of the uranium mine area now looked like a Friday-night high school football game.

The mysterious motorcycle driver followed a trail leading to the bank of an old creek bed. "Madden, get off and go down to that dry river bank. I'll meet you there, hurry!"

He quickly found a position on the bank and watched as the driver grabbed some packs from the motorcycle and quickly placed them next to Madden, followed by the motorcycle.

"Who are you and what're you doing?" Madden asked the DEA agent, who seemed oddly familiar.

"Rob, later. Just stay where you are and take cover. Now!"

Finding cover, Madden lifted his head above the edge of the bank and watched the action at the security complex, feeling relieved to be in the safety of the dry creek bed with the mysterious driver. Madden watched the driver open some of the packs and make some adjustments. When she appeared to be satisfied, she ordered Madden, "No bullshit, Madden. Stay down, and don't look at the security complex, do not look at the complex."

Madden nodded his head and was hunkered down ready for what he now knew was coming. The driver grabbed a small device from a pack and joined Madden lying on the bottom of the dry creek. She pressed some switches on the device and added, "Get ready, stay down, and hold your ears."

The explosion was sudden and violent with dirt and debris flying everywhere. Madden and the driver continued to lie low and cover their heads while explosions rocked the security complex sending debris everywhere. Soon the wailing of the emergency response and law enforcement vehicles could be heard racing toward the mine blast, filling the horizon with the brilliance of the responders' flashing emergency lights.

At that point, Madden and the driver rose and dusted off the dirt caking their clothes and faces. The driver rapidly packed her equipment on the motorcycle and advised Madden, "We better get out of here while the getting's good."

Once on the motorcycle, both Madden and the driver took a short glance at the complete destruction of the complex noting that the entire side of the cliff was now on top of the old mine entrance. The driver put her night-vision goggles back on as they drove down a trail to depart the uranium mine area. Several miles away from the mine, two vehicles were waiting for them. The driver parked the motorcycle while two large men immediately picked up the bike and placed it in the back of a large SUV.

After the driver removed her night goggles and black ski mask revealing her penetrating green eyes, an astonished Madden said, "Bonnie McCord?"

"Well, Rob Madden, glad to have run into you tonight. Might even say I saved your life," smirked a pleased McCord.

"Nice work, Bonnie. And thanks for your help, Rob," added Agent Webb approaching them from an old, rundown pickup truck—like those that are so familiar around Calico County.

The DEA and FBI teams professionally secured the area and removed any telltale signs of activity. Webb handed Madden a gym bag with a change of clothes and said, "Rob, we need to get you cleaned up, changed, and back to your trailer immediately."

Dazed and still confused, Madden asked, "What about my Honda parked at the mine entrance? They have me identified as coming in the area. Couldn't that be a major problem?"

"No problem, Rob. We thought of that a while back." Webb continued, "We had an agent, who looked and dressed like you, leave the mine entrance parking lot in your Honda. It'll be sitting in front of your trailer when we get there.

"It's completely documented," Webb explained, "that you went out to see Hemrod at his office to say goodbye and reconcile any differences, and you got the hell knocked out of you for your effort. Of course, you left prior to the explosion, which is, again, fully documented."

Webb winked at Madden smiling, "Looks like you left right in the nick of time. Okay, Rob, please get changed and take a seat in the pickup. We're off to your trailer now."

Madden thought, *I'll get answers from McCord later,* as he quickly changed in the dark while several agents were preparing their reports to their directors, who would be pleased. "Shit, pal, couldn't you make the ride a little more comfortable," Madden mused as he rode toward his trailer in the old, rusted pickup that had seen better days.

"Rob, now listen," Webb briefed, "when you get to your trailer, you'll find the agent who took your place is gone and a nurse will be waiting there to patch you up. If anyone asks about her, we recommend you say she's an escort from the casino. After the night that you had with Hemrod, you needed some company."

"I'll be all right," Madden replied as the agent escorted Madden into his residence and introduced him to the nurse who began caring for his wounds.

Madden realized that in a few minutes, local area, state, and federal law enforcement agencies and investigators would be contacting him about the mine explosion and subsequent deaths.

CHAPTER

34

"Sir, it's been confirmed by Special Agent Webb and his team: at exactly 2005 hours on Thursday, 24 May, known terrorist Humza Aldawasari and his three cell members were killed in a blast at a uranium mine in New Mexico," the security communications coordinator relayed to the joint task force at the National Counter Terrorism Center. "Also, sir, known drug producer and distributor William Hemrod and eight of his employees were killed in the same mine explosion."

Reviewing the current situation in a secure conference room, FBI Special Agent Jim Stock, DEA Special Agent Carl Brown, and CIA Agent Vernon Tobey were all pleased with the final outcome.

"What a coincidence that one of the most-wanted terrorists in the world would stumble into a working meth lab and all of a sudden there's a catastrophic explosion that kills everyone. What a perfect storm," commented Stock.

"Outstanding work by your agents on the scene in New Mexico. Who were the key players down there?" Stock asked Brown.

"Jim, the on-scene agent in charge was Steve Webb with undercover work by DEA Special Agent Bonnie McCord. We're also grateful for logistical support provided by CIA Agent Wayne Wentz—the team could not have worked better." Brown explained, "The logistical support included four professional snipers: marksman, who were covering the mine security facility at various hidden locations—a little safeguard for Madden in case the operation failed.

"I know Webb from past field operations, but I've not had the pleasure of meeting Bonnie McCord," Tobey noted.

"Ah, yes, McCord is our rising star and she sure deserves the title. She's been working undercover in Tres Rios as a blackjack dealer at the local casino for the past year to monitor Hemrod's drug operation," Brown explained.

"As an attractive casino dealer, she was able to give us the complete details on Hemrod's operation at the mine's security office, including all of the specifics about his production labs. Most interestingly, she was able to penetrate the network and learn where Hemrod hid the fail-safe explosives around the labs and, most important of all, locate the control box, which she used to destroy the lab operation that evening."

"How in the blue blazes was she able to do that?" the impressed Stock asked.

Brown controlled his laughter as he continued, "One of Hemrod's employees bragged to McCord at her blackjack table one night about how rich he was from the work he did for Hemrod. He was pretty liquored up and literally panting over McCord to impress her. She did her best acting and went out with him after her shift with the intention of getting a lab tour. McCord played him like a fiddle and got the tour, while her new friend bragged about his importance at the lab and showed her how everything worked. She was then able to provide us with the necessary layout," Brown summarized.

"One other point I think you'll find interesting and amusing," Brown relayed, "is that just prior to Madden's school year, Hemrod and his crew made a little payback visit to him at the school and were just about to take a baseball bat to Madden."

"What saved him?" a curious Tobey asked.

"This is where it gets good," Brown mused. "McCord got wind at the casino that Hemrod was bragging about the broken arm he was going to give Madden; so she left work, hid her cross-country motorcycle in a ravine near the school, and watched events unfold. When she noticed things were looking bad for Madden, she raced into the cab of Hemrod's pickup, gunned the engine in front of Hemrod's crew, and waved the finger at them while she sped off toward to an old mine quarry."

"What happened to Madden and the pickup?" Stock laughed.

"Well, Hemrod's crew dropped everything including the bat and tried chasing after the pickup, which left Madden unharmed. That must have been a site," mused Brown. "The pickup was found in an abandoned mine complex a few miles from Tres Rios. Before leaving the pickup truck, McCord left a personal letter on the dashboard addressed to Hemrod."

"I got to know. What was in the letter?" asked Stock.

"The letter was from one of Hemrod's many, ahem, 'lady friends.' It stated she did not like Hemrod being married and fooling around on her. In other words, she was a jilted lover who was just trying to get Hemrod's attention—and gosh did she ever."

"Quick thinking and solid work by McCord. She saved Madden, saved our cover, and placed the stolen pickup on one of Hemrod's illicit squeezes. Brilliant," Tobey acknowledged.

Brown added, "One more thing. You talk about coincidence; Rob Madden had saved her life in Colombia several years ago while she was in training." Stock and Tobey looked puzzled by this statement. "Madden was an Air Force combat controller assigned to train our agencies in tactical deployments against the bad guys there. McCord was defending a helicopter-landing zone that was being overrun by FARC terrorists. Madden somehow got to her position just before the terrorists dragged her off, and they were both wounded in this action."

"Relieved to hear McCord was able to pull Madden out of this operation just in time. How is he?" Stock asked.

"We don't have all the details yet, but according to initial reports, he was badly beaten by Hemrod and his gang, but is being cared for now—nothing major. He sure took a hit for the team, though, wouldn't you say?"

The agents smiled and nodded their heads with Tobey asking, "So what does Madden's future hold now that this is over?"

"Sergeant Madden will complete his teaching obligation at the Tres Rios Rural Elementary School next week and then work on his doctorate in education at Stanford University on a full scholarship." Brown added, "We asked him to join the DEA several years ago, but he was focused on teaching school."

"However, I had recently been informally notified that there was a major break in the investigation of the terrorists who murdered Madden's family," Stock informed his team. "When Madden is updated on this development, he just may postpone Stanford and join our terrorist task force, just maybe."

At the end of the classified conference, Stock commented, "We were lucky here, real lucky!"

The next morning, Madden was approached by an endless barrage of questions from law enforcement regarding his visit to Hemrod's security office at the mine. He provided the same testimony to each local agency: "I merely took two cases of beer out to Hemrod and his employees as a little going-away gesture of good faith. We'd had our conflicts in the past and I wanted to reconcile with Billy before I left. Well, my gesture was clearly not appreciated, because he beat the hell out of me while his crew held me down. They let me go when they'd had enough, and, as you can see, I took a lot of hits. I barely made it to my Honda and back home. That's all I know. Any further questions?"

Madden called Dr. Kramer early that same morning. "Good morning, ma'am. I'm sorry for troubling you so early but I have an important request."

"Rob, are you okay? I just heard about the explosion at the mine," Dr. Kramer answered, shaken by the news.

"Yes, the explosion occurred right after I left the mine." Madden's reply was getting pretty standard and routine now. "I'm truly lucky to be alive, I know."

"What can I do for you, Rob; are you hurt?" a very sympathetic voice asked.

"Dr. Kramer, Billy and his crew worked me over, and I need a few days to recover," came another boilerplate reply by Madden. "I'll be there next week to complete the school term. Is that okay with you?"

"Of course, Rob, and please let me know if I can do anything for you."

"Yes, ma'am, two things: have Hank open the school this morning and have him tell the leaders that they will be responsible for the conduct of the class."

"Rob, are you sure about this? We can cancel classes with no problem," offered Kramer.

"No, this will give the leaders a chance to show their stuff without me in their shadows," Madden reasoned.

"All right, Rob, I'll back your judgment on this, and your next request?"

"Dr. Kramer, would you please contact Dr. Lightfeather and ask him if he wouldn't mind making a house call to my residence. I need his healing talents on a few cuts and bruises."

"Sure, Rob, I'll get a hold of him immediately. Oh, and Rob, I'm …" Kramer stopped for a moment and reset her thoughts. "We'll talk Monday about your departure, okay with you?"

"Be glad to, Dr. Kramer," said Madden anxious to get off the phone and get some rest—it had been a very long night.

An hour later, Lightfeather knocked on the trailer's door, "Hey, Rob. Good morning, and are you okay?"

"Yeah, yeah, I'm coming. Give me a minute," he said waking from a deep sleep. Madden slowly opened the door.

"Rob, I came as soon as I could," Lightfeather hurriedly said. "*Dios Mio,* what happened to you? I heard about the mine explosion and that you were there."

"Doctor, come in, come in, and thanks for coming."

Lightfeather immediately directed Madden to the small kitchen table where he began an examination of Madden's wounds, cuts, and bruises. Opening his rather large medical briefcase, Lightfeather went to work attempting to identify any major problems. During his examination, he noticed several wounds had already been addressed quite well.

"Rob, it appears you did a rather good job of caring for your wounds last night or was someone here to give you first aid?" Lightfeather looked suspiciously at Madden.

"Please, Doc. Just help me now and get me going as soon as possible." Madden added, "We'll talk outside as soon as you finish, okay?"

Nodding his head and with a stethoscope wrapped around his neck, Lightfeather spent over an hour administering to Madden's health. He finally said, "Rob, this isn't the whipping you received when you first got to town, but it's pretty close. You'll be okay, but I'd like to take some x-rays ASAP; there's a couple of ribs I'm concerned about."

Both men walked out to the handmade wooden chairs next to the trailer. Lightfeather brought out some coffee and donuts as they enjoyed the bright, brilliant New Mexico morning, listening to the loud chirping of birds in the nearby tree. Both remained with their thoughts.

"Rob, who worked on your wounds last night? It was good work."

Trying to protect Lightfeather from knowing too much information on the true circumstances of the mine explosion and the deaths of Hemrod and his crew, Madden stuck with the official version that some nice lady from the Flying Buffalo Casino had stayed with him and cared for his wounds. After the explanation, Madden winked at Lightfeather.

"Rob, I still don't understand how you got mixed up with Hemrod at the mine."

"Doc, because of this ridiculous do-gooder mindset of mine, I thought it best to make amends and reconcile with Hemrod before I leave next week. You know—let bygones be bygones. To show my good faith, I even took a couple of cases of beer to share with Billy and his crew. Apparently, he and his people were not in a forgive-and-forget mood. In fact, given all the booze and drugs, God knows what kind of mood or mindset they were in. All I know is that Billy and his crew were killed in a terrible mine explosion, and I got out just in time. No good deed will go unpunished."

Lightfeather was convinced after his observations and he listened for what Madden did not say—that the explosion was no accident and Madden was just a player in a much larger mystery. "Okay, Rob, whatever you say," Lightfeather acknowledged sitting back relishing the time he had spent with this crazy gringo.

CHAPTER
35

The following Monday morning at exactly 0700, the Tres Rios Rural Elementary School's bell rang out and the American and New Mexico flags were raised into a calm wind. The routine procession of students arrived at the school and were met by a rather scratched, bruised, and aching Madden. It would be one of their last days together as a class.

Entering the school, the students stared at Madden with all of his bruises and bandages covering his head and arms. "I guess he won't be tangling with Billy Hemrod anymore," one of the older students said.

Madden heard the comment and replied, "Robert, you are correct," he said with a quick laugh.

Ramon Rodriguez was also smiling and in better humor hearing the fate of Billy Hemrod at the mine's cave-in.

The leaders now took responsibility for opening the class while Madden sat back and monitored their instruction, as he'd done for the past few months.

Alan Moore held an elementary discussion about computer programming and the importance of mathematics that nearly brought Madden to tears. He could see that he was no longer required and it was time to move on. God, he and his students have come a long way this year.

On Madden's last night in town, Señor Ramos Arroyo raised his glass and announced, "A toast to my good friend, Rob Madden, *salud!*" at Madden's going-away reception in Arroyo's *Café & Cantina*. The little cafe was filled with Calico County school administrators, teachers, local law enforcement officers, and the parents/guardians of the students at Tres Rios. With plenty of food, beer, and wine, the reception turned into a grand party celebrating the success and achievements of the Flats and Tres Rios.

Besides saying their final goodbyes to Madden, the major topic of conversation was the explosion and cave-in at the uranium mine and Madden's miraculous escape. Still looking a little battered from his ordeal at the hands of Billy and his goons, Madden was asked hundreds of questions regarding the incident and his involvement.

Giving his standard, pat response, "I'll tell you, I went to the security office of the mine to make peace with Billy and his crew and say goodbye with no hard feelings. Apparently they have a real different way of saying so long." All laughed and saw the humor in his "blessed be the peacemaker" response.

While putting down his third beer and his fifth taco and sharing a joke with a grateful parent, Sheriff Wells asked Madden to meet with him and the other law officers outside.

"Thanks, Sheriff, and I hope this meeting is nicer than some of the other meetings we've had in the past."

"Smartass," Wells jokingly replied as he and Madden moved through the parking lot filled with police patrol cars on to Madden's nearby trailer.

The smiling law officers gathered around Madden and patted him on the back. Each officer shook hands with Madden and awkwardly thanked him for what he had accomplished at the school and in the community. Most believed that Madden had something to do with the mine explosion and, without ever admitting it, they were happy and relieved it had occurred. The deaths of Billy Hemrod and his crew ended the drug manufacturing and trafficking business in Calico County and northern New Mexico. And to all of the law enforcement officers, it also buried the financial records of Hemrod's drug operations—their payoffs. It was finally over.

"Rob, I am not going to bullshit you, I'm going to tell it to you straight," Wells began. "Thanks to you and your actions, we all have a new start here and don't have to work under the thumb of Hemrod and his gang anymore. Unfortunately, too many things happened in the county that we had to ignore. We wish we could undo the past—especially with you," Wells admitted. "So on behalf of all of the law enforcement officers here in Calico County, New Mexico, I'm presenting you with an honorary deputy sheriff badge and certificate. Congratulations."

The officers were now applauding and clapping while Madden thought, *I'd rather piss on this certificate—what a bunch of bullshit.*

As a tribute to Madden, the Calico County officers had arranged for Madden to have a police escort up to the Interstate and across the county line.

"Come on, Rob. We don't have all day," yelled Sheriff Wells waiting for Madden to depart.

"Thanks, Sheriff, be right there," Madden shouted out the door of the trailer.

His last few minutes were filled with packing his final personal items and books into his Honda Element and trailer for the continuation of his trip to Stanford. With the Element filled and the trailer empty, Madden recalled his first days at Tres Rios and prayed to the Almighty for his protection and grace. As he checked one last time in the trailer for anything he might have forgotten, his phone rang loudly.

"Rob, this is Bonnie McCord. We know who killed your family. The FBI just raided a sleeper cell in Florida and one terrorist provided credible evidence about the explosion."

Madden stood silent and motionless while trying to grasp what McCord was saying.

"Do you hear me, Rob? We know who killed your wife and daughters and where they are."

ABOUT THE AUTHOR

Growing up in the oil fields, John Witzel served in the U.S. Air Force as a navigator and was a volunteer in the Iranian Rescue Attempt in 1980. Appointed and served as Director of the Strategic Air Command Airborne Command Post, Witzel retired after 22 years of service. Following the service, he served as an accountant at a national bank and was subsequently asked to return to the military as a defense contractor/consultant. Currently, Witzel is serving his 12th year as a School Board Director and YMCA Board Member.

9957538R00176

Made in the USA
San Bernardino, CA
02 April 2014